OUT OF ORDER

PHOEBE ATWOOD TAYLOR

OUT
OF
ORDER

An Asey Mayo Cape Cod Mystery

A Foul Play Press Book

THE COUNTRYMAN PRESS
Woodstock, Vermont

This edition is published in 1988 by Foul Play Press, a division
of The Countryman Press, Woodstock, Vermont 05091.

ISBN 0-88150-105-0

Printed in the United State of America

OUT OF ORDER

1

"ONE hundred and sixteen?" Williams from the coat room stared incredulously at Mr. Root, for thirty-eight years as much of a fixture in the Hybrid Club lounge as the mahogany desk behind which he presided. "One hundred and sixteen telegrams, every last one alike?"

Odd things happened on the night of the Big Game, even in the Hybrid Club, but this, his tone indicated, was too odd.

"One hundred and seventeen, now," Mr. Root said. "The last was a cable. And every one said the same thing. They said," he lowered his voice to a dramatic whisper, "'DO NOT FIGHT WITH HARPER DIXON!' His wife's work, I understand. Betsey Porter."

The Hybrid Club staff was not given to gossip, but it had

followed three generations of Porters through Porter carriages and bicycles to the famous Porter Sixteen cars, and it took an intense and fatherly interest in all Porter affairs.

"His wife's work, eh? She's a one, that girl." Williams approved of Betsey. "It's a good plan. Mr. Bill hasn't fought Harper Dixon yet, and Donald tells me he hasn't touched a drop. Not a drop! This'll be the first time in six years those two haven't fought on the night of The Game."

"Maybe." Mr. Root pursed his lips. "May*be*, Williams. But just you listen to these three cables that Sampson mislaid in the drawer. All from Mr. Bill to Asey Mayo in Jamaica—"

"That would be the detective from Cape Cod he brings here once in a while?"

"Exactly. He's wintering in Jamaica. I—er—I expect to spend my own vacation there, later on in February." Mr. Root coughed elaborately as he adjusted his pince nez. "Here's the first, written this noon. 'MAYO, RETROP, JAMAICA. OKAY SALES, CARBURETOR PIP, SWELL SALES. BILL.'"

"That's just about the new model. It don't mean—"

"Wait. The next was written at five-thirty. 'WE LOST. BILL.'"

"Just telling him about the game," Williams said. "I don't see those prove—"

"But the third makes my point. Look at the writing." Mr. Root put the yellow blank down on the desk. "See. Sprawled and careless. No cable address. 'ASEY MAYO JAMAICA. PLEASE COME TO BLIGHT.' Now, what d'you make of that? Does that sound as though Mr. Bill hadn't bent an elbow? Why, he's even signed it 'X.' Not even with his name, like the others."

"What's it mean?" Williams wrinkled his forehead. "What's the 'X' for? What's Blight?"

"The last cable Mr. Bill got," Root explained, "was from Asey Mayo, see? D'you see it now? Mr. Bill's mad, and sent him this answer. The 'X' is probably meant to be funny."

"Funny? It don't make sense," Williams protested.

Mr. Root took a beautifully pointed pencil from his vest pocket, crossed out the word *come* and wrote *go* above it.

"Now d'you get it? 'PLEASE GO TO BLIGHT.' Go, not come. In other words, Go to Hell. That's not a message from Bill Porter in his right mind. He is very fond of Asey Mayo. Yes, Williams, I think before the night is over, or the banquet, we'll have to get Sullivan up from the boiler room to separate Mr. Bill and Dixon, as usual. Dixon," Mr. Root sniffed, "was in a terrible state, even before luncheon. Mr. Peter Dixon was having a time with him. And it looks to me very much as though Mr. Bill was on his way to a fight, if he can send a cable like that to Asey Mayo. After all, Williams, that Porter-Dixon fight is almost a club tradition!"

But Bill Porter, sober as a judge and mad as a hatter, had firmly made up his mind that the Porter-Dixon fight was going to be filed in the legend and not the tradition class.

Alone with his hundred and seventeen telegrams and cables, he sat in a dim corner of the club's fourth floor writing room, waiting for ten-thirty to come. At ten-thirty he would rush in and give his promised speech at the banquet, and then he would grab the midnight home, and fool everybody.

DO NOT FIGHT HARPER DIXON!

Bill sighed at the sentence that leered up at him.

What Betsey and Asey and everyone else couldn't be made to understand was that he never really wanted to fight Harper

Dixon, either the first time or later. Harper goaded him into it. Or some of Bill's old team did. Six years might have passed since the November afternoon when Harper Dixon cuddled a football under his arm and raced forty-two yards to plant it on the wrong goal line, but to the elephants of that team, it was practically only yesterday.

So Bill was hiding as much from the gang as from Dixon, and in an hour he'd be away from both, and on his way to the station. That was that. Tomorrow he would compose a hundred and seventeen nose thumbing answers to those messages. A neat but caustic rhyme would do the trick. Idly, he started to pencil a first line on the back of Betsey's telegram.

A man stumbled into the writing room and lurched to a seat at one of the tables near the door. Bill ducked back farther into the shadow. If it was someone he knew, he'd have a barrel of explanations on his hands.

Twin desk lights clicked on, and Bill almost broke down and wept.

Harper Dixon.

It would be, Bill thought bitterly. Forty rooms in this club, all of Boston outside—all the whole damn Eastern seaboard, as a matter of fact. But Harper would pick this spot. Bill gritted his teeth until his jaws ached. He couldn't get out without being observed, even if Harper was back to him. Well, he'd chuck the banquet and wait. After all he'd gone through to keep out of a fight, he wasn't going to start one now. Not if he had to wait there till Monday morning.

The first fifteen minutes passed quickly, but the next half hour dragged. Finally eleven o'clock chimed.

Bill raised himself up in his chair and peered around to see if Dixon might be sleeping it off. But Dixon was awake, sitting there scattering cigarette ashes and butts all over the rug. Burning butts, too. Some, Bill noticed with growing irritation, were scorching holes in the deep piled broadloom.

Broadloom. Bill leaned back. This—yes, sir! This was the rug he'd paid for himself, last month! Forty-two square yards of crimson broadloom, dyed to order, at twelve dollars the square yard. Plus labor. And Dixon was burning it up. Forty-two yards of broadloom meant nothing to him, no more than his forty-two yards to the wrong goal line.

Peeking around again, Bill saw another burning cigarette plop on the carpet.

"For God's sakes!" he couldn't hold in another second. "D'you have to ruin that rug, Dixon? Can't you use an ash tray?"

Without displaying the faintest trace of surprise at Bill's presence or his question, Harper turned around and yawned.

"Cat had your tongue, Bill? I've wondered."

Bill went hot and cold all over as he suddenly realized that Harper had known all the time that he was in that corner. That mirror. That damn mirror! Bill could have kicked himself in sheer exasperation. All the time he'd been crouching there, Dixon was watching him in the mantel mirror!

"That's a new rug!" It was a thoroughly inadequate answer, but Bill was too wrathful to care.

"It's a damn ugly rug."

"It happens," Bill rose from his chair, "to have cost twelve dollars a yard for forty-two yards, and it happens that I paid for it, see?"

"Forty-two," Harper observed thickly, "isn't your lucky

number, is it, Bill? Did you get that hired man of yours—what's the name? Asey Mayo? Did Asey Mayo track the rug down? I won't suggest where. Couldn't get that color red in a virtuous establishment. Tell me, d'you sub—" he cleared his throat, "subsidize that phoney sleuth, as well as club carpets?"

Bill took two steps forward, then jammed his hands into his pockets and forced them to remain there. Harper's eyes were glazed black slits under his heavy caret-like eyebrows. He had that over-boiled lobster look. The man was out cold on his feet, even if he could talk. But then, Harper could talk a streak even when he had to be carried.

"That's right," Harper said. "Can't biff drunks. Do you subsidize the phoney sleuth, Bill? You know. He gets mixed up in a murder on your old Cape Cod, and solves it in a Porter sixteen roadster. Nets you a tidy sum, I suppose?"

"NO!" Bill started past Harper to the door. "NO! Asey Mayo isn't subsidized by me or by anyone else, and he's no phoney—ooop!"

He thudded down on the crimson broadloom as Harper's foot shot out and tripped him.

"I won't tell a soul," Harper said. "Not a soul. Had me fooled, though. I thought you were sober."

Bill got slowly to his feet, and thrust his hands behind his back.

For the first and only time in his life, he really wanted of his own accord to tear Harper Dixon apart, limb by limb. The only time, except for a split second six years ago when he realized that Harper had lost The Game, and nothing could save it.

"Ah, the Porter fighting face," Harper said. "Jutting jaw, and everything. Clean limbed America!"

Bill ignored him. "I'm sober, and you know it. And the next time I find you sober, Dixon, if I ever do, I'm knocking the daylights out of you. Not for spilling me, but for calling Asey Mayo a phoney. Does that percolate?"

Harper laughed that grating, irritating, superior laugh of his that always infuriated Bill.

"Come off, Porter! It's the swellest stunt any car maker ever pulled. Homespun sleuth in custom Porter! Clever of you to keep him on the Cape. Once he got away, the poor hick would be sunk. Does Betsey prompt him?"

"Nobody prompts Asey Mayo!" Bill shouted. "He solves his own cases! He—"

"That hick couldn't solve a grocery order, and you know it! I'll bet you—"

"Listen, Dixon," Bill said, "do your damndest, but I'm not going to fight. Get it?"

"Who said fight?" Harper retorted. "I said, I'll bet you— well, I'll bet you five thousand dollars he couldn't even solve my Aunt Eugenia's grocery order! He couldn't—"

"What do you mean, grocery order? Are you being funny? Do you—"

Out in the corridor, a chorus boomed unevenly.

"We want PORTER! We want POR-ter! We want Bill!"

Harper laughed softly. "The Mighty Porter! Go along and be a hero. Bill's all grown up, now. Won't bet, won't fight—"

The chorus from the corridor invaded the writing room, considered the scene for a second, absorbed it, and set up a happy din. Sammy Forsythe clambered up on a table and took charge.

"Yah, fight! Fight! Roll up the rug, boys! Here they are! Fight, fight, fi-ut—"

"Shut up!" Bill ordered. "There's not going to be any fight. Get down, Sam. Dixon—"

He broke off and changed his mind about making the statement he intended as he saw the face of Peter Dixon in the doorway. Poor Pete, he spent half his time getting Harper out of scrapes, and the rest of it listening to people fuss about him.

"Say, Harper," Pete began soothingly, "let's—"

"This is my business." Harper somehow got to his feet. "Shut up. Keep out of it."

It was amazing, Bill thought, how different the Dixon brothers were in build, coloring, disposition and everything else except those bushy angular eyebrows. Harper was a big brute, and his dark hair and dark eyes accented his perpetually sullen expression. Pete was half his size, and light, and pugnosed and freckled.

"Come on," Pete tried again. "Let's us go—"

"Touch me," there was something sinister in Harper's drawl, "and I'll smash you to a pulp. I can do it. Or don't you remember?"

Sammy Forsythe didn't in the least understand the finer points of what was going on, but to him the situation still had possibilities.

"Fight!" he piped up hopefully. "Fight! Roll up the rugs! Fight! Come—"

"It's about time you shut up, too," Harper said. "This isn't any fight. It's a bet. Get down before I—"

"What's the diff?" Sammy hated Harper. "It's you against good ole Bill, ain't it? Come on, gang. I bet with Bill. Who's betting with me for good ole Billy Porter against Dixon?"

2

Betsey Porter surveyed her husband quizzically the next morning at breakfast, and looked once more through the slips of paper.

"Those are just copies," Bill said in a weak voice. "Forty-nine thousand, nine hundred and fifty. That's—"

"Darling," Betsey said, "don't crab over fifty dollars. Call it an even fifty thousand. Bill, you nut, couldn't you just have *fought?*"

Twice Bill opened his mouth to tell her everything all over again, and twice he closed his mouth. What was the use? Neither Betsey nor anyone who hadn't been there could ever understand how those bets accumulated, with Sammy Forsythe egging the crowd on, and Harper with his slit eyes and boiled expression, keeping on to annoy Pete, who was having kittens, and—oh, you couldn't explain!

"I'll cable Asey," Bill said.

"You'll do nothing of the sort, if you haven't."

Bill stared at her. "Huh? Why, Bets, Asey'll be glad to—"

"To let you walk over him with a steam roller in either hand," Betsey said. "I know. He'd love it. And he undoubtedly could solve Harper Dixon's Aunt Eugenia's grocery order, too. Grocery order! What's he mean, grocery order? Does he mean a real grocery order, or is it just a figure of speech? Or what?"

"I don't think so," Bill said unhappily. "I mean, I just think he meant grocery order. You know, like a grocery order. Why can't I cable Asey?"

"Bill, you fool! You—oh, listen to me! Asey adored your

father, and because he did, he's taken on all your troubles, and your brother's, and your factory, and—well, everything! And for those very reasons, you simply cannot ask him to get you out of this mess!"

"But Betsey—"

"Very well." Betsey shrugged her shoulders. "Send him a nice cable. 'Dear Asey, I bet a drunk you could solve a grocery order. Just leap up from Jamaica and tend to it, will you?' Sounds nice, I think. Wire Geoff at the factory to mind the furnace this week, while you're at it. Maybe he'd take out the garbage, too. He'd be glad to oblige your father's son, I'm sure."

"You mean," Bill looked dazed, "you—but—hell, Betsey, I never thought it would be insulting! I never—I mean, I just wanted Dixon to eat his words, and have Asey show his stuff! I—my God, I never thought of that angle!"

"Consider it," Betsey's cool voice was loaded with sarcasm, "now."

"The money. What about that?" Bill demanded.

"Sammy Forsythe," Betsey said, "has his first job in three years. You let him bet a thousand dollars. You let those kids in for it. Wrote the bets, even. You know perfectly well most of those fools haven't a cent. Consider that angle, little one!"

"I—"

"The Porter sixteens can take it," Betsey said. "And they're going to. Next year," she slid an arm around Bill's shoulders, "you can take me to the game, and we'll have a nice coca cola afterwards, and come right home on the street cars or something."

"I know, but—"

"They were all squiffy, and backing you against Harper.

You've got," she picked up one of the slips, "three months. 'On or before February 28.' Just about three months. Let it ride, and quiet down, and on February twenty-fifth, send your check to Harper. It's up to you to take it on the chin. If Harper has a shred of decency, he'll send the check back. Tell the boys it's been called off. And Bill—"

"Uh-huh," Bill said. "You've hammered it home. You're right. You—"

"Next year, perhaps you'd better just listen to the game, don't you think? Over a nice radio?"

But Bill's thoughts were already settled on the forty-nine thousand, nine hundred and fifty dollars due in February. Call it February twenty-first. He pulled a notebook from his pocket and flipped through the pages. If anyone but Harper Dixon had forced him into this, he'd laugh if off without losing face. After all, the night of the big game was the night of the big game, and a lot of funny bets got made. But rather than give Dixon any opportunity of calling him a welsher, he'd pay twice fifty thousand, with pleasure. He could take it.

He scanned the notations already down on the February pages of the notebook. Yacht club dues, country club dues. See about bunker on 9 at mtg. February 18: life ins. due. Steel board. February 21: Porter directors mtg. Wire Asey full report.

Under the latter he wrote, "Pay Dixon," and put the notebook back in his pocket. That, he supposed, was that.

3

On February twenty-second, Asey Mayo sat on the hotel verandah with a code book in his hand, and translated from

Bill Porter's lengthy cable the account of the Porter directors' meeting the day before.

A cruise ship had just docked, and already there were crowds of American tourists flocking through the Kingston streets. The hotel was overrun. Judging from the noise, most of the men had already set to work sampling Southsides at the bar, and all the children were whooping it up in the palm fringed hotel pool. Everywhere Asey looked there seemed to be an eager eyed elderly woman armed with a camera. Two women, after a loud discussion of his white linen suit and sun helmet, had even taken pictures of him under the impression that he was a typical English planter.

Asey forced himself to concentrate on the cable, and was even getting the sense of it when someone pulled out the wicker chair next his, sat down and began to cough. After struggling with "odium oiled" for five minutes, Asey glanced down at the end of the message. "Betsey's bodice"—he grinned. "Betsey's" meant "Betsey says," but "bodice" was a new one. Probably some personal touch.

He glared at the fellow next him out of the corner of his eye. In another minute he was going to buy him cough drops. Tourists were a necessary evil; but he disliked them at home on Cape Cod, and he found no reason to change his mind about the Jamaican variety.

Still, there was something familiar about this dapper old gent, swinging his pince nez on the end of a black ribbon. Boston, most likely. Asey turned to meet a timid smile.

"Mr. Mayo? I—er—" the fellow beamed nervously. "You may remember me at the Hybrid Club? Mr. Porter said—"

"Sure." Asey extended his hand. He didn't really know the

man from Adam, but if he was a Hybrid Club friend of Bill's, he had to be played up to. "Sure. Just in, Mr.—Um?"

"Root. Yes, we've just got in, and I wonder if you would recommend a good guide, Mr. Mayo? Mr. Porter said I mustn't fail to see Spanish Town and the Botanic Gardens, and—"

"Tell you what." Asey closed the code book and looked at the tourists milling around. "I'm just in town for a day or so, but I feel I won't get much done today. S'pose I show you the sights, myself?"

"Oh!" Mr. Root's face lighted up, and then a shadow crossed it. "Oh. But I belong to the *staff* of the club, you know!"

Asey grinned. "I always thought more of the staff of that place, Mr. Root, than I did of most of the members. Come 'long. I'll get my car."

Not until he had reached the last course of a strange luncheon containing every Jamaican dish Asey could think of, did Mr. Root venture to ask the question that had been worrying him and the club staff for weeks on end.

"I suppose," he inquired diffidently, "you ran up and settled Mr. Bill's bet?"

"Bet? What bet?"

"Oh, maybe I shouldn't have mentioned it. I'm sorry. I really shouldn't have brought the matter up. But I put the bets in the safe that night, and nothing had been done about them as far as I knew. I'm in charge of such matters," he added parenthetically.

Asey looked at him. "Will you sort of delve into this, Mr. Root? What bets of Bill's went into your safe when? Don't squirm, now. This sounds interestin'."

Syllable by syllable, Asey dragged from Mr. Root what little he knew of the affair.

"I—really," Mr. Root was almost in tears. "I—"

"So Bill," Asey said, "an' his friends, they bet with Harper Dixon last November that I could solve a groc'ry order, did they? Harper Dixon. Huh. I've met him."

"From Blight," Mr. Root said. "Among the staff, we often call him that. The Blight. We—"

"Blight?" Asey leaned forward. "What's that you say?"

"He comes from Blight. That's a part of the town of Monkton, Mr. Mayo. The first settlers called it that. From the Indians, and the sickness, and the floods, and—hasn't anyone told you about this, Mr. Mayo? Didn't Mr. Bill say a word about it all?"

"Huh," Asey said. "So that's what that last wire I got that— Root, you say they bet fifty thousand, like fifty thousand dollars?"

"Yes. But I can't understand why Mr. Bill didn't let you know."

"He did, in a way," Asey said. "That same night. An' then— sure, I know what happened. Betsey found out an' give him blazes. An' Bill d'cided to take—well, well! You through, Mr. Root? Let's get goin'."

At an incredible speed, Asey drove the big open Porter through the crowded streets of Kingston, weaving around donkey carts and horse drawn cabs, and groups of calico clad native women with tall stacks of fruit on their heads. He was so absent minded about it all that Mr. Root finally shut his eyes to the scene and prayed.

The Porter drew up at a dock. No, Mr. Root corrected himself. A seaplane landing. Asey jumped out, buttonholed a young man in uniform, and talked to him for at least five minutes without seeming to stop for breath. The young man nodded, called out some orders Mr. Root couldn't understand, and instantly the place was in a turmoil.

Asey tossed his sun helmet on the car seat and buckled on a leather flying cap.

"Say, what was that date? The twenty-eighth?"

"Yes, Mr. Mayo. I—"

"Drive a car?"

"Yes, but Mr. Mayo, I—where—"

Asey thrust a key ring into his hand. "Catch hold of these. When you're ready to leave, stick the car in the hotel drive an' tell 'em to take care of it. They'll find a guide to go to Castleton. Don't buy any fake silver bracelets. Worse than usual this winter—"

"Mr. Mayo!" Mr. Root screamed for the first time in his life. "Where ARE you going?"

"Out of order," Asey told him gravely, "cometh chaos. Or maybe it's the other way round. Anyhow, it's in the Bible."

"Where—" Mr. Root was in no mood to enjoy puns.

"I'm goin'," Asey grinned as he put on a leather coat, "to Blight. So long, Mr. Root!"

2

IN a snow drift up to his knees, and with snow biting at his hands, Asey scraped away the ice that had formed on the windshield of his Porter coupe, and made violent mental additions to his list of flaws in the new model.

The so-called de luxe heater with all its fancy gadgets was bunk, plain bunk, and about as much use as two candles from a kid's birthday cake. The defroster was a joke. And the genius responsible for the thing pretending to be a windshield wiper was going to take a spin through a factory window on the toe of Asey's boot.

Brushing the snow off his white shoes and linen trousers, Asey climbed back into the car. He really had no business to find fault with such comparatively minor items, for the trip thus far had panned out pretty well. Eric Fennell had flown him to Newark before the blizzard stopped the plane, and a special train had ploughed through to East Whitefield, the station nearest Monkton and within sixteen miles of it. The Porter dealer from Whitefield Center had done his dazed best to fill Asey's order telegraphed from Miami.

"All the samey," Asey murmured to himself, "it looks like the last ten miles was goin' to be the hardest."

He pulled a map from the dashboard compartment and switched on the top light. Thank heavens, the lights and the battery were up to Porter standards. If they gave out, ten miles from Monkton and Blight, and apparently a thousand miles from anywhere else, he was going to be sunk. With his hand-me-down overcoat provided by the car dealer, and a visored cap filched from the train conductor, he was hardly equipped to struggle with blizzards.

The map was clear enough, and by now it was etched on Asey's brain. Monkton, South Monkton and Blight might have been a corner of his own back yard in Wellfleet. It was a swell map, only in this swirling blinding storm, no fences or houses or signs or landmarks existed. The roads hadn't been touched by a plough, and driving through them was more like swimming in cornstarch pudding. But in spite of the storm, he intended to keep on with his original plan of breaking down in front of the Dixon house and easing himself that way into the family circle. If that didn't work, something else would turn up to gain him entrance somehow.

Fifteen minutes later—his speedometer told him he had progressed just two miles,—he jammed on his brakes as a freak drift loomed ahead, spreading from one side of the road to the other. He surveyed it for several minutes before it dawned on him that it wasn't a drift but a large bus that had got stuck when its driver tried to turn it around. They might, Asey thought, at least have had the decency to leave a flare, or something to mark the thing before they abandoned it.

He leaned on the wheel and considered. This meant trouble. He couldn't get by, and if a bus had given up, his own prospects might briefly be summed up as hopeless. If only he had a shovel, he might dig enough to turn the Porter back. But Porters unfortunately no longer included shovels as standard equipment, as they had in the old days.

"Next time I get phil'nthropic an' try to save someone fifty thousand dollars," Asey announced, "I'm goin' to take a few years off first an' fit me out a caravan. Huh!"

He jerked the flashlight from its stand next to the fire extinguisher. The dealer, or someone, he noticed indignantly, had substituted a cheap light for the regular powerful model which he himself had specified.

Snapping it on, he dove out into the storm and started for the bus. With luck he might find something inside with which he could try to dig.

He ploughed around past the back of the bus to the door on the far side. The door was open, and there were fresh prints in the snow.

"Huh," Asey said, and swung his light toward the engine in time to pick up a figure darting away.

He called out, then turned and followed his own prints to the back of the bus. The Porter headlights outlined the slim figure of a girl hastening through the drifts.

"Wait!" Asey said, starting after her. "Ahoy there! Wait up! Any shovels on board of that craft?"

She stopped as he drew near.

"Are you—oh." There was relief in her voice. "I—oh. I thought you were someone else. What did you say?"

The flashlight disclosed the snow covered figure of a girl, blue with cold, shivering from head to foot. Her pert, rather pointed face looked frozen under her tight fitting beret.

"Any shovels on the bus there? I—say, you the only one there? You look perishin'—here. C'mere. Get into my car an' perch over what they laughin'ly call a heater. Hustle!"

No gloves, he noticed as he raced the engine, trying to get up some heat. No gloves, no overshoes. No wonder she was jittering like that!

"Where's the driver?" he demanded. "Who left you alone like this? Ain't there a heater on that bus?"

"Tim Sparks," her teeth were chattering, "went for help about three years ago. Or three hours, I guess. Gee, this is swell. This is wonderful!"

"I s'pose," Asey said, "this is about the only time anyone could honestly praise that heater. Anyhow, it's better than nothin'. Did you say they was a shovel on that bus? I was aimin' to get to Blight, orig'nally, but I'd just like to get turned around, now."

"You're a couple miles off the main road," the girl said. "You missed the fork, same as Tim. This road here leads right back to Monkton. If you could turn around and get back to the fork, you might get to Blight. There is a shovel on the bus, and a sort of little plough thing, too. The kind you hitch onto a bumper."

"Why on earth," Asey asked, "didn't your driver use it? Well, anyhow, this sort of gives me hope. Sit here an' warm yourself while I see what can be done."

"I'll help," the girl said. "Maybe it'll warm me up to move around."

It took nearly an hour before the Porter was headed in the

opposite direction, with the small plough lashed onto the bumper.

"There," Asey said. "Your driver may not like that much, but it's his own fault for leavin' things b'hind. Crazy sort of fellow, pullin' into that drift when he could have stuck this thing down an' kept on goin'. May not work for us, but it's nice to know we got it. We can always push it by hand, an' now with the wind b'hind us, maybe we'll blow to Blight. Say, Miss—what'd you say your name was?"

"I didn't, but it's Gerty McKeen," the girl lighted a crumpled cigarette. "I'm so used to being known, I forgot you was a stranger. Everyone knows me. I run the beauty parlor in Monkton, Mr. Mayo."

"You—how'd you know who I was?"

"Aw, I know you all right. Your clothes put me off for a while. In pictures you always wear a Stetson and a flannel shirt and a coat with a lot of pockets. But I know you. I got three pictures of you in the shop. I've got you, and Gary Cooper, and the Prince—I mean, the King of England."

Asey threw back his head and laughed. "Tough on them, ain't it?"

"Not the way you mean," Gerty returned. "You see, I—well, I got a sort of inherited yen for detectives. My father used to be on the force in New York. Hey—here's the turn! We was nearer it than I thought. Say, what're you doing in these parts, Mr. Mayo?"

"I been wonderin' myself for the last few hours," Asey neatly evaded her question. "Where was you bound, on the bus?"

"I was going to the Dixons to doll their Aunt Charlotte—that's Mrs. Babb—up for some party."

"Dixons, huh?" Asey's eyes gleamed.

"Swells," Gerty said. "All of Blight is swells. Big places. So swell they don't allow stores, and keep the roads bad on purpose to keep the hoi polloi out. You know."

"Dixons," Asey said. "Huh. Seems to me I heard of—two boys, ain't there? Harper an' Pete? An' an aunt named Eugenia?"

"That's the ones," Gerty said. "Only Aunt Eugenia—Mrs. Crane, that is,—she died about a year and a half ago."

Asey whistled under his breath. From what Root had told him about this fool bet of Bill's, he understood that his job was the comparatively simple one of translating a grocery order belonging to Harper Dixon's Aunt Eugenia. It had sounded too foolish a thing to waste fifty thousand dollars on. Go to Blight, see the aunt, solve whatever puzzle it was, and get back to Jamaica. That had been his plan. Somehow it had never occurred to him that Aunt Eugenia might be dead. Root hadn't said so, but then, probably Root hadn't known.

"So Aunt Eugenia," Asey said, "has passed to her r'ward, has she? I didn't know that."

"Oh yes. She got flu, and then something else, and then her heart give out. Wasn't she a pip?"

"I never met her," Asey said.

"Didn't you? She was tall and skinny, and her face was so bony it hurt to give her a facial. She was the only woman I ever knew that never forgot a single thing, and always did what she set out to do. Mrs. Babb's so different! She's short and fat, always on the go. She's steamed through three husbands. People say they just wore out. Nothing new gets by her, whether it's something you should eat or something you should think."

Asey laughed.

"That's right," Gerty insisted. "Last time I went to the house to do her, it was around lunch time, and she asked me to stay. Guess what we had! Snake meat salad and vitamin pills!"

"Huh?"

"That's the truth! Lucky for me, I ate all the salad I wanted before I found out, but honest, I wiggled for a week afterwards. The rest of the meal was in pills. They," Gerty made a face, "tasted like sawdust."

Asey grinned. "Aunt Charlotte sounds entertainin'. Does she rile Harper? As I r'call him, he riles easy."

There must have been some reason, he thought, behind that bet of Harper's. Perhaps he might get a new slant on the man from this youngster.

"He's not so bad." Gerty rose to the bait. "Not as bad as people make out. Of course he drinks too much, and he's always getting wound around phone poles in accidents, but he's not so bad."

"I thought Pete was the nice one," Asey said. "I never heard anyone stand up for Harper before."

"Pete's nice. Of course, he's not big like Harper, nor as good looking. He's engaged to Suzanne Vail, did you know? She's another swell."

"Want me to leave you at Dixons'?" Asey admired the deft way in which Gerty turned the conversation away from Harper. He had a feeling that for all the ease with which the girl chatted, she was not easily pumped. "So as to show'em that nature in the rawr don't hold you back?"

"You talk Cape Cod like, just as the papers always say, don't you? I like it," Gerty remarked. "Sure, we could stop there a second. I forgot and left my bag in the bus, but anyway it's too late to do Mrs. Babb now. She's probably gone on to the party. But it'd please her to know I come. Then I guess you better take me to my cousin's, and I think you better stay there too. Even if that plough works, you can't get anywhere on the Blight hills, and there's no hotels nor nothing."

Asey nodded. He was going to have a reasonably legitimate reason for getting into the Dixon house, and that was what counted.

The Porter slewed on through the snow, its engine purring away. Bill hadn't let anyone tinker with that. It was the same old engine, able to take it.

"Hey!" Gerty spoke as Asey braked. "Somebody's waving on the side of the road—"

A man, whose face looked even colder than Gerty's had, came panting up to the window Asey let down. Over his head and his wet, snow covered evening clothes was pinned a scanty blanket.

"I wonder," he began, "if you could—oh, Gerty! Thank God it's someone I know! Gerty, would your friend take me and my sister to the Dixons'? *Could* you crowd us in? We started out three hours ago for Sue Vail's party, and the car's stuck over—"

"An' you're freezin'," Asey said. "Sure we can take you! Where's your sister?"

"Mulling around a drift. She's all in. I saw the lights coming up the valley, and raced ahead to get you before you passed. I—"

"I'll help you get her over." Asey took the flash, and got out of the car. "No, you stay here, Gerty."

His jaw sagged when he saw the woman. She wasn't any young thing like Gerty, either! She was more than middle aged. Over her draggled evening dress was a short fur wrap, and tied around her shoulders was the man's overcoat. His felt hat partially protected her white hair.

"God A'mighty!" Asey said. "Here—let me help. You win Gerty's place over the heater!"

The woman managed a smile. "Isn't this perfectly foolish? I feel like Lincoln Ellsworth being rescued at the South Puppole."

"No overshoes, no gloves, no—hustle!"

"It's a relief," the man said, "to hear someone tell us we're fools. We've religiously refrained from making any personal comments. Gerty, if you rate my lap, it's going to be an awfully damp seat!"

"Don't you mind me," Gerty said. "Mrs. Westcott, let me take those pumps off, and you put your feet right over this heater. Oh, I wish I had a towel! Mr. Mayo, this is Mrs. Westcott and her brother Mr. Thorn. They live in the next place beyond Dixons'. What happened to you two?"

"It was just sort of snowing casually when we set out for Sue's," Mrs. Westcott said. "Then all of a sudden it was a blizzard. We ran out of gas at the foot of her road. We tried to walk it, and we tried the back way, too, but the drifts in those back valleys are terrific. I'll bet Sue's Cousin Ernest is marooned for weeks in that cabin of his. Oh, Hank, isn't this nice? Being rescued, and all?"

"Considering we were going by dead reckoning, when we saw the car lights, I do think it's rather nice. I was beginning to long for one of the Phyfe-Jordan St. Bernards."

"Don't you want me to take you to this Vail place?" Asey asked, as they started off.

"You couldn't," Mrs. Westcott said. "You couldn't, I assure you. And I have an intimate knowledge of conditions. Dixons' is nearest, and the snow fence keeps this road beyond passably clear. The Dixons can bed us down. Mr. Mayo, are you really Asey Mayo?"

"Why—"

"My dear man, everyone who goes to Gerty's stares at your face by the hour. Oh, isn't this splendid, Hank? Really, I was terribly scared."

"So," Hank said briefly, "was I."

"Me, too," Gerty said, "before he rescued me. What's the matter? Why're you stopping again?"

"Seems to be another wayfarer," Asey observed, "hoofin' it —hey, mister, want a lift?"

He leaned out the window and called again.

"What's that? Lift? Thank you, no," came the polite answer.

"Hank," Mrs. Westcott said, "that sounds like Sue Vail's cousin, Ernest! Professor Vail, is that you? Hank, it is! Get out and pull him in by the ear—wait. I'll talk to him. Professor Vail! Come here! Here, the other window! Now, just where do you think you're going?"

"Why, I—oh. Mrs. Westcott." Asey was surprised to find that the professor was young, younger than Hank Thorn by his looks. "Why, how do you do, Mrs. Westcott? Quite a little storm, isn't it?"

"Quite a storm indeed! Professor Vail, where are you going? Where do you think you're going?"

"Why, it's quite interesting, really." Asey stifled a chuckle as the man leaned on the window ledge and unconcernedly, as though the blizzard didn't exist, started to explain. "I never thought I should need it, so I left it in Cambridge. I remember asking myself whether or not I might find any use for it, and decided that I should not, so—"

"Ernest Vail," Mrs. Westcott said, "what are you talking about?"

"The proverb anthology. You see, I left mine in Cambridge, and I remembered this evening that I had seen a copy in the Dixon library, so I thought I'd stroll over and ask if I might borrow it."

He appeared slightly bewildered by the laughter that followed.

"Get in," Asey said. "Get in. Curl up on the floor."

"Oh, no. No, really. Thanks for the—but really, I've had no exercise today, and I find this brisk walk very stimulating. I—"

Gerty giggled helplessly.

" 'Fessor," Asey said with ominous firmness, "if you don't get into this car this minute, you're goin' to find somethin' a lot more stimulatin' than a no'theast blizzard hittin' you plonk on the top of your cranium. Get it?"

The professor got in, and once again they proceeded on their way. Asey sighed with relief when they finally reached the gates of the Dixon estate.

"Lighted up," Hank said. "Apparently Char and Pete and Harper got back from Sue's, somehow. I don't see how they did. Here's the drive turn—"

Asey smiled to himself. Around here was where he had planned to pull his fake accident. Perhaps it was a good omen, being able to drive to the front door. The Dixons couldn't do much but take him and Gerty in with the others.

The car stalled suddenly, and Asey waited for the automatic starter to show its stuff. Instead the motor coughed and died, and the lights went out.

"D'luxe bat'try," Asey's irony was elaborate. "Oh, my, oh

my my! Poor Bill Porter! I guess we just get out an' hoof it. An' golly, that dum flash's gone, too!"

All of them were nearly exhausted before they reached the front door at the head of the curving drive.

Asey banged a lusty tattoo with the round iron knocker.

"I'll bet," Mrs. Westcott's teeth were chattering, "that they all stayed at the Vails', Hank. The servants are probably sound asleep in the wing. Or else Char's let 'em go to the movies. She does that when—oh, Asey, bang again! Someone must be here!"

"Let's," Hank said after Asey had banged for ten minutes, "let's try the back doors."

To Asey, hungry, chilled to the bone and far more tired from his hectic trip than he realized, the wing seemed a vast distance away. He turned the door knob, knowing full well that the door wouldn't give, but wishing that it might.

He was intensely surprised when it did.

"Well, I never!" Mrs. Westcott said. "How peculiar!"

They stepped into the brightly lighted hall, and instantly all the lights went out.

"Wah!" Gerty squealed.

"Hold still a sec," Asey said.

Under his cold wet feet, the carpet was soft and squashy and quiet. In his brief glimpse of the hall, he recalled that the carpet covered the stair case, and in all probability it covered the next floor landing, too. But in spite of all that silent soft carpet, it seemed to him that he heard footsteps somewhere.

"Ahoy!" he called out. "Can you help us, please?"

No one answered.

"This is perfectly foolish," Mrs. Westcott said. "I—call again.

Here, let me. Edward! Oh, Edward. Martha! This is Mrs. Westcott, with Mr. Thorn! Come here, please!"

"Let's go out," Gerty tugged at Asey's arm. "This is spooky! I don't like this!"

"Prob'ly we scared a maid," Asey said, lighting a match. He hunted up a wall switch, and snapped the lights on. "P'raps they're automatic," he continued reassuringly. "P'raps the lights work when the door opens. That is, if they're off. We r'versed it."

"It appears to me," the professor said matter of factly, "as though someone had deliberately turned them off."

"Let's go back!" Gerty said. "Let's—"

"Not with a phone b'fore my eyes," Asey told her. "I'll try a g'rage—"

"And I'll call Sue," Mrs. Westcott said, "and tell Char we're staying here. I'm not going to cope with any more blizzard tonight—what's the matter?"

"Guess the phone wires is down," Asey said, replacing the receiver. "Say, I sort of think dry clothes is indicated. Is that a closet at the end of the hall there?"

"It's an entry." Mrs. Westcott removed Hank's coat from her shoulders. "With a powder room on one side, and a closet and men's room on the other. I don't like the thought of pulling people's houses apart, but I think even Mrs. Post would consider this an extenuating circumstance. Let's see if there's not something there."

She waited, Asey noticed, for him to lead the way up the long hall, and en route she looked nervously toward the dark rooms on either side.

"I say," she paused with her hand on the door knob of

the powder room, "come in and see if—and turn on the lights, will you, Hank? I feel scared, somehow."

Asey laughed what he hoped was a hearty and carefree laugh. In a sense he shared some of her trepidations. He wasn't afraid, as she and Gerty obviously were, but this whole business was screwey. There was something queer feeling about the house,—doors open, lights popping, footsteps sounding, phone out of order.

"The Dixons," he said aloud, "can hardly grudge us dry clothes, can they? B'sides, whyn't their door locked proper? Gee!" he blinked as he snapped on the switch and got the full effect of Charlotte Babb's chromium and glass powder room. "This is what they call modernistic, ain't it? Now I know how gold fish feel."

"Oh gee, it's keen!" Gerty said ecstatically. "Some day, I'm going to have a shop that looks like this! See the coat racks, you wouldn't know they were coat racks, would you?"

"No," Asey said with complete honesty, looking at the strange maze of chromium rods running along one side of the room, "you wouldn't."

"What are those things?" Professor Vail demanded. "Those glass things?"

"Why, dressing tables!" Gerty said. "Powder tables. Come and look. The chairs are glass, too. And see how the mirrors reflect—they're—they—they—"

Pointing at the center mirror, Gerty and Mrs. Westcott simultaneously emitted screams that sent shivers running up and down Asey's spine.

3

"WHAT'S—"

Before Asey could finish his question, the door behind them into the entry slammed shut, and a lock clicked with definite finality.

Asey strolled across the room and tried the knob.

"Y'know," he said casually, "that ain't good manners, attall. On two counts it ain't. It ain't p'lite to slam doors in the first place, an' where I come from, it ain't c'nsidered good manners to treat busted down travellers like they was a bunch of horrid rude burglars, even if they *are* callin' sort of informal like. I think—"

"For—for the love of soup!" Gerty crumpled onto one of the glass chairs. "Did you see that hand—that—that hand? I seen it in the mirror. Just like a movie, or something! Honest, I couldn't make words come out of my mouth! I—how can you act so calm—didn't you see that hand, Mr. Mayo?"

Asey chuckled. Now that he knew for sure that something screwey was going on, he was beginning to enjoy himself. Someone was obviously rampaging around the house, but not necessarily with motives dangerous to this crowd. They were all safe enough, locked up, with the rampager on the outside.

"I missed the hand, Gerty," he said. "I was too busy wonderin' which I'd grab b'fore you d'solved onto the floor—you, or Mrs. Westcott. What was the matter with the hand, did it have six fingers, or what?"

"Oh, no," the professor said. "No, indeed. It was a normal hand, although strange. Unusual, I should say. Not that the hand was unusual," he added hurriedly, "I do not mean to give that impression. It was a man's hand—"

"Man's hand, nothing!" Gerty interrupted indignantly. "With them bright red fingernails? You're crazy."

"That is why the hand was unusual," the professor remained unmoved. "Very few men I have known ever expressed favorable opinions on the feminine practice of painting fingernails with red paint. The majority dislike it intensely. That is why I consider it unusual for a man to have red fingernails. That is, to paint his fingernails red."

"The unusual part of it all as far as I'm concerned," Hank Thorn said, "is that I'm dead sure I wrote something like this, once."

"You write?" Asey looked with new interest on this tall young fellow with the keen grey eyes and long nose. On the whole he had liked most of the writers he had met. Some of them were queer fish, but they never seemed to require as many explanations as other people.

"Well, I think I write, but it's not a universally accepted fact. Really, I'm positive I wrote something of this sort, but I can't for the life of me remember how it turned out."

"It was a woman," Vail said, "pretending to be a man. She used modelling clay to create an impression of size and strength in her fingers, but she forgot the red painted nails."

Hank crossed the room and shook the professor's hand warmly.

"My public!" he said. "Nell, d'you hear that? Isn't that superb? I've met someone literate who reads what I write! It's a red letter day! It's—"

"It's going to be a red letter night if we don't do something about this idiotic situation," Mrs. Westcott returned. "It's going to be the night that poor Nelly Westcott, Thorn that was, caught that nasty pneumonia. Mr. Mayo, can't you do something about all this?"

"Some scared servant watched us come in," Asey said, "an' was too panicky to answer when we called out, an' now she— or he's—locked us in while the chance was there. Can't hardly blame a body for gettin' scared at us. We ain't exactly a high class lookin' crew."

He surveyed the group with amusement. They were a scraggly appearing lot. Mrs. Westcott's white hair was plastered in strings to her face and neck, giving her a half drowned look. The lace skirt of her black evening dress sogged in folds to the floor. Every few seconds she pulled at them to let the water run away from her stockinged feet. Her pumps, soaked to a pulp, made little puddles under the dressing table before which she sat. Gerty's practical tweed coat had protected her to some extent, but her feet were dripping, too. Hank

Thorn was soaked to the waist. Rivulets of water trickled from the professor's plus fours and plaid mackinaw.

"You, yourself," Mrs. Westcott informed Asey, "are no one to make any comments. Aren't you just a wee bit tropical under that overcoat, with all your white linen? And that cap—when did you take up with the New Haven? No overshoes, either. In fact, you're loads worse than I am, and that's a lot."

Asey admitted it. "I wish old door-locker had tossed in some dry things. Awful thoughtless critter."

The professor pointed to the small door beside him.

"What's this?"

"Shower and bath," Mrs. Westcott said. "It doesn't lead any—"

"You're wettest," Vail said. "You're first."

"I—what?"

"Why, really," Vail looked at her, "I do think that you are the wettest. Of course, Mr. Mayo is really wetter than you, but ladies are first."

"What on earth," Mrs. Westcott demanded, "do you mean? That—"

"We are wet, and we are cold," Vail said. "And there is a shower bath, and I can hear a steam radiator sizzling. It seems foolish not to take advantage of them."

"But—"

"Come along, Mrs. Westcott," Gerty took her arm. "I'll help you, and maybe you'll dry out some."

Asey eyed the professor with a certain amount of respect. There was one thing you had to admit about these literal-minded, direct-thinking fellows. They went to the point.

"Ernest," Hank said, "how come you're not at your cousin

Sue's party? The professor," he explained for Asey's benefit, "is living in a cabin on the Vail estate. It's his sabbatical year. He's writing a book—what's it on, now, Vail? I can't ever remember."

"I'm tracing the history of the vowels, with special reference to the eleventh century vowel shift," the professor supplied the information in an offhand manner. "Very interesting. I do wish I'd taken my chance to step into the library and get that book. It's just a matter I want to clear up in my own mind. Nothing to do with my work."

"What was the proverb?" Asey asked. "I've picked up a few on the Cape, and round about. Maybe I could help."

"Ungodly oysters." Professor Vail put on a pair of nose glasses and looked at Asey with mild academic triumph gleaming in his eyes. "I doubt if you—"

"You can't stump an old Wellfleet oyster man," Asey told him. "Thoreau couldn't."

"Then what—"

"Oysters is ungodly," Asey said, "b'cause they're eaten without grace. They're uncharitable b'cause they leave nothin' b'hind but shells. They're unprofitable, b'cause they got to swim in wine."

The professor took off his glasses and put them back in his pocket.

"He's got you," Hank said. "Own up, prof!"

"A very unusual piece of information for an ordinary—I mean, for an average—that is, for—really, Mr. Mayo, it is indeed unusual to find a—"

"Let it go at that," Hank patted the professor on the back, "before you get in any deeper, Ernest. Nelly, you're not dried out already?"

"Mostly, my dear. The things that matter, anyway. That radiator is crackling hot, and there are towels galore. Gerty's going to fix my hair. You're next, Mr. Mayo—"

One by one, the men dried themselves out.

"Now," Mrs. Westcott said, "now what? Do we just sit and—what's that object on the floor?"

"Nutmeg," Asey told her. "Must have come from my pocket—"

"Nutmeg? D'you carry nutmegs around, like horse chestnuts for rheumatism, or something?"

"Well," Asey said, "I only left Jamaica yesterday around noon—say, what's the time?" he changed the subject not so much to divert their exclamations of amazement at his journey as to get a few seconds of unadvertised silence while they all consulted time pieces. It seemed to him that he heard footsteps again outside the door.

"Two o'clock," Hank said. "D'you suppose we've got to spend the night in this place?"

"Harper," said the professor suddenly, distaste vibrating in his voice. "Harper!"

Mrs. Westcott nodded. "I thought of that. It's just the sort of thing he'd think terribly funny, if he were a bit tight, or tighter than usual. But he should be at Sue's. He and Pete and Char all intended to go."

Thinking of that hand with the red fingernails, Gerty opened her mouth to contradict, but she changed her mind. This was no place to uphold Harper; the professor loathed him, Mrs. Westcott wrinkled up her nose when she mentioned his name. It was better not to say a thing.

Asey watched her in the mirror as he walked over to the entry door.

"Let's try it, for fun," he said.

The door opened easily.

"It's Harper, all right," Mrs. Westcott said grimly. "For once in my life, I am not going to restrain myself. I am going to tell that fellow exactly what I think of him. Come on, all of you. Let's present him with a few home thrusts!"

As they trooped out into the hall way, the front door opened, and Harper Dixon entered, tossing a pair of snowshoes down on the carpet.

For a full minute he stared at the group without speaking, and Asey took advantage of the silence to look the fellow over.

His face was wet and red with cold, and his heavy eyebrows were crusted with snow. His high boots were snow covered, too, and so was his dark blue ski suit and cap. Apparently it had not been Harper who had done the door locking job. No red paint on his fingernails, either, Asey noticed as Harper pulled off a pair of wet mittens. He didn't look drunk, or even as though he had been drinking. In fact, he seemed more than slightly amused.

"Hullo, Nell. Hi, Gerty. Hi, Thorn. And my old pal of the winsome intellect, Professor Vail! How's the old vowel shift these days? And—as I live and breathe, if it isn't the homespun sleuth in person. Look, it's next week. My birthday, that is. I'm thirty on the first of March. You're a bit early with your—"

"We've all been marooned," Thorn interrupted, "and Asey rescued us—"

"Why, the old rescuer!" Harper said. "I suppose, Mayo, you always wear white linen during blizzards? Protective coloring, no doubt. Or is it the spirit of Mark Twain? Anyway, if you've come about that bet, I'm awfully sorry."

The others were as flabbergasted as Asey by Harper's breezy geniality.

"I mean it," Harper went on. "I'm truly sorry about that bet. I was drunk, and I apologize. I intended to hang off until the last moment, and then take my licking. I've got a letter all written to the Mighty Porter."

"Then that order," Asey said, "was a figure of speech, as you might say?"

Harper hesitated. "Well, yes. I thought Porter understood. I never expected he'd drag you from the tropics to—I say, you all look terribly washed out. What happened?"

"Harper," Mrs. Westcott's voice sounded uncertain, as though she couldn't make up her mind whether or not he deserved the talking to she intended to administer, "what's the meaning of all this? Where've you been the last few hours? Haven't you been in the house?"

"No, mam. I've been out in the greenhouse since eleven o'clock. Something's gone wrong with the heater. Before then I was at Sue's—"

"Then what," Mrs. Westcott said, "is behind all this senseless horseplay and stupid practical joking that's been going on? Who's been turning out the lights and locking us in and all?"

"What—what d'you mean?" Harper demanded. "The servants are at the movies, but Char—where's Char?"

"She's not here. And the front door was open, and men's hands with red fingernails—"

"Wait," Harper said. "Let me get this straight. Mayo, what's the story?"

"We got m'rooned," Asey said, "an' come in when we found your front door open. We yelled, but no one come, an' when we ruthlessly entered your powder room to forage for dry duds, someone with red nails slammed the door on us, after playin' tag with the lights. Just now we found the door unlocked again, an' come out—"

"But Char's here!" Harper said. "She—haven't you seen her? She decided the storm was too much for the car, so she stayed home. Pete and I went to Sue's on snowshoes. Haven't you seen Char?"

"No," Mrs. Westcott said, "we haven't seen anyone or anything but that terrible hand—"

"Come upstairs," Harper said. "I'll wake her and get you people some clothes. She's probably asleep. Sleeps like two logs. Sat in the front row and snored right through Wagner last season. Come on, Nell."

Thorn nudged Asey as they followed the rest up the curving staircase.

"This amiability of Dixon's," he whispered, "has got Nell on the ropes. I think it's your influence. I never saw him like this before, in all the years I've known him. He was the fellow who lost the nineteen-thirty game, remember?"

Asey grinned. "I can give you pointers on it," he said.

"Well, this is a miracle, that's all I've got to say," Thorn told him.

On the second floor landing, Harper stopped.

"Nell, come with me and—my God, her door's open and the lights are on—Char! Aunt Char!"

Asey watched Harper's face as he strode to the doorway. Mrs. Westcott and Vail could sniff all they wanted to, but the fellow's surprise was genuine enough. You couldn't just assume any expression like that.

Harper walked into the room, stopped short, and then called Asey.

"Come here, will you, Mayo?"

He pointed to the door of the bath on the left of the room.

"I—I—I don't—something's wrong. She's in there, seated as though she were washing her hair. She—"

The two of them hurried across the soft green carpet and then paused.

"Char!" Harper said. "Aunt Char!"

Mrs. Babb, fully dressed, with a towel around her shoulders, sat in a straight backed chair, her head forward over the wash bowl, her startlingly red hair almost totally immersed in soapy water.

"She—her face is in the water," Harper said. "She—Mayo, is she dead?"

" 'Fraid so. I—I'm sorry, Dixon. See all them bottles an' soaps an' things. She was shampooin'—"

"Oh!" Gerty appeared beside them. "Oh, she—oh, that's awful, that's—Harper, it must have been another heart attack like the one she had last Saturday in the shop. When I called you and Dr. Stern. It—"

"I'll go over to Vails' on my snowshoes and get Pete," Harper said. "Mayo, will you wait here until I get back? I shan't be long."

Asey watched Harper closely. The boy was stunned.

There wasn't any acting about his grief. There was even something leaden about his walk. Bill Porter and almost everyone else might call him an unfeeling, irresponsible brute, but no one could prove it by Harper's actions in the last ten minutes.

Mrs. Westcott, the professor and Hank Thorn came in, looked at the scene for a moment and then went back into the hall. After a few minutes, Asey and Gerty followed. Mingled with the grief on her face, Asey noticed, was an odd expression that he couldn't quite place. It was almost absent minded.

"How awful!" Nell Westcott said. "There we were downstairs—and all this up here! When d'you think it happened, Asey?"

"Some hours ago, I think."

"The—the poor dear! She has a bad heart, you know. All her family have. And she didn't take the care of herself that she should. Three weeks ago at the club concert she had an attack. She was such a human dynamo. That day she'd done all the decorations, and supervised the food, and had a dinner party for twenty odd, here. She'd just come back from a week's shopping trip in New York, too, and she'd gone to eight theaters in that one week besides. Isn't—I mean, wasn't she active, Gerty?"

"Yeah," Gerty said. "She was."

Mrs. Westcott looked at her curiously, and Gerty flushed.

"I'm sorry, that didn't sound right, did it? I—I—well, I can't hardly explain. You see she wasn't just one of my best customers. I liked her a lot besides. She was good to me, and she was good fun, too. I got a lot to thank her for, and now I can't." Gerty pulled a package of cigarettes from her pocket, and lighted one. "I guess I was just thinking of that, and all, and not paying much attention to what you were saying. Here—hey, Asey! You better get the prof a glass of water, or pat him on the back, or something. Look at the guy, will you?"

Asey whistled softly. The professor's cheeks, originally whipped to a fiery red by the storm and then made even redder from his shower—those cheeks were now the color of the snow from Harper's boots, melting on the green carpet. It was an odd gray-green hue, like sea sickness, Asey thought.

"Chill?" he asked sympathetically. "Hank, pop down and see if you can find something to lay it—"

"It is not a chill." Vail spoke with difficulty. "It is nothing at all, nothing at all, I assure you. Nothing. Dear me, no. Really."

"Nonsense," Nell Westcott said. "Go on, Hank. Here, I'll come with you and Ernest. You too, Gerty. We'll break into the cellar. I'm sure the Dixons won't mind."

"That's right," Asey said. "Go with 'em, p'fessor. Do you good. This storm, an' one thing an' another is prob'ly more d'mandin' than you figger. Takes more out of you than the—what was it? Vowel split?"

"Shift," the professor corrected him. "If you mean my—"

"Okay," Asey said. "Shift it is. Ain't you goin' with'em, Gerty?"

She shook her head. "I think I'll just sort of sit here in the hall with you. I'd like some coffee, but that can wait."

In the silence that followed the departure of the others, Asey paced in a small circle at the end of the landing, and Gerty curled up on the window seat.

In his own mind, Asey wondered about the reason for the open front door, and the footsteps, and the man's red nailed hand that had pulled to the power room door, and locked them in, and all the rest.

And Harper, now. He couldn't understand why Harper should call off that bet and expose himself so casually to the loss of so many thousand dollars. No one threw sums like that around as a gesture these days, even folks as rich as the Dixons were supposed to be. Why had Harper changed his mind, and why had he changed his manner? Why was he suddenly so amiable? He had been, Asey remembered, a fine athlete, but on the argumentative side. He was more unpopular with officials than among his own team mates. At the Hybrid Club he was endured. Even that old fuddy-duddy Root had called him The Blight. Yet tonight he had been almost pleasant, so much so that Thorn had commented on it.

"What come over Harper?" he asked Gerty.

"I told you," she said, "he wasn't as bad as some people thought. I guess it boils down, Asey, to your taking him as he is, or taking him the way people say he is."

There was something in her tone that made Asey feel rebuked. Still, Bill Porter's judgment on people was usually reliable, and Bill's opinion of Harper Dixon was unprintable. On the other hand, Asey admitted to himself, his own opinion and Bill's didn't always coincide on people they both knew.

"Huh." Asey turned and paced in the opposite direction. In the middle of his circle, he stopped, went into the bedroom and looked at the still figure once again. Rather to his surprise, Gerty followed him.

"Asey."

"Uh-huh." Things were finally beginning to click in his mind.

"Asey, isn't someone," Gerty's voice wasn't steady, "going to be awful sorry we come?"

"What's that?" Hank Thorn came quietly up behind them. "What's that?"

"I think," Gerty repeated, "someone is going to be awful sorry we come here tonight."

"What d'you mean? Look, you can't—no. Of course you don't mean that. It's absurd."

"Bunch of monkey wrenches," Asey said, speaking apparently to himself, "that's what we was!"

Mrs. Westcott and the professor joined them and overheard Asey's statement.

"Your faces!" Mrs. Westcott said slowly. "You—what awful looks you all have on your faces! I—what's the matter?"

"Er—well, you see," the professor began, "this—that is, it wasn't heart trouble. That's it, isn't it, Mr. Mayo?"

"But that's perfectly foolish!" Mrs. Westcott said. "Of course it was her heart, Ernest! Everyone knows she had a bad heart. We—why, everyone knows! You're mistaken, Ernest. It was her heart."

"But I'm right," Vail said simply. "She was murdered, wasn't she, Mr. Mayo?"

"I'm sort of inclined to b'lieve," Asey said, "that maybe p'raps you're pos'bly speakin' the truth."

4

"MAYBE," Nell Westcott said stubbornly. "Maybe. But I continue to say what I said last night. Charlotte Babb had heart trouble, and she died of heart trouble. Why, even to think anything else is diabolical!"

"But Nell," Hank said, "diabolical things do happen, you know. They—"

"They do in your stories," Nell retorted. "Only this isn't something you're writing! This is life! I think it's perfectly horrid of all of you."

It was the following afternoon, and the five who had been marooned in the Dixon house sat before the log fire in the Westcott pine panelled living room.

"Horrid," Nell repeated. "Perfectly horrid!"

"We know how you feel, Nell," Hank said. "We feel that

way ourselves. It's a hideous thing to contemplate. But it happened, don't you see?"

"She had heart trouble, and she died of heart trouble—"

"She had heart trouble." Hank's patience was wearing thin. "That's just it, don't you see? Someone knew it, and took it for granted that people would think her death at any time was simply due to her heart trouble. They took advantage of the fact and built the whole scene up to it. They'd have got away with it, too, if we hadn't been keyed up and noticing more than usual, after that hand and all. Matter of fact, I think they'd have got away with it if Asey and Gerty hadn't been there. I might have wondered, but I wouldn't have said anything. Like you, I'd have thought it was heart trouble."

"I don't see what the scene has to do with it," Nell remarked. "When a person has heart trouble, and dies, they have it and die. They can't exactly choose the place! Look at your Uncle Henry Cabot! She—"

"Uncle Henry—she? Oh, come, Nell, what do you mean? Uncle Henry, she! Uncle Henry," Hank said, "was a very masculine man. I resent that. So would he."

"This is no time to joke," his sister reproved him. "I was going to say, Uncle Henry died in an elevator on his way to the poultry show to see about Buff Orpingtons. But no one called that murder! As for Char, she came from a family that all died of heart trouble. It was unfortunate that she had to die while shampooing her hair, but I can't see why you have to say it's murder. No more than Uncle Henry in the elevator!"

"White Faverolle," Hank said, "not Buff Orpington. It was Cousin John Henry who liked Buff Orpingtons. Uncle Henry never had one—"

"He was going to that poultry show," Nell said, "to see about Buff Orpingtons. I guess I know! White Faverolles nothing! He—"

"Look," Gerty interrupted the incipient row, "look. About Mrs. Babb. I knew as soon as I got over the shock of seeing her. She never used soap shampoo in the winter for fear of catching cold. She always used a dry cleaner sort, always, all winter, until it got warm. Always! And you certainly can't call last night warm!"

"No, but—"

"And there was that soap shampoo out, and the water all soapy. And her nails—"

"Exactly," Hank said. "All the polish and oil and everything, all out. She'd just done her nails. And Gerty says, and even I know—"

"You wouldn't shampoo your hair last," Gerty said. "You'd do it first, and your nails later. Now, Mrs. Westcott, don't your nails get done after your shampoo, if you're doing both yourself?"

"I was fond of Charlotte Babb," Nell said. "I've known her all my life. I know that she rarely if ever followed logical methods in anything. I can think of her shampooing her hair after doing her nails just as easily as before. And if she made up her mind to use a soap shampoo, instead of the other, she would have."

"Well," Gerty said, "we all noticed the nails. And Asey caught on to things we missed. No spray out, no tumbler, or dipper, or anything to rinse with. No towels laid out. Just that little one over her shoulders, and that was the wrong kind. A face towel. Nothing absorbent. And Asey caught on about her dress. Would you of washed your hair in that dress? You can say all you want to about her being different, but she wasn't that different."

"Charlotte Babb—"

"Look," Gerty said, "that was a brand new dress she bought in New York. She told me all about it. She was saving it for Sue Vail's dinner, she said. She was proud as anything of that dress. It was a real Chanel."

"Ah, well," Ernest Vail felt someone should do some oil pouring, *"quot homines, tot sententiae."*

Gerty stared at him.

"He means," Asey told her, "everyone in Christendom's got a thousand opinions on the same thing, roughly speakin'. The Wellfleet Academy Latin teacher," he added, "boarded to our house winters. Cram full of tidbits like that, he was. Well, after all, we ain't really sure yet. It's just a lot of figgerin'."

He stifled a yawn. They had sat up the rest of the previous night at the Dixon house until the courageous milkman who arrived in a pung at six o'clock had carted them with difficulty to the Westcott place. The professor had wanted to go to his cabin, but the milkman refused even to try to take him there. He had already attempted to deliver his milk at the Vails', and found the roads completely blocked. Gerty had come along, because the roads back to Monkton were impassable.

Asey couldn't hold the next yawn in. Mrs. Westcott's beds were soft enough, but he'd sort of got out of the habit of sleeping in the last couple of days.

"I'm glad it's Sunday." Gerty hated the long brooding silences that fell and hung like clouds over everyone the instant the conversation stopped for two seconds. "I'd hate to lose any business. And I sure hope I get back by tomorrow. Miss Enderby has had the Monday nine o'clock for six years. Monday's always a dull day, so I give her half prices."

"I wish—" Professor Vail began and then stopped.

What he wished was true enough, but it occurred to him it might not be a very tactful remark. Ordinarily he didn't bother to cloak his words in any mantle of tact. It seemed such a stupid waste of time, bothering to say what you meant in such a way that it still conveyed your meaning, but didn't exactly sound as though it did. And it was particularly important at this point for him to guard his tongue.

Just the same, he would have preferred to have remained at the Dixons'. Not that the library here wasn't large, or comfortable, but it consisted almost entirely of fiction. The discovery that so many romantic love stories had been written in the past twenty-five years came as a distinct shock. Why, there wasn't even a standard encyclopaedia, or a dictionary!

A harassed looking maid fairly leapt into the room.

"Well, Ra—I mean, Rochelle?" Nell Westcott always stumbled over that. The girl had been just plain Rachel until the last month, when she'd embraced numerology from a magazine article. Some pulpy magazine Hank wrote for.

"Well?" she repeated. "If it's that tooth aching again, I'm sorry, but you'll just have to put more of that stuff on it. As soon as the road shows any signs of being passable, Mr. Thorn will drive you to—"

"It's the Dixons, Mrs. Westcott."

"What's the matter with the Dixons? Did they phone? Is the phone working again?"

"Well, the Dixon boys, they're fighting on the front door step, Mrs. Westcott. I opened the door, and they started fighting over the threshold, so when I got the chance, I just shut them out again."

"Quite right," Nell said. "Harper broke the grandfather's clock while you were away, did I tell you, Hank? He paid the repair bill, of course, but I'm not going to have it happen again. Let me know when they're through, Rach—, I mean, Rochelle."

Asey inquired drily if this were their regular method of approach.

"It's not in the least unusual," Hank told him. "It means either that Harper is drunk, and decided to come and call on us, and Pete's trying to keep him out, or else that Pete came to call and Harper is drunk and insisted on tagging along. If you see what I mean. I do feel for Pete. He has his hands full most of the time, and he takes it a lot more philosophically than I should."

"Sometimes," Nell said, "I think he's altogether too philosophical about it. I do feel it's such a pity Pete couldn't have been the athletic one, for everything would be so much simpler then."

They could plainly hear the sounds of the fight, now. Thuds and bangs and a lurid flow of language.

"That's Harper, outdoing himself," Hank said. "Nell, hadn't I better go? It seems as though Pete needed help. And I always learn such a lot listening to Harper. My golf talk is good, but Harper gets right back to the primordial slime and works up."

"Pure stable," Nell said. "Horrid. Yes, I suppose you should go, Hank, but it embarrasses Pete so, and Harper does get so mad if anyone interferes. Asey, you had a miraculous effect on Harper last night. Why don't you go see what you can do?"

Asey grinned and departed.

In the hallway he dismissed Rochelle and the other maid who were staring out the window with their noses pressed against the glass.

"I'll cope with'em," he said. "Run along. This ain't hardly your line of work."

He threw open the door and surveyed the scene before him.

On the top step the two Dixons were going at each other noisily and viciously. Pete's nose was bloody, one eye was closing, and he was using a snowshoe alternately to beleaguer Harper, and to defend himself from the shower of blows coming at him. Harper might be drunk, Asey thought, but there was nothing wrong with his sense of timing.

Watching his chance, he grabbed Harper by the collar and held him off long enough to yank Pete inside and into the hall.

"Get in," he said, "quick!"

In a second Harper was after him, but Asey put the flat of his palm against Harper's chest, and pushed.

Harper reeled backwards into a snow drift, and came up like a rubber ball.

"Stay there an' keep on sputterin'," Asey said. "Next time I'll hurt."

"Stay here like hell! I'll—"

"Listen," Asey said. "Bill Porter can lick you, an' I can lick Bill with one hand tied b'hind me an' the other in a sling. I didn't learn my fightin' on a nice soft mat in some gym. I learnt it in a series of fo'castles. Want to get hurt?"

"I don't fight old men—"

"Cherish that kindly thought," Asey advised, "until you're wanted. You—"

Harper started up the steps, and Asey waited for him, hands in his pockets.

"C'mon, start somethin'. Don't let the grey hairs bother you."

"I'll smash you—" Harper lunged forward.

A split second later, with a cry of anguish, he thudded back into the drift.

"Oh, boy!" Pete said. "What happened then? If I could do that just once—just once! I'd feel my life had been a complete success."

"He'll come to pretty soon," Asey shut the front door and bolted it. "Only maybe he won't feel so awful good at first. Nasty comb'nation, knee an' fist. Now, what's this all about?"

"If I could get cleaned up," Pete said, "I'll tell you. It was you I came to see. If I can ever see anything again, out of this eye—"

Later, with a piece of steak over his eye, and splotches of court plaster on his face, Pete leaned back in one of the library easy chairs and sighed.

"Sometimes," he said, "I wish—you know, Asey,—I mean, Mr. Mayo—"

"Make it Asey. I ain't used to bein' mistered."

"Well," Pete tried to grin, "sometimes I wish those ads worked. You know. 'Let Us Make a Man of You. Are You a Weakling?' Know what I mean? I wish they worked. I knew they were fakes before I was ten."

"You're no weaklin'," Asey surveyed Pete professionally. " 'Bout five-eight an' a hundred an' forty, ain't you?"

Pete sighed again.

"I'm five-six and a half, and one-thirty-eight. But Harper is six-four, Asey, and weighs two-thirty. He doesn't look that heavy. It's the way he's built. And more than that, it's coordination. He—well, let's not go into that. Asey, Dr. Stern came over, and he says what we thought is so. She was murdered.

There's water in her lungs. She didn't just die and slump forward. Someone held her head in the water."

"Can you think of anyone you might suspect of doin' it? Anyone with any sort of motive?"

Pete shook his head. "That's just it. Char was such a swell! I liked Aunt Gene, but it was Char who brought us up, really. She was active, and she—well, she was eccentric, but she was just different enough, and funny enough about the differences, so that everyone liked her. She got on well with Harper, and I'll say for him he was decent to her and Aunt Gene."

"Did the doctor say when it might have happened?"

"Around eight, he thinks. She was well enough when we left. Both of us went up and spoke with her. That was around seven-thirty."

"Did you shut the door behind you?"

"Banged it," Pete said. "I banged it myself. I can't understand how in the world it was unlatched when all of you people came. And all this business about men's hands, and lights snapping off. Someone must have been in the house, but who? And why? That was hours after eight. You came around ten-thirty, I think Hank said."

"Nearer eleven, or after," Asey corrected him.

"About the time Harper got to the greenhouse," Pete said thoughtfully. "He left Sue's around ten, after a slight squabble. Asey, I don't know how to go about asking you, but will you take this business on, and name your own figure? I know," he added hastily, "how you've always refused to go off the Cape to solve things, but—honestly, I don't know which way to turn—"

He fumbled for a cigarette, lighted it, and went on.

"Dr. Stern is over there now, waiting for the local men to come with the plough, if that ever gets this far. We phoned 'em long ago. Stern used snowshoes, and I think they might have tried 'em, too. Somehow neither Stern nor I've got much faith in their abilities."

"The state police," Asey began hesitantly, "are—"

"Fine men and all, but damn it, it just wouldn't seem right to leave it to them, don't you see? I couldn't stand it, not taking any action on my own hook! It's—well, disrespectful is the only word I can think of! It's as though I didn't care! And I do! Thank God, I was—Harper and I were together from the time we left the house until ten. Publicity will hit us, of course, it's bound to. But we're innocent and we've got alibis, and witnesses, and all the rest. If only we could get you to—"

"To d'sperse the pub'licity?" Asey inquired. "Sure, I know what you mean. But I'm just ole home week to the r'porters. Why, if I said a millionth of the smart things they say I say, I'd be coinin' money on the radio. Maybe even in Congress. Jokin' aside, Pete, I know how you feel, an' I see your side, but I don't think I'm up to tacklin'—what's that?"

There was a hideous crash out in the back of the house, followed by an assortment of screams and feminine shrieks.

"It's Harper," Pete said with resignation. "Anything that sounds like that is Harper. You'd best lock the door."

Grinning, Asey got up and turned the key.

"What's eatin' him, anyhows?"

"You mean, in general, or right now?"

"Both," Asey said.

"Generally, I don't know. Aunt Gene used to call it natural perversity. She said it was a family trait."

"How do you cope with it?"

"I try not to take it seriously," Pete said. "When it gets too annoying, I ignore it. That's how Harper always made Bill Porter mad to the boiling-over point. He leads Bill on till Bill can't ignore it."

"Ignorin'," Asey said, "ain't one of Bill's strong points. But what's Harper got against me t'day? Last night, him an' me was pals. Got along like beans an' brownbread."

"That," Pete answered bitterly, "was last night. I told him I was going to ask your help, and he flew off the handle. Went berserk."

"Did, huh? Say, what was all this business of the—my, my!"

"Let me in!" Harper, out in the hall, banged furiously on the library door.

"What about that bet he made with Bill?" Asey paid no attention to the noise. "That grocery order business. What about that?"

Pete shrugged. "If you could only find out about that list! You know, before all this happened to poor Char, when I first saw you last night—I mean, before we knew she'd been killed, I intended to ask you to find out about it, anyway. The grocery business."

"Find out anyway? What d'you mean?"

"The whole business," Pete had to raise his voice to make himself heard above Harper's bellows, "is a blank to me! I don't know what he meant, or what he intended, or anything!"

Asey stared at him. "But he wouldn't of been so crazy as to bet all that for nothin', would he?"

"I don't know," Pete said. "I hoped Bill would hold him to it, and ask you here, and teach Harper a lesson he damn well needs. And—"

"But Harper told me last night he was goin' to give up, an' pay Bill," Asey said. "What d'you make of that?"

Pete drew a long breath. "I don't know. I—oh, I can't say anything one way or another without seeming—I—" he stubbed out his cigarette and lighted another. "As a matter of fact, when Harper said you were here, when he got me at Sue's, I decided I'd ask you if you wouldn't get to the bottom of the thing, if there was a bottom. No matter what happened to the bet. I'd like to know for my own information just what he meant by Aunt Gene's—well, the list. And your solving it. I've racked my brains. I don't know what it's all about."

"He told me last night it was a figure of speech," Asey observed. "Like saying I couldn't solve a laundry list, or somethin' of the kind, I gathered. Fifty thousand's sort of a high price to pay for any figure of speech, though. Too high for a lot of whimsey."

"That's just it!" Pete had to yell again to make himself heard. "Will you—"

"Wait up," Asey said, "he's goin' to smash in that door if I don't let him in. Seems to me Thorn an' Vail might stir their stumps an' stop this—"

He crossed over to the door and jerked it open suddenly, but Harper didn't fall in head first, as Asey had rather hoped he might.

For a second he stood there, glaring. Behind him were Thorn and the professor, Gerty and Mrs. Westcott, and all the maids. Even a chauffeur, Asey noticed.

"Mayo," Harper said, "let me get this straight. You're not going to mess yourself into this business of Aunt Char, see? No bloody goddam publicity with your filthy Porter sixteens, see? I don't care a damn what my worthy brother's got to say.

You're not going to set foot inside my house. If there's anything to be solved, the proper officials will solve it. No field day for you!"

"That," Asey said, "is a clear an' I should say compellin'ly c'mplete statement. Anythin' else?"

"Just this." Harper was breathing hard. "My aunt has been murdered. It is not fitting that her unfortunate death should be put to the advantage of the Porter factory. It's a beautiful opportunity, and might sell Bill Porter a lot of cars, but you do no homespun sleuthing on sixteen cylinders in this particular case. And as your dear friend and employer Mr. Porter once asked me, does that percolate?"

"I gather," none of those present knew Asey well enough to grasp the implications of that soft purr, but Hank Thorn and Gerty looked as though they guessed, "you think my d'tectin' is hooked up with Porter cars an' sales?"

"Of course it is," Harper said contemptuously. "You can't deny it. Bill Porter couldn't. He as good as said that he and Betsey fed your lines to you."

Asey swung around on his heel and turned his back on Harper.

"Pete," he said, "you have hired what the papers are pleased to call a d'tective. You may have to hire me bodyguards, too, from the looks of—"

"Asey, that's—"

"Hold up," Asey said. "I don't often get mad, but I'm sort of riled, now. I come here intendin' to solve that gro'cry order in time to save Bill fifty thousand dollars. I'll do it in time, an' for good measure, I'll solve this case for you, too, unless the p'lice beat me to it. An'," he continued in the same soft purring voice, "we'll leave Porters out of it. I'll use a hoss an' buggy, if you like. An'—don't butt in yet. If I solve things by Thursday, all well an' good. If not, I'll pay Bill's bet, an' the other bets, to Harper. Got that, Harper?"

Harper swung on his heel and left abruptly without saying a word. Gerty followed him.

Asey grinned suddenly. "What was that crash, anyway?"

"Harper," Nell said succinctly. "Harper, entering through a closed French door. Asey, will you stay here till Thursday? And anything Hank or I can do, let us know."

"You can't do this, Asey," Pete said unhappily. "He goaded you into it. If you take this on, I'll pay—"

"Hank," Asey said, "dig .ne up a vehicle, will you? An', if you all don't mind, I'd sort of like to set an' brood some. Thanks."

Alone in the library, he sat down in an easy chair, filled one of Thorn's pipes and lighted it.

"Dum fool!" he said. "You dum fool, you!"

He didn't mind losing the money—and there wasn't any doubt in his mind that the fifty thousand was as good as gone. It was a foolish gesture of his. He was foolish to lose his temper, foolish to think that he could solve this mess in a place he didn't know, among people he didn't know, and all the rest. On the Cape, he'd already have a batch of ideas about this. Here—why, he didn't even know what lay beyond the curve of the road outside. All of these folks were strangers. He didn't know them. There weren't any lifelong friends, or relations, to help him know them, to help him drag out the thousand and one things he ought to know. No chubby faced Dr. Cummings, with his pithy, helpful cracks.

And it was all his own fault for losing his temper. First time in years he'd ever been so mad. So mad that he banked on his own ability to pull himself out of a hole a mile wide that he'd gone and dug himself into.

The professor edged into the room.

"Sorry," he apologized, "to bother you, but I left my glasses here. My reading glasses. Er—he hurt her badly, you know. I resent it very much."

"What?" Asey demanded. "Who hurt who, and who do you r'sent?"

"Harper Dixon," Vail said. "Brute. The utter brute! A large welt on her cheek, where he struck her!"

"You mean he hit Gerty?"

The professor nodded. "She hurried up to her room. She wasn't crying, but she probably is now. I—it is none of my business, Asey, but I do think that you should look very closely into the matter of Harper Dixon and his desire to have you ignore this case."

"I intend to," Asey said. "Say, when you got so sort of clammy an' jittery last night, after we found Mrs. Babb, did you guess she'd been killed?"

"Well, yes and no." Vail was choosing his words with care. "No, because it seemed, as Mrs. Westcott said, that if she had heart trouble, she died of heart trouble. Yes, because—well, you were there. It was the sort of thing that might have happened in one of Mr. Thorn's stories, if you see what I mean."

"For all that yes an' noin'," Asey remarked, "you sure took on somethin' awful, all of a sudden. You," Asey hesitated and then, startled by the look on Vail's face, shot wildly into the dark. He was going to have to take a lot of wild shots if he expected even to get to first base in this business. "Say, p'fessor, you wasn't there b'fore, was you? B'fore we picked you up?"

"Why—er—but she was alive, really! She was alive when I saw her at nine! She was. I assure you. Really, she was alive!"

5

WITH infinite care, Asey knocked out his pipe, returned it to the rack, and settled himself back in his chair.

"Well," Vail watched Asey's deliberate movements and wrongly interpreted them as concluding the conversation, "well, here they are. My reading glasses, I mean. I'm sorry to have bothered you. I can quite understand how you might desire to consider in solitude the various items you must have in your mind. I—"

"Professor," Asey said in admiration, "if it's an act, it's a wonder. If it ain't, you're a wonder yourself."

"I fear I don't understand—"

"Set," Asey told him gently. "Set, an' make yourself com-f'table, an' b'gin at the b'ginnin', an' go right through this business of what you done last night b'fore we picked you out of the bosom of that storm."

"Why, certainly." Obediently Vail sat down and folded his hands in his lap. "I'd be glad to tell you, in one sense. It has been making me uncomfortable, although I cannot exactly see why it should. Withholding the information, I mean. On the other hand, I was not, strictly speaking, withholding information, since until now no one requested it. At the same time, I felt I should say something about my previous visit. But—"

"But on t'other hand," Asey said, "you didn't want to get mixed up in this. Is that it?"

"Exactly. In a—er—in an eggshell."

"Make it a great auk," Asey said, "an' I might agree. First, why'd you go, why'd you leave, why'd you go back?"

"I told you. I went for that book."

"But you knew, didn't you, that your cousin Sue Vail was givin' a dinner? Didn't you know Mrs. Babb an' the Dixons would be there?"

"I didn't think of that until later," Ernest said. "I—I just went. The door was unlatched, and I opened it as you did later—"

"Didn't think it was funny, findin' the door open?"

"I didn't consider the matter. I rarely lock doors myself," he explained, "because it's such a nuisance, remembering keys. After I got inside the hall, it occurred to me I ought to summon someone, so I pulled the bell cord, but no one came. There was a light on upstairs, so I started up—"

"But the li'bry's downstairs, ain't it?"

"Yes, but it was dark. There was a light shining into the hall from Mrs. Babb's room, so I went to the doorway and knocked. Then I looked in and saw that she was shampooing her hair, so of course I quickly went out of the room and down the stairs again."

"Why?"

"Why?" Vail looked reproachfully at Asey. "Why, you see—really, it would hardly be polite to interrupt a lady under the circumstances! It's—as though she were dressing!"

"And you're sure she was alive? You seen her move?"

The professor blinked behind his glasses.

"Now that you mention it, I really don't know if I just got that impression, or if I really saw her move. I didn't exactly linger, or stand and contemplate the scene. I—why, I simply assumed that she was alive. Why not? There was no reason to assume anything else. One hardly expects to find murdered women when one calls. I just—er—took in the situation, and left."

In his own mind, Asey had a flickering picture of the professor dashing like a scared rabbit away from the vision of Mrs. Babb apparently *en dishabille,* washing her hair.

"I see. So you just took it for granted she was alive, huh? Then what?"

"Well of course," Vail said lamely, "by then I felt reasonably certain that the servants were out, and that Mrs. Babb was alone in the house. I was sure that Pete at least would be at Suzanne's dinner, since he is her fiancé. Of Harper, I was not so sure."

"Why?"

"In the few months I have spent in Blight," Vail said, "I have learned that Harper Dixon, in addition to being one of the most unpleasant young men with whom I have ever come in contact, is also one of the most unpredictable. At all events, I had no desire to meet him under the circumstances."

"Don't get on with Harper, I take it?"

Vail didn't even bother to answer Asey's question. He brushed it aside like a troublesome fly.

"So," he said, "I left. I admit that I wanted to slip into the library to verify that proverb, but I decided not to. I left."

"Yup, you left," Asey agreed. "You was so dead bent on leavin' that when we found you, you was headed back in the same d'rection. Just what was the line of reasonin' there? Don't tell me you took to broodin' about them ungodly oysters again, Vail. I don't think I could swallow that oyster line again."

"You know," Ernest said, "if you'd said, swallow *them*—"

"It'd win a dollar in the worst pun contest," Asey finished up. "I get it. Why was you headin' back to the Dixons' place, willy, as you might say, nilly?"

"Why, you've already guessed. I decided that Mrs. Babb might be through her—er—ablutions, and so I was returning. That's it. In—"

"An eggshell. I know. P'fessor, tell me about yourself. Will you? Like your age, an' teachin' an' all."

"I'm forty," Ernest said. "At the beginning of life, as you might say. I was graduated when I was nineteen, but I had begun my work as assistant in the department the previous year. I have remained there ever since, giving instruction in the summer school as well—"

"Twenty-one solid years?" Asey sounded a little horrified. "Winter an' summer, both?"

"Except of course for sabbaticals, and a brief period during the war when I became a second lieutenant, in the Army. I was in charge of File Office 32-A-69. I—did you say something?"

Asey shook his head. "Just a cough, like. Go on."

"Well, I have every reason to believe," Ernest said with quiet pride, "that my work has met with some favor and that my position may be considered a reasonably permanent one."

"I guess," Asey said, "you have. Huh. Whyn't you tell us you'd been to the Dixons' earlier, an' all?"

"Many people," the professor told him, "seem to find a certain humorous aspect in my work and my preoccupation with it. I try very hard not to be classified as a—er—comic supplement variety of absent minded professor. I—er—"

"Didn't want to lay yourself open. I see. Well, thanks. That'll be all for now."

Asey felt somewhat defeated. You couldn't doubt the professor's honesty any more than you could deny his naïve simplicity.

"I feel, Asey," Ernest looked at him seriously over the rims of his glasses, "that your impression of me is quite possibly not entirely accurate. I am no cloistered scholar. By no means! I enjoy a number of outside interests. The chess club, for example. And I collect stamps. Twice a week I attend swimming classes at the pool. I belong to a group of rifle enthusiasts, and I am qualified as an expert rifleman."

Asey nodded with the proper amount of respect. He wasn't interested in rifle experts right now. What he needed more than anything else was a drowning expert.

"And," Vail continued his recital, "I have three life saving medals, for saving the life of three children who would have drowned without my aid. That is," he added, "one child on three separate occasions. Not of course the same child, but different children. That is—"

Asey looked at him thoughtfully.

"I get what you mean," he said. "Uh-huh. An' yet you got jittery last night b'cause you decided right plumb off the bat that Mrs. Babb had been murdered, an' you didn't want to get mixed up in the mess. That it?"

"Well, I didn't want to be accused of being her murderer," Vail said. "That's it, I think. In books, people in my position are always accused of the murder."

"If my friend Doc Cummings was here," Asey remarked, "this is where he'd haul off an' say he was speechless, in somethin' less than six hundred words."

"If he were speechless," Vail pointed out, "he would hardly —I mean, six hundred words is not being speechless. Far from it. I—"

"That's so, ain't it?" Asey tried to figure out for the twentieth time in as many seconds what was really going on behind the professor's mild blue eyes. It didn't seem possible that one man could be quite so humorless, or leave himself so wide open to misinterpretation.

"Yes, you see, Asey—"

"I see," Asey said. "Now, I wonder if you'd do me a favor an' ask Gerty to come here?"

He sighed to himself as the professor departed, and amended his former opinion. With a literal man like that you could do one of two things. You could say that he was the original honest man that the old duffer waved the lantern for, or the candle, or whatever it was. Or you could take the reverse side and call him a very smooth article. Either way, he more or less had you.

And now there was the problem of Gerty.

Perhaps it wasn't quite accurate, calling her a problem. She was more of a puzzle, in one way. Not that he didn't like Gerty. You couldn't help liking her and her easy running flow of words, the same sort of professional chatter that most barbers and dentists affected. But for all her chattering, she didn't let things slip if she didn't want them slipped. Gerty was nobody's fool. She was as keen as her name. And she was, he thought to himself, the ideal sort of person to provide him with the information he needed.

Asey smiled as he recalled an uncomfortable hour he had spent the previous autumn, waiting for Betsey Porter to come out of a beauty shop. The only bright spot in those sixty long minutes was overhearing the conversation of the four women who had passed through the booth against which the back of his chair rested. Four haircuts. And the way those women had talked to that girl was an eyeopener. They talked about everything from Haile Selassie and Greta Garbo to the noisy children next door, and what might best be summed up as delicately and entirely feminine problems. Betsey had laughed when he commented about it to her.

"Asey, I grant that you know a lot about mankind, but women are different. A woman will tell a manicurist six reasons why she should divorce her husband before the girl even has her nails shaped up! And as for a permanent—!"

Yes, Gerty was the ideal person for pumping purposes, but the question was, would she be pumped? She was obviously a loyal little soul, and there was obviously something going on between her and Harper. She wouldn't refuse to give information if Asey wanted it. He felt sure of that. She wasn't so dumb. But he wondered if she wouldn't be inclined to color her stories to Harper's advantage. Of course, Harper had just biffed her one, and that might change matters. But Asey wasn't so sure.

He could see the welt across the side of her face the instant she entered the room. She might have been crying, but if she had, she had also expertly removed all traces of her tears. The whites of her eyes were a little pinkish. But so were Asey's own. And Mrs. Westcott's, and Thorn's and the professor's. Might just be a lack of sleep.

"Wonder," Asey said, "if you'd be a one to help me, Gerty?"

"Sure I will, Asey. Only I don't think I can add very much. We was all there together, and we gone over every single thing about fifty billion times already."

"I don't mean about last night so much," Asey said. "I mean about Blight, an' the folks, an' these folks here, an' all."

"And maybe Harper?" Gerty suggested.

"Mebbe." Asey grinned at her. "You got to admit he ain't been very charmin' t'day."

Gerty flashed him a smile. "In a cold cream booklet I read last week," she observed, "they said charm was elusive. I guess the professor could say it nicer in Latin, but you know what I mean. If you're wondering about this biff on my face, I asked for it, and I got it. I don't often stick my head into other people's business, but I did, and that's what I got."

"Advisin' Harper?" Asey inquired. "I call that a brave an' courageous undertakin'."

"I told him," Gerty said, "he should own up about his part in last night's goings on. The fingernails and the locking part, and that."

"You think it was him?"

"I didn't at first, then I thought it over. Harper was in my shop one day last week when some salesmen come in, trying to sell detachable fingernails. He—"

"With what?" Asey shook his head. "By gum, you-say, that's somethin' new, ain't it?"

"Not very. These was sort of cellophane like things you stuck on. Different colors, in sets. Harper thought it was a great joke, and bought a set of bright red ones. Now maybe you didn't notice, but in Mrs. Babb's room—"

"Her polish was all ladylike an' light an' pinkish," Asey said. "C'nserv'tive, almost. Yup, I noticed. So you think Harper stuck'em on last night, an' then fooled around with us? But he looked pretty snow covered when he come in that front door, Gerty."

"One roll outside would of done that," Gerty said. "In that weather."

"Huh." Asey considered for a moment. "But why'd he do it, Gerty?"

"Search me! I thought I knew Harper better than some people do, but I'm beginning to wonder if—well, your guess is as good as mine. I told him to clear it up before you did the clearing, and he got himself into trouble, and so he biffed me."

"You don't seem to be takin' on much about it," Asey commented. "Most women would yell their heads off at bein' smacked like that. You seem sort of satisfied, almost."

"You," Gerty said briefly, "should ought to see Harper Dixon's face!"

She looked down at the sharp points on her own well cared for nails, and smiled.

"I get the impression," Asey said, "that you did a little clawin'. Good for you. Stick around. I may need you to claw a bit for me. Gerty, did Mrs. Babb have any enemies?"

"None I know of. She was a great one for losing her temper in a second, and blowing sky high. Had a lot of spats, but they didn't mean much. With the grocer, and delivery boys, and the like. With her own kind, she had little fights about gardening, and flowers. They go in for flowers in a big way in Blight, you see. That is," she added honestly, "they all buy big hats and gardening clothes in New York, and then they tell men where to move bushes. You know."

"Gardenin' by proxy," Asey said. "I seen it done. Gerty, think the Dixons had anythin' to do with this?"

"Not a chance."

"How about the p'fessor?"

"Him?" Gerty sniffed. "He hasn't gumption enough to kill a fly. He's not exactly stupid, though. He knows a lot. He ain't slow, exactly. But he seems both, somehow. He's so interested in what's going on inside his own mind, he don't have time to think of anything outside."

"A nice summin' up," Asey said. "Well, I guess I'll go see if Hank's found me anythin' I can plough over to Dixons' in. I somehow don't feel snowshoes is dignified for a man of my years an' standin'. In fact, I don't think I'd have any standin' left."

"Say, how old *are* you?" Gerty blurted the question out as though she had been holding it in for some time.

Asey chuckled. "You're in the business of addin' an' subtractin' age. Guess."

"I did," Gerty confessed. "So did Mrs. Westcott. We argued a solid hour about it this noon."

"My age," Asey said, "is my own secret. I don't mind tellin' you most folks give up. They b'gin at forty an' guess to sixty, an' then b'gin all over again. Don't worry none about my age. I don't. Come 'long an' let's git the transportation problem settled."

Mrs. Westcott was poking at the maple log in the living room fireplace.

"Why this thing won't work with an east wind," she said plaintively, "is one of the major trials of my life. There's so much east wind, it seems. The mason wants to rebuild it again, but I can't bear the thought. Last time he pulled it down, thousands of squirrels entered by it, and made themselves at home in the attic before we found out. I'd always thought squirrels were such nice animals, too. Before. Asey, can you do anything about this smoke?"

Asey looked up the fireplace and pulled at the draft lever with a poker.

"There. That seems to help. It's sort of usual to keep that open, you see," he explained gently.

"My dear man! I've seen that thing and wondered what it was. You know, sometimes I wish Hank were more practical minded and a bit less creative. Two of the windows in my room stick, and two clatter, and Hank won't do a thing! Won't even try to attack them. And the electric plugs, too. It looks so simple when the man comes, but Hank won't learn which wire goes where."

"I'll give you a day's labor," Asey told her, "b'fore I go home. Where is Hank?"

"Finding you sleighs, and all. Did you see Ernest going out for a walk? He's disgusted with the reading material I provide, I'm sure, but he just stops short of saying so. He thinks I'm light minded. Why don't you go and see if Hank's found anything—"

"I have." Hank came in. "It was where you thought it might be, along with Aunt Matty's golden oak in the shed. Asey, it's a superb sleigh. Puts me in mind of the one hoss shay that lived a hundred years and a day. Remember?"

"On the whole," Asey said, "maybe I better snowshoe."

"Oh, it's not that bad. It's shayish, with runners, and it had a name painted on the dash, all surrounded by a wreath of flowers. Very tasty. It's the 'Daisy-Belle.' Frank has got it out, and he's giving it the once over. He says that Robin will draw it nicely. Robin," Hank laughed, "is a horse."

"Robin an' Daisy-Belle. Sounds," Asey remarked, "kind of lush, an' verdant, an' chipper. Is Daisy a two-seater?"

Hank nodded. "And very snappy, too. Hand carved whip sockets, even. Frank—he's groom as well as chauffeur,—he's leaping into the spirit of the thing. He's found a plush blanket, or lap robe, and for all I know, he'll dig up tassels for Robin's ears. Asey, what about clothes? Come up and let's go through my wardrobe."

Mrs. Westcott protested indignantly when Asey returned half an hour later, dressed in a slightly motheaten raccoon coat and a yachting cap.

"Hank Thorn, get him something else! It's—"

"It's the only heavy coat I've got that fits him, Nell. He's terribly broad shouldered. I say, doesn't he look the rugged individualist? Back to the horse and buggy days. The spirit of mothballs. The—"

"You," Gerty said, "would look awful foolish in that outfit, Mr. Thorn, but Asey doesn't at all. He looks solid and dependable."

"An' I feel," Asey said, "like somethin' that might of walked out of Noah's ark b'tween the dodo birds an' the laughin' hyenas. Now, let me get my route straight. I turn—"

"Follow where it's ploughed," Hank said, "if you can find it. It's a very superficial ploughing we got, and I fear Rochelle's tooth is doomed to oil of cloves until tomorrow. Frank says it's senseless to take a car out. Here. I'll draw a map."

"No, you don't!" his sister said. "Let me! You got the Slingsbys to North Whitefield with the last map you drew, and they spent weeks hunting us. See, Asey. It's very simple."

He pocketed her sketch.

"Fine, an' now can I have some sugar lumps? I want Robin to think well of me. I was just figgerin', the last hoss I drove was in 1909. 'Course all cars then was virtually hoss pulled most of the time, but I sold my last critter then."

He strode out to where Frank was waiting with Robin and Daisy-Belle. He hoped that he looked confident. He didn't feel that way.

"It's sound, Mr. Mayo, as the day it was made, and I've put in snowshoes, as Mr. Thorn advised. You'll have no trouble with Robin. He was a trotter. Mrs. Westcott often uses him with an old buggy, summer times. She likes the back roads, and there's a lot here you can't get through in a car."

"Okay," Asey said, "but just the samey, Frank, if Robin trots home without me, you better do some mighty tall hustlin', snowshoes notwithstandin'. What's this?"

He pointed to a water pistol sticking out of a worn holster hung over the dash.

Frank smiled. "Mr. Thorn's idea, sir. He said it was as near as the place could come to providing you with a forty-five Colt, like you always have in the papers. There's a lantern, too, Mr. Mayo, and a flash. It'll be dark before you get back."

"Thanks. Wheee, the springs in this seat is springs, all right!"

With his silver mounted whip, he saluted the group waving at him from the living room window, and then jogged down the driveway to the road.

He chuckled to himself. After years of tearing around in Porters, he had almost forgotten how scenery stood out when you just bobbed along. Gave you plenty of time to stare at each snow laden tree, and beyond them to the rolling hills.

Something was bulging in the pocket of his coat. He investigated and discovered a small pair of binoculars in a worn leather case. Probably a relic of Hank's college days, like the coat itself. When he got to the next hill, Asey decided, he'd stop and make use of the glasses. That was what made him most uncomfortable about this business of tackling the Dixon troubles,—his ignorance of the lay of the land. Not knowing what lay behind the hills, or even on them, bothered him tremendously. It was worse than not knowing the people. You could make up your mind tentatively about people, but you couldn't be as casual with your surroundings. Just saying, this is hilly country, didn't get you anywhere.

"Whoa up, Robin," Asey said. "That's it. Jam on the brakes. Good feller. Don't need no sawin' or pullin', do you? Hydraulic, practic'ly. Yessir—"

He leaned forward to wind the reins around the whip, and at the same instant a shot rang out.

Asey slumped over the dash.

6

THE next fifteen minutes were never entirely clear in Asey's mind.

That shot had been fired with him as the target. On that point there was not the slightest doubt. He had heard the whine of the bullet, almost felt the breeze as it passed through the space where his head had been a split second before.

That much he understood perfectly.

But what went on in Robin's head was something else.

Apparently the shot had taken him back to his trotting days, and the track. Joyously, he bounded off down the long curving slope of the hill.

His knees sliding on the bottom of the sleigh, Asey clung to the dashboard with his fingertips, and tried to climb to his feet.

The first curve nearly threw him out head first.

As Robin swerved around the second, Asey heard something snap. Before he had time to figure out what it might be, they were half way down the hill, and Robin and Daisy-Belle had parted company entirely.

Asey forced himself to relax as he felt himself hurtled through the air.

"N'en, all of a sudden like," he told Hank Thorn later, "there I was, chewin' snow in a drift, with the sleigh cocked on a slant b'hind me, an' that painted name an' wreath of flowers leerin' at me sideways over my head."

He blinked rather dazedly at the wreath of flowers surrounding the name. Mixed flowers, Hank had called them, and Hank was right. Things like that never grew on land or sea.

As he started to get up, another shot rang out.

Asey winced as the second bullet whined near him.

"Polishin' me off!" he murmured indignantly to himself. "Huh!"

He lay back motionless in the drift. This required considerable thought. He and Daisy-Belle were a good half mile away from where the fellow had shot first. But this last had not been any casual, stray bullet. This one had his name on it, too, and very nearly his correct address.

Someone, he decided, had—well, maybe a 30-06 with telescopic sights. He was on the hill across the valley, popping away in a restful and leisurely manner. That was the only explanation. The fellow couldn't have been near at hand, for the second shot had sounded in the same general direction as the first. Besides, considering Robin's burst of speed, someone near at hand couldn't have caught up as quickly as all that.

He closed his eyes and tried to think back to the scenery he had been watching as he and Robin jogged up that hill.

There had been a cabin there, a log cabin. Not someone's house, but one of those expensive little shacks people put up even on the Cape, and called play houses. He remembered recalling the one back home on Carter's estate when he first noticed it.

Well, it was clear that someone there didn't like him. When you took to such accurate shooting with the sort of weapon that fellow had, you meant business. Whoever it was had apparently been sitting there and waiting for Asey to come.

There was only one thing to do: lie there and wait until it got dark, and then sneak off back to the Westcotts'. Always providing that the fellow didn't decide to march over and finish him up.

More than anything else in the world, Asey wanted to crawl back to the shelter of the sleigh, but he didn't dare move an eyebrow. There was no use to invite any further fusillades.

The greatest thing in his favor was the setting sun. Even now it was beginning to darken up, and from where he lay he could see the long shadows creeping up the snow covered hills.

If only this expert, he thought, would come over and investigate in person, without further shooting! That would be a fight to look forward to.

"Expert!" Asey spoke out loud. "Expert—an' that fool p'fessor went for a walk, didn't he?"

But he dismissed the idea of the professor's shooting at him almost as soon as it entered his mind. Ernest Vail had no gun with him, and you didn't carry a 30–06 around with you in any offhand fashion, anyway. Still, for all Asey knew, that cabin beyond the valley might be Vail's. Even if it weren't, the professor had had ample time to go there and pick up any possible gun, no matter whose cabin or whose gun it was.

Asey brooded about Professor Vail and his qualifications as expert rifleman as he lay there and watched the sky streak over with grey. He listened, too, with all his might and main. The expert might well decide to cross the valley, skirting around the pines. Someone on skis or snowshoes could cover that distance in no time at all.

Who in this benighted town of Blight would want to shoot him, anyway? Only a handful knew he was there. The professor was more or less out of the question, although the whole thing smacked of the professor's direct-thinking mind. If Vail decided to kill anyone, Asey decided, he would go at it in just such a business like way.

There was always Harper. If Gerty was right in thinking that Harper had been the one fooling around with the lights, and locking them all in the powder room—if she was right, Harper had a lot to explain. Perhaps his tirade this afternoon had been a preliminary warning, and these shots were driving the warning home. When someone missed hitting you as narrowly as whoever fired those shots had, you might almost figure that it was a purposeful miss.

Pete said that Mrs. Babb had been killed around eight o'clock. Yet Asey's friend Dr. Cummings back in Wellfleet had always sturdily insisted that no one could tell with any degree of exactitude the time of a person's death, unless the person was actually present at the time.

"Only in detective stories," Cummings had said it scornfully, time and time again, "only in detective stories can any doctor point to a corpse and say, 'This man died this morning at four-forty-one and three-eighths!' It's all a lot of nonsense."

Supposing that this Dr. Stern was wrong. If she had been killed around nine o'clock, the professor was involved. He had no way of substantiating his silly story about the ungodly oyster proverb; Asey smiled to think what the mere mention of it would do to a jury. If Mrs. Babb had been killed later on, Harper came into it with a bang. They had nothing but Harper's word that he had been in the greenhouse since eleven, and had come to the main house for the first time around two.

Taking it by and large, Harper seemed the best bet.

Why, Asey wondered, had they been locked in that room and then let out? Could it have been for someone to gain time, to dress up that enameled bowl with all the bottles of shampoo, and the rest, so that Mrs. Babb's death might seem natural?

It was almost dark enough now for him to begin edging under the sleigh. Half an hour more, and he'd try to get away, but first he wanted to paw around. With luck he might find the lantern, or the flash that Frank had put in, although he hardly dared use either. The snowshoes had been in the sleigh up to the time it tipped; they should be around somewhere.

He closed his eyes and listened. Somewhere, far off, a dog was barking. Near at hand the evergreen branches rustled. The wind was coming up strong again. Little particles of snow were blowing against his face. His left foot was asleep, and he was colder even than he had been the night before. Probably, he decided, if someone didn't wing him before this business was over, he'd die naturally of pneumonia. He didn't know what might have happened to that horse, but by rights Robin ought to have trotted clear to Monkton and back to the Westcotts' by now. If that broken harness didn't bring that bunch on the jump, nothing would.

There was another sound, now. Something—yes. Snow was crunching. Someone was coming toward him on snowshoes.

Asey opened his eyes wide and began to wiggle his left toes

frantically. If this was old thirty-oh-six, he didn't want to be hampered by any sleeping foot.

Whoever it was came nearer, stopped for a second, and then slowly advanced.

Asey's hand closed over the binoculars still in his pocket. If someone would only lean over him and try to finish him off, those glasses in their heavy case would serve nicely as a blackjack.

The figure was nearer, only a few yards away.

Asey closed his eyes and waited. If this were anyone out looking for him from the Westcott house, or some casual passerby, either would have spoken long before this. Thank goodness for Hank's muffler, he thought, wound high up around his chin. That would hide any telltale puff of breath and prevent the fellow from finding out that he was alive. He would hardly touch what seemed to be a dead body, but there was no telling what he might decide to do if he thought Asey merely unconscious.

A cold hand brushed across his cheek.

It rested there only a fraction of a second before it was withdrawn, but to Asey it seemed like twice his life time.

During the brief silence that followed, in which the person seemed to be considering the situation, Asey felt the perspiration trickle off his forehead. If that man lighted a match and peered down at him now, the jig was up!

Finally the person turned and went away, and Asey allowed himself to take into his lungs some of the air for which they had been bursting. His heart was thudding and thumping, making so much noise that it didn't seem possible that the man wouldn't hear it.

When his ears finally stopped pounding, Asey tried to listen again for the crunch of the stranger's snowshoes, but he couldn't hear a thing. Possibly the man had stopped, and was awaiting developments at a distance. Perhaps he had covered the ground so rapidly that he was out of earshot. Asey couldn't tell.

He forced himself to count. One minute. Ten. Half an hour. Then he edged toward the side of the sleigh.

He almost yelled out loud for joy when his hand closed over the flashlight. And mixed up with the plush lap robe were both snowshoes.

Buckling them on, he gripped the flashlight and took one step toward the road. Then he stopped.

The logical move was to return to the Westcotts'. But with the increasing wind, there would be no visible tracks tomorrow around that cabin opposite. And if anything really was going on over there, now was the time to investigate, while the fellow who had been doing the shooting still thought himself successful.

"Just for fun," Asey said, "I guess I'll meander over that way!"

Hank's comic water pistol went into his pocket before he started off, awkwardly, toward the valley. He didn't in the least feel at home on his snowshoes, and Hank's long coat was a nuisance, flopping around his ankles.

Somewhere ahead, he caught a glimpse of a tiny light that flickered, went out, and then came back again.

"Huh," Asey said. "Match!"

Cautiously and quietly as he could, he moved toward the spot as the match lights continued to flicker. Not much of an outdoor fellow, Asey thought, not having sense enough to face into the wind!

He was near enough before the man finally lighted his cigarette to make out the visor of a cap.

The professor wore a cap, a particularly ill-fitting thing of some violent plaid. Only the professor, by his own admission, shunned cigarettes. But Harper, both that afternoon and the night before, had worn a small blue cap with a visor, the sort of thing skiiers affected. And Harper was a chain smoker, lighting one from the other.

Here, Asey thought with pleasure, was his opportunity to get started. After all, Thursday was his deadline, and he couldn't waste any more time waiting for others to follow up their offensive. Now he'd start right in being offensive, on his own hook.

He started forward, when someone beside him spoke in a voice that was probably audible in the next township.

"Lost?"

Asey swung around and snapped on his flashlight, directed it to the face of the young fellow standing almost on top of him.

His first impression was of teeth, large numbers of tombstone like teeth. They were surrounded by a face that somehow seemed of secondary importance.

"Lost?" the boy asked again.

"Lost," Asey said bitterly, "what?"

"If you're lost, I'll show you the way back to Monkton for a dollar."

"I ain't lost. Just ole op'tunity," Asey said, trying to catch some sound of the person who had been so nearly within his grasp. "She's lost. That's all. Good night."

"Stranger here?"

"No." Asey figured that he had a very comprehensive knowledge of Blight, considering the time he had spent there.

"*I* never seen you before."

"It'll be okay with me," Asey observed, "if fate says thumbs down on the future. Listen, son, I ain't lost. An' furthermore—"

"For fifty cents," the boy said, "I'll show you the road back. I—"

Asey sighed. "Listen real careful, Wallin'ford. Listen hard. I am not lost. I know where I'm goin', an' if left to my own d'vices, I'll get there. Puttin' it another way, it's been fun havin' this little chat with you, an' it pains me to leave you so soon. 'Night."

"Oh, I don't have to go," the boy said. "I don't have to leave. I'll come along with you. Perhaps you'll get lost, an'—"

"What kind of a racket is this?" Asey demanded.

"Oh, the snow trains come up around here every Sunday," the boy said airily. "Lots of folks get lost. I lead 'em back to town, and charge 'em a dollar apiece, and then Tim gives me a dollar apiece more for bringin' 'em to him. He drives 'em over to East Whitefield for ten dollars a head, and they take the last train in. It's a regular trip Tim makes anyhows, only they think it's special. If there's enough to bother about, ma makes up packets of sandwiches, and I—"

"Let me guess," Asey said. "You peddle 'em for a dollar a head. I know. Huh." He thought for a moment. Gerty's bus driver the night before had been named Tim. Tim Sparks. "Well, Sparks," he continued, "you don't make a red cent on me. I ain't lost, nor hungry, nor desirous of reachin' Whitefield. No p'centage attall. So you just pop along an' see who else you can find. If there was a snow train t'day, you ought to be able to dig any number of city slickers out of drifts. 'Night."

"They wasn't no train, but some folks they come anyways. Say, how'd you know my name?"

"I'm psychic," Asey said. "Go 'long. Scat. I'm sure there's someone else around. I seen 'em. Maybe they're lost."

"It's only Harper Dixon," Sparks said. "I already met him."

"Cherub," Asey said, "are you sure 'twas Harper?"

"Say, I guess I know him all right!"

"Would you," Asey demanded, "like to make five dollars?"

"Five? Say, sure! Sure I would!"

"Here's the five. You find Harper Dixon again, an' go up to him, an' say 'Pooh!' Got that?"

"Pooh? What d'you mean, Pooh?"

"Pooh!" Asey told him, "as Pooh, in Winnie the. Pooh, as in he who laughs last laughs best. Pooh. Plain pooh. Now, get going!"

To his intense relief, Sparks strode away. Asey waited a moment and then continued towards the place where the match-lighter with the visored cap had been.

By the aid of his flash, he found the exact spot, surrounded by quantities of half burned matches, and two match flaps. And —Asey crowed as he bent over to pick up a cap.

Only, it wasn't Harper Dixon's cap!

That plaid wasn't something you could make a mistake about. That cap belonged to his old friend of the vowel shift, old honest Ernest, old trusty brains, the rifle expert!

Asey stuffed it in his pocket, took his bearings by the dim stars, and plodded on down the valley. He lost the marks of the snowshoes, but that didn't particularly disconcert him. He was more than ever convinced that the solution to all this lay in that cabin on the hill.

It took him nearly half an hour to reach it, and for several minutes he stood in the shelter of the tall pines and listened. There wasn't much to hear but the wind howling, but for all he knew there might be any number of people around. People lurking around seemed to be one of Blight's strongest points.

He strode toward the cabin; this time at least it was his first turn.

Thin, hair like strips of light appeared in the center of the three windows facing him. Probably, like the Carter's cabin on the Cape, this one also had inside wooden blinds which pulled across on either side like old fashioned folding doors.

Cautiously he walked to the nearest window and tried to peer in, but the crack was too narrow for him to see more than a brief streak of grey fieldstone fireplace, and a piece of gaily colored Navajo rug in front of it.

He circled around to the back door, gripped the knob and began slowly to twist it. Blight didn't seem to be much of a door locking community, and probably—yes. The door gave as the latch drew back.

It occurred to him suddenly that he was in no condition to engage in physical combat with anyone, and certainly that water pistol was small protection.

"Come, come," he admonished himself, "this ain't the proper spirit!"

But somehow, in the last few days, some of his proper spirit had dissolved. Perhaps it was due to the change from the tropics to this frigid blizzardy weather. Perhaps it was the result of being locked in rooms, and being shot at, and all the rest. Maybe it was lack of sleep.

"Your own fault," he said, "for stickin' your nose into gro'cry orders. Gro'cry orders! An' to think I thought I come here on account of a dozen of eggs an' a box of tapioca!"

Stepping out of his snowshoes, he thrust open the door and entered the kitchen, dark except for a beam of light that came from the living room beyond.

The blaze of heat made him hesitate momentarily, and he quietly slipped off the raccoon coat. Then he crept to the living room door and peeked in.

For several minutes he stood there, staring at the figure back to him, and then, with a grim expression on his face, he crept back and salvaged the water pistol from his coat pocket.

It looked very much as though he were going to need it.

7

"UP!" Asey stepped into the living room. "Up, if you don't mind. Just reach your hands up an' keep 'em there!"

"Why! Why—why," Ernest Vail said blankly, "I never expected ever to see *you*—"

"Again? Nope, on the whole, I don't s'pose you did," Asey said as he walked over to the professor and took possession of the 30–06 that reposed on the latter's lap. "Nun-no, I didn't s'pose you did. Now, little vowel splitter, just you crawl out of this, will you?"

The professor viewed Asey at length and in silence.

"It's the vowel shift," he said, "shift. Not split. You know, you look quite sane. I—"

"Where's your cap?" Asey demanded.

"Cap? Oh, my cap. I lost it. A gust of wind blew it off my head as I came along the valley."

"What you doin' here? Whose cabin is this? Yours?" Asey spat out the questions.

"I believe that it is actually Harper Dixon's. That is, he owns it, but while I am occupying Sue's cabin, he allows her to use this for her—er—sculpting." He waved a hand casually toward the end of the room. "You will find all her things there. Clay bin, and what not."

"What you doin' here now?" Asey asked. "Why're you croonin' over this gun?"

"Well," Vail said, "it's rather a long story. It goes back to a slight argument I had with my cousin Sue last week. She was very rude. I am afraid that I said some rather sharp things myself, and since that time I have not seen her. But she had borrowed a book of mine several days before our—er—tiff, and I've wanted very much to get it back. It was a book on art, and I felt sure she would have taken it over here. When I started out to walk from the Westcotts' today, I had no intention of coming here, but I saw the cabin, and thought of the book, so I came over here to get it. I—er—picked it up, and read. My, my," he looked at his watch, "it's quite late, isn't it?"

Asey sat down in a leather chair. "Pos'tively amazin'," he said, "how it gets late ev'ry day about this same time. What about this gun, now?"

"A fine weapon," the professor said heartily. "I've never been over here before except in Sue's company, and I've always wanted a chance to look that weapon over at my leisure. It hangs, as you may have guessed, over the fireplace. That is, it hangs there regularly. A fine weapon," he repeated, "but it really should be given a modicum of care. When Sue and I meet again, I shall certainly suggest that she take it to her gunsmith. Look at the rust! And that trigger! Really, it's disgraceful, allowing a fine thing like that to go to rack and ruin!"

Asey looked more closely at the gun, and then he stared at the professor.

"By gum," he said, "you're right. That barrel—why, this gun ain't been fired in weeks! P'fessor, I hate to say this, but I take it all back."

"Er—what? What's that? What back?"

"Wa-el," Asey drawled, "someone's been pottin' at me. Tiresome, kind of, lyin' in snow drifts, waitin' to see if you'd be a bull's eye. N'en—"

"You," excitedly, Vail took off his glasses and put them back on again, "you don't mean that someone has been shooting at you? Oh! Oh, I see. I see. Doubtless that explains your peculiar actions when you first came in. Were you shot?"

Asey nobly refrained from saying that he was riddled with bullets and dead in a snow drift that very minute.

"I feel," he observed, "like ole Hezekiah Hopkins. He had a habit of talkin' to stone walls an' door knobs an' other such like inanimate objects. No, Ernest, I ain't shot, but I've had a very rilin' evenin'."

"Tell me all about this shooting affair," Vail said. "If you think it was a 30–06, I may inform you that Harper Dixon owns one. He's rather a good shot."

Briefly, Asey told him of his attempted trip to the Dixons with Robin and Daisy-Belle.

"And you say you met someone just now? Who was it?"

"Kid named Sparks. I gathered he was the brother of the local bus driver. Know him?"

"Tch, tch," the professor made a clucking sound with his tongue. "I should say I do! A most repellent adolescent. A pathological liar. A—"

"Liar, huh?"

"Exactly. The very first day I was here, I met him out in the hills. He asked me if I were lost, and said that for—"

"I know. For fifty cents he'd show you the road."

"No, a dollar. I assured him I required no assistance, but he was most persistent. Finally, in order to get rid of him, I—"

"You gave him a dollar. Uh-huh. So young Master Sparks is a liar, is he? You mean, he lies steady an' constant, or he just tells an occasional whopper?"

"Both," Vail said. "He tells the most fantastic and outlandish stories. Whether one wants to or not, one is practically forced to listen to him. He is virtually unquenchable. They aren't just little falsehoods that he tells. They're connected stories, complete in all details, but patently untrue. Impossible. After several encounters with the boy, I met and talked with one of his teachers at the high school. She said he was a problem child, with an immediate background best described as unfortunate. His mother is dead, and her husband, who—uh—my informant did not consider a very able type, runs a pool hall."

"Huh," Asey said. "But say. He said somethin' about 'ma' puttin' up food for tourists."

"His step mother. I—er—purposely said, his mother's husband, instead of his father, because there appears to exist some doubt as to the two being—er—synonymous. Leon—the boy's name is Leon,—has told me some really outrageous stories. I remember one about a man setting fire to an empty bucket that was really something for a case book. Fancy anyone carrying a bucket for miles, and then setting it on fire! He made it quite dramatic, though, Leon did."

"Well, it's one way to cart kindlin'," Asey said. "An' if Leon chases around after tourists, you can expect almost anythin'.

Why, one day last summer on Cape Cod, I waked up to find a tourist in my bed room, almost in the act of r'movin' my spool bed from underneath me. He'd peered in the window, an' he thought it was a nice old fashioned bed, so he come right in to get it, quick. Y'know, p'fessor, I'm sort of sorry Leon's a liar. He'd give me some mighty encouragin' news. I—"

"I'm far more interested," Vail interrupted, "in the matter of the cap you found, and think is mine. As if I weren't sufficiently involved, having gone to the Dixon house earlier last night! This upsets me, Asey. I don't understand it. I don't like it. D'you have the cap here with you?"

Asey went and got it from his coat pocket.

Ernest examined it with great care.

"Ain't it yours?"

"Strange," Vail said. "Very strange. Very strange indeed. I quite agree with what Nell Westcott said. This actually might be something written by her brother. You see, that is my cap. But it is not the cap I lost this evening. It's the one I lost a long while ago, shortly after I came here. I can tell by the lining. The lining of the cap I lost tonight was badly soiled. This is quite clean."

Asey nodded.

"You don't appear to be a bit surprised," Vail said. "I am. I am exceedingly surprised."

"Oh," Asey told him casually, "I left off bein' dumbfounded an' s'prised several hours ago. Two camels an' Charley Ross could walk straight through that front door at this point, an' I wouldn't bat an eyelash. I don't—"

Someone was at the front door, stamping snow from their feet.

"Well, well," Asey continued, unmoved, "comp'ny."

He settled back in his chair, folded his arms and waited.

"But who—" the professor was almost twitching with nervousness, "who is it?"

Asey shrugged. He had reached the state where he felt that he owed it to himself to sit back and enjoy things.

The door opened, and Leon Sparks walked in.

He looked from Asey to the professor and back again.

"Hm," he said. "I *thought* there was somethin' funny about. I thought there was somethin' funny goin' on."

His remarks were received with polite silence. Asey agreed entirely with the boy, and Ernest Vail didn't know how to answer.

"I said, I *thought* there was somethin' funny goin' on." Leon raised his voice.

"We heard," Asey said.

"Well, what you going to *do* about it, huh?"

"Do about what?"

"Breaking and entering, that's what!"

"Breaking and entering, nonsense!" Vail said. "No one has broken or entered anything!"

"This ain't your house! You broke in! Yes, sir. There's too many funny things goin' on around this town. What are you goin' to *do* about this?"

"My boy," Vail said, "I think it would be a part of wisdom for you to leave."

"Listen," Leon said, "for ten dollars, I might promise not to tell on you. But—"

Asey chuckled. "Shylock, you've had your fun for the day. Vamoose."

"But this is Harper Dixon's cabin!"

"An' the p'fessor," Asey said, "is Harper Dixon's brother Pete's fiancé's cousin. Tell me, did you meet Harper again?"

"Yes, I did. But you—"

"D'liver my message? What'd he say?"

"Well, he cussed," Leon said frankly. "He cussed to beat hell, an' I run off before he belted me one."

"Seemed to know who the message was from, didn't he?"

"He didn't name any names, but I guess he did."

"D'you s'pose," Asey turned to the professor, "that Leon really did say 'Pooh' to Harper for me?"

Vail shook his head. "Of course not. Asey, tell that boy to go. Tell—"

"Say," Leon stared at Asey, "say, are you Asey Mayo? The Asey Mayo? You look like the pictures. Say, I bet you are. Say, what do you know about that? Say, ain't—"

"Oh dear." Ernest sighed. "Now we'll *never* be rid of him! Leon, get up out of that chair and go home. Instantly! Go this minute! Go at once!"

Leon ignored him. "Say, there *is* something funny going on, huh? What is it? Is it a murder? Who's murdered? I knew there was—"

"Yup," Asey said, "you knew. Now, please be so kindly as to beat it b'fore I beat you. If—"

There was more thumping and rattling at the front of the house.

"Give me the Grand Central station," Asey murmured. "Or Times Square. What the town of Blight needs is a nice quiet r'treat."

"Asey! Asey Mayo!" It was Hank Thorn's voice that bellowed outside. "Asey, are you there?"

"Come in," Asey called, "we can 'com'date about—well, make it hommes forty, hosses eight. Come in, Hank!"

Thorn burst into the room.

"My God, Asey! Are you all right? Let me tell you, virtually the whole countryside and both the local constables are out—"

"Scouring the vicinity in high powered cars?" Vail asked eagerly.

"What?" Hank stared at him.

"In your stories," Vail defended himself, "people always scour vicinities in high powered cars, but I suppose that the snow—"

"Asey," Hank threw himself down on the couch, "what happened? Robin came bobbling home with half the harness trailing around him, and a sort of triumphantly diabolical look on his face! Gerty and Nell and I went frantic! And then Pete Dixon started calling up for you. And then we all bustled around organizing rescue parties—Nell even called up the Phyfe-Jordans in Whitefield. For their dogs!"

"Come," Asey said soothingly. "Come, come. This'll pass. This—"

"I mean it! They're St. Bernards, you know, and Rochelle forgot her toothache, and she and Lena went scurrying around emptying all the mouthwash and vanilla and things in bottles and filling 'em with whiskey—"

"To tie on the St. Bernards?" Asey leaned his head against the back of his chair and chortled. "Oh, my!"

"No, so that each rescuer would have something to rescue you with! I tell you, we've been in a frenzy. What happened? And where'd you come from, Ernest? And oh, my God—Leon the leech! Leon, go home. I can't stand any more. Put him out,

Asey. I'm too exhausted to move, and I've got a million things to tell you, and if that child hears—"

"I ain't a child," Leon protested. "I'm nearly eighteen."

"That," Hank said, "is what you think. Look, here's a dollar. Go harry someone else."

Leon remained silent, and seated.

"Well," Hank pulled out another bill from his wallet, "make it two. Scram!"

"It's worth at least ten—"

Asey got up, and stretched. He strode over to Leon, clasped one firm hand on the boy's collar and drew him out of the arm chair. Before Leon quite understood what had happened, he was on the front porch.

"There." Asey shot the bolt. "Hop around to the back door, Ernest, and lock it tight. What's up, Hank?"

"Well," Hank pulled off a coat and two sweaters and tossed them on the hearth, "they got the Brandts over. They're the Monkton law, or something. Really they run the fish market. You could tell it at the first sniff. Anyway, they moseyed around—say, we ought to get back, Asey, and let 'em know you're safe. There was a regiment around that sleigh. And what did happen to you?"

"First tell me the news, Hank. B'sides, I ain't rested up enough yet to tell my yarn over again, or even to think of puttin' on them infernal machines an' settin' out over all that snow."

"Well, the Brandts really crashed through. They found a back entry window unlocked, and in a place where the snow swirls and there's no drift, and someone could have got in with ease. And then they sensibly asked where Char's jewels were, and Pete and Dr. Stern and Edward—he's the butler. All four servants are back, by the way. Anyway, they all hunted, and it seems Char's jewel case is missing. And it seems that on Tuesday, Char went to the bank and dragged the whole collection out of her safe deposit box, because there was a mess of parties coming. When the boys left last night, all the jewels were in her room. Nell's remembered she was at the bank Tuesday while Char was there, and Nell berated her for taking out so many valuable things, and being so careless about them. So they've figured out how someone got in, and why they killed her. And I gather all they want now is for you to come and tell them who."

"That so?" Asey grinned. "Ain't that nice. That all your items?"

"Oh, we've got a reporter, too."

"Not so soon! Not already!"

"Oh, it's just a local boy, from the Blight 'Bladder.' I forgot to tell you about the Blight 'Bladder,' Asey, when I gave you the low-down on Blight. I only hope I'll have a copy with me if I ever get cast away on a desert island—is that Leon, howling like a dog? How'd he enter into this?"

Asey told him, and summed up his own story.

At its conclusion, Hank looked at him reproachfully.

"No fairs," he said at last. "No fairs. There's enough competition in the writing business right now!"

"There." Ernest Vail appealed to Asey. "There. See? I told you so! I said it sounded as though he wrote it!"

"If you think, Hank," Asey said, "that my story is any crazier than phonin' for St. Bernards, an' fillin' mouthwash bottles with whiskey!"

"You haven't heard it all yet," Thorn said. "Nell's got a stretcher lashed onto her car, just in case you need it, and her plans for coping with you if you're really incapacitated are so complicated that I didn't pretend to grasp 'em. I heard her muttering about ambulance planes on skis, if worse came to worst."

"What about Gerty?" Asey inquired. "Is she managin' to bear up?"

"Her faith in you," Hank said, "is practically boundless. She has four hard boiled eggs and two ham sandwiches in her pocket, and she confided to me that she didn't think you'd really even need them. Oh, another thing. Edward, the Dixon butler, is awfully upset about the decanters. He accused me. Me, mind you!"

Asey wanted to know what happened to the decanters. "Did you tell 'em about the St. Bernards, or did they get up on two legs an' do a tango?"

"They're empty. Edward thinks we threw a horrid party there last night, I'm sure. Nell lost her temper at him. Said we took four tablespoons of brandy to revive the professor, and his insinuating anything else was going too far, and it was horrid brandy anyway. But Edward just looked at her with one of those 'Very-well-but-I-know-better' looks. He thinks we're a pack of booze hounds. Asey, we ought to get going. And that young leech is outside, waiting to fasten onto you. I can hear him. I strongly suggest that you make every effort to nip him in the bud."

Asey brought in his snowshoes and his coat and began to get ready for the trip home.

"I wish," he remarked, "that your sister had done more plannin' on what to do with me if I was alive an' well. Didn't she give you orders to carry me back, no matter in what c'ndition you found me? Honest, I sort of hate to go out. Both of my ankles feel like they b'longed to some other feller, an' him kind of ailin'."

"Cheer up," Hank advised. "With the crust coming on this snow, you may be able to sit on the hill here and reach the valley with one push. Say, have you seen any matches around?" He pulled an empty flap from his pocket and tossed it on the table. "I've just exhausted my supply. Six of those flaps have got used up since I set out on the A.M.R.P. Number One."

"The what?" Asey asked warily.

"The Asey Mayo Rescue Project Number One." Thorn laughed. "Maybe it should be the P.D.A.M.R.P. Number One, now I think it over. Nell was referring to you as Poor Dear Asey Mayo when I last saw her. She—"

"Matches are up there." Asey pointed to the mantel, and casually picked up the flap which Thorn had discarded. "Mind if I keep this cover, Hank? I got a friend home who c'lects these empty flaps. Got eleven thousand or so, all mounted like butterflies. This looks to me like a sort of a rare specimen."

"Sure, take it. He won't have a duplicate of that, I know. Lad I know in the advertising business sends me a year's supply every single Christmas. All tastefully and specially decorated. He makes up different ones for all his pals. See the quill pen motif? That's his conception of the writing business, the boob. Quill pens! I use a super-noiseless typewriter that looks like a Mogul Mallet engine, set in a rubber composition table. Quill pens!"

"Don't you find," the professor asked interestedly, "that the —er—mechanical detail, as you might call it, interferes with the—er—creative process?"

"My creative processes," Hank informed him, "are curiously hardened. I hired an office, once, and a secretary, and took to dictating like a business man. I had to give that up because I couldn't find a sufficiently mechanical secretary. Then I went and bought me a dictaphone."

"Didn't that work?" Asey asked.

"Beautifully, but I got carried away by the sound of my own voice, and found myself orating and telling jokes—you don't know how free you feel, telling jokes to a dictaphone. I went back to typing. Probably the only writer in creation who uses all ten fingers— Asey, you seem entranced by that match flap."

"Nice design," Asey said. "Kind of int'restin'. Say, did you hear Leon while you was roamin' around, huntin' for me?"

"I thought I heard him yell and ask if I were lost, but I didn't wait to identify him. Leon the leech isn't one of my passions."

"Int'restin'," Asey said. "Huh. Put on your cap, Hank, an' let's go."

The more he thought about Hank and the match flap on the long trip back to the road, the more interesting both became. For the flap Hank tossed on the table was an exact duplicate of the two which Asey had picked up in the snow bank near the sleigh.

8

ASEY was whistling cheerfully as he got dressed the next noon. Ordinarily he owned to a profound scorn for the type of person who rose at noon, and he could recall without effort any number of scathing comments he had made to such individuals at odd times. Today, to him, it all seemed very sensible and proper.

In fact everything seemed sensible and proper, for a change, beginning with the clear bright blue sky. His room glowed with blazing sunlight that had melted every last icicle outside his windows. Patches of gravel showed down in the driveway, and gargantuan piles of snow on either side of the main road demonstrated that at last some proper ploughing had been done.

Perhaps it was just that he had finally got some sleep. Disregarding the pleas of Pete Dixon and the entreaties of the

Brandts, and ignoring the time element that had been worrying him so, Asey had gone directly to the Westcott house after leaving the cabin the night before, and gone to bed.

Now his promise of action by Thursday no longer ground into him like something on the end of a dentist's drill. It was a sporting proposition. He had risen to the occasion before, and it was possible that, with some luck, he might ring the bell again. The facts of his not knowing Blight, and what scenery lay beyond its hills, of not knowing the people involved and what thoughts lay in their heads—all that had ceased to bother him.

Asey tied Hank's gaily striped tie and put on Hank's coat. He rather wished that Hank went to a different tailor. Not that the coat was badly made, but for his part Asey preferred smooth tweeds. Hank had commented on his wardrobe while picking things out for Asey.

"I can walk anywhere in the country, or play golf on any continent, but they'd shoot me on sight in the city as an escaping hairy ape from the zoo. I hadn't realized I'd gone so country."

Asey grinned at himself in the mirror. He'd made a mistake in calculations there, too. Hank was younger than Ernest Vail. His grey hairs made the difference. He liked Hank, in spite of the match flap problem, and he liked Nell Westcott, too.

"Just," he murmured to himself as he started down the stairs, "just ole Pollyanna Mayo. That's what."

He found Hank and Nell beginning their breakfast.

"Mornin'. Where's Gerty?"

"Gerty," Nell said, "has gone to town to 'do' Miss Enderby. Doesn't it sound—well—"

"Immoral?" Hank suggested as she paused for a word.

"Well, something like that. I mean, I always think of Gerty 'doing' me, but I never thought of being 'done' by her, if you see what I mean. She's promised to quit work for the afternoon, and Frank's bringing her back when he brings Rochelle from the dentist's. Then you can take her over to Dixons' with you. I'm hurt, Asey, that you should ask Gerty and not me."

"Come along," Asey invited. "More the merrier. I just wanted the shampoo expert around. Did Pete call?"

"Did he call? My dear, he began phoning at six-thirty this morning, and he's not stopped yet. He—"

"Nell!" Hank reproved her. "You know perfectly well that the phone hasn't rung all morning! At least, I haven't heard it."

"Of course you haven't!" Nell retorted. "At eight o'clock, after Gerty left, I went through the house and took the receivers off. Asey needed some rest, and so did I. Ernest Vail thought of it. He said he always keeps his receiver off when he wants to work in peace, and the telephone people in Cambridge got very annoyed about it. Had the police out, to see what foul play had gone on."

Asey and Hank laughed.

"I think it's a very sensible plan," Nell said. "Possibly it's the sun shining again, but it seemed to me that Ernest was brighter this morning than I ever gave him credit for being. He's gone home, but I don't see how he can stay there. Sue told me last night when she phoned that the storm— Asey, your toast's about to pop."

Asey jumped as the slice of toast hit him on the cheek.

"Them machines," he said with a grin, "that hurls toast through the air like jugglers always scares me half to death. Betsey Porter give me one a couple years ago that's as near to bein' human as anythin' I ever seen. I used it just once an' then went back to the old fashioned fork over the coals. Almost soothin', 'twas, not havin' to dodge around."

"I met Betsey Porter once," Nell said. "Charming girl, I thought. Asey, isn't it nice that this horrid business is all over?"

"Over?" Hank said. "Nell, what do you mean, over?"

"Of course it's over, Hank, don't be so obtuse! We know it was some tramp or someone after dear Char's jewels, and you can find out who this afternoon, can't you, Asey?"

Asey said that he had a few doubts.

"But it's perfectly clear! I told Char at the bank Tuesday— Gerty was there, making a deposit, and she heard me. I told Char she was the most careless thing I ever knew about her jewels. Imagine, bringing them up from the vault in her muff! Then leisurely—leisurely is the only word,—stuffing them into a knitting bag! Right there in the bank, in plain sight, without a lock. That is, on the bag. Why, every bum in town saw her!"

"So folks know about her jewels, do they?"

"Can they help knowing," Nell said, "if she flings them around casually in knitting bags, and wears them to church suppers, and things? That horrible thug who drives the bus— Sparks. He was there, and let me tell you, his eyes were sparking. So was that nasty gas station man with the squint. The fiend who said he filled the tank in your car, Hank, and he couldn't have put in half a pint, to have the thing run dry last night! Really, Asey, the wonder of Char's jewels is that no one's tried to steal them before."

After breakfast, Asey asked if he could use a phone.

"Want to make some calls to Boston," he said. "Would you mind? I'll find out how much they come to, an' pay you in a lump before I go."

"My dear man," Nell glanced at Hank, "I'd die of the shock if you did any such thing. Hank has a friend—"

"Nell, can't you—"

"A friend," she continued, "who has a girl in Hollywood, and he calls her every night at least once, and sometimes twice or more. Hank says I shouldn't be carping about him, because he's a vegetarian and is cheap to feed, but I tell him I could stuff the fellow with Porterhouse until his eyes bulged, three times a day, forty times on Sunday, and still save money. And all he ever says to that girl is 'Darling, are you well?' and 'Darling, is it raining there?' and—"

"He's a genius," Hank said. "You should take that into account before you carp—"

"If 'Darling, are you well' and 'Darling, is it raining' are any signs of genius," Nell said, "I am Einstein. I am the Brains Trust. I—"

Asey left them wrangling amicably, and went to the phone to call his friend Steve Crump. Half of the Hybrid Club depended on Stephen Crump to settle their legal difficulties, and if he didn't have a finger in the Dixons' business, he could tell Asey who did. And Asey wanted a little information which he hesitated to request directly.

After all, he thought as he waited for someone to page Steve, someone profited by Mrs. Babb's death. The Dixon family was even wealthier than he thought. And whereas she might have been killed for her jewels, it seemed to him an awfully pica- yune motive. There was a lot more going on than met the eye. A common tramp or some native Blighter would hardly have potted at him the night before, so carefully. They wouldn't even have known of his presence. A common ordinary mur- derer would set to work covering up his own tracks if he thought there was any possibility of someone uncovering them. He wouldn't attempt killing off the uncoverer.

Yes, Gerty had been right. Someone was already sorry that he and she had landed at the Dixons' at that particular time. They regretted it intensely.

He spoke at length with Steve Crump and then strolled back to Hank and Nell.

"Going to take Robin again today?" Hank asked. "The harness is mended."

"No," Asey said, "nun-no. I think I'll take a nice safe car. Leastways, an engine won't run away from me, or pulverize my ankles—"

"Did you use that stuff on them?" Nell interrupted. "That liniment?"

"Mrs. Westcott," Asey said, "I intended to. I honestly did. But I took one sniff of that concoction an' give up."

"I shall get it right now," Nell said firmly. "Hank can massage it in. I—"

Hank came to Asey's rescue. "Hank will do no such thing," he said, "and besides, here's Gerty. There's no time. Hurry and get your things on, so Asey can start off. Asey, what car will you use? Pete had your coupe fixed and sent over. Want that?"

Asey hesitated. "I'm sort of duty bound," he said, "not to use Porters. I see that big car of Mrs. Westcott's is one, too. Guess you better drag out that ole beach wagon—"

"It's a thousand years old," Nell said, "and it's more of a· menace than Daisy-Belle—"

"It couldn't be," Asey said. "Have Frank get it, anyway. It'll do."

Mrs. Westcott absolutely refused to go anywhere in the beach wagon.

"It's unsafe. And it bounces so! And really, I do think you ought to go in a nice warm car! Think of your poor ankles. And if you'd only rub some of that—"

"Nell," Hank said. "Nell! No. Asey isn't your poor long suffering brother, and he's not one of your long suffering infants. Asey, I give you my word, when her three offspring were in their first flush of youth, they spent half their life wandering around potted palms in hotel lobbies, trying to find where they'd parked their rubbers and overshoes!"

"It never hurt anyone to bundle up some—"

"Then you go bundle up this minute!" Hank shooed her out of the room. "Asey's ready and waiting! Gerty, did you do the Enderby up brown?"

"Uh-huh." Gerty said. "Say, Hank, I want to say some things to Asey. Will you—thanks. Asey," she led him over to the window as Hank obligingly left, "Harper came to see me this morning. He—"

"That why you look so dourish an' tired?"

"Maybe. Look, I don't know what to do. I'm going to tell you and let you figure it out for yourself. He says he won't stand for your butting in, and—well, he didn't exactly make any threats, but—"

"But you gathered it wouldn't be exactly healthy like for me to hang around, huh?"

Gerty nodded. "Truly, I don't think it was him that shot at you! Only—"

"Only," Asey said, "he warned that I'd already got a sample, an' told you to get it into my bean that home was sweet. Or words to that effect?"

"Yes. I don't understand anything at all, but Asey, will you be careful?"

"I will," he promised. "Did Harper say anythin' about sockin' you?"

Gerty smiled. "Believe it or not, he apologized. But I didn't. I said that for two cents I'd scratch him again, and if he did a single mean thing to you, I'd scratch his eyes out. I would, too!"

"Come on," Asey said. "Hank says he's goin' to protect me with a gun, an' Mrs. Westcott wants to protect me with liniment a hoss wouldn't stand for, an' you got your nails ready. Looks like I was set."

There were two state troopers outside the Dixon house, and half a dozen reporters.

"Westcott," Hank told a trooper. "Dixon wants us."

The trooper waved them on, and the reporters paid them scant attention. Asey, almost hidden from sight in the back of the beach wagon, chuckled happily.

"Lots of advantages," he said, "b'tween drivin' Porters, an' bein' driven in beach wagons. They'll never spot me in these here hairy tweeds, anyhows. Good as a fancy dress costume. My, I'm goin' to enjoy this."

They were met at the door by Pete Dixon, the two local constables, and more state police.

"Thank God you're here," Pete said. "Asey, this is Watson and this is Vito. You know the Brandts. First of all, they can't find any fingerprints."

"Not even on the door that was pulled shut on us?"

"Clean as a whistle," Brandt said. "Now, will you come and—"

"Wait." Dr. Stern, whom Asey had met the night before, joined the group. "First of all, I want him. I didn't have a chance to talk with him last night. And I'm due at the hospital. Can I have him first?"

Pete sighed. "Go on. We've waited around so much that a few minutes more won't matter. Only, do hurry!"

The doctor and Asey retired to a small sitting room off the main hall.

"First," Asey began, "I'd—"

"I know." The doctor's eyes were twinkling. "Of course I can't tell you the exact time she died, but I'm sure it was around eight. You see, she'd been in to see me Saturday morning, and her blood pressure was soaring. I told her to go home and go to bed, and she politely told me to go to blazes. Saturday afternoon I heard the radio report of the coming storm, and I called her and told her again to stay home. I knew there'd be a lot of excitement at that party—Sue's parties are very Roman things. And I didn't want Char hung up, either coming or going. But she told me—"

"To go to blazes some more?"

"Just about. Well, she was on my mind. I called her once after seven-thirty. I don't know how much after, but it was after the radio news, anyway. The line was busy. Then I called later—exactly at eight, for the hall clock struck as I picked up the phone. They rang and rang, and no one answered. So I called Sue's, and they said the Dixon boys had just come, but Char was staying home. At that point, I sat down and played bridge, happily convinced that Char had finally taken my advice and gone to bed."

"But," Asey said, "maybe she was alive then, and just didn't come to the phone. Think of that side?"

"Out of the question entirely," Dr. Stern assured him. "You

didn't know Char. She couldn't bear to hear a phone ring without finding out who was calling. She was—well, she was the sort of person who always asked what the name of your book was, if she found you reading. She forgot the title at once, and the information meant nothing to her, but she just wanted to know. When she asked what you'd been doing since you saw her last, she expected to be told. You couldn't just say that you'd been working. She wouldn't let it go at that. I had to recite every blister, every stomach ache, every item you could converse about politely."

"I see," Asey said. "Well, that bein' the case, it sort of settles the time angle. That helps. Of course, the op'rator might of rung the wrong number, or somethin'. But if we delve into that, we won't even have a startin' place. Now, they's no chance she wasn't drowned, is there?"

The doctor shook his head.

"Not a chance. And," he got up and paced around the room, "I might as well admit this to you, because it's the truth. I wouldn't tell those oafs from town, or the cops, on a bet. But you're different. You see, Mayo, I've been looking after Char and her heart for ten years or more. If the Dixon boys had called me when they found her, and if you and Gerty and the others hadn't been around, and using your heads, the chances are ninety-nine out of a hundred that I'd have said, 'Heart,' and let it go at that."

"You'd have been within your rights," Asey returned. "You'd seen her pr'fession'ly within twenty-four hours, an' she was a patient under your care. An' someone was bankin' on just that."

"Furthermore," the doctor went on, "I'm acting medical examiner for this region at the moment. Unless the Dixons had requested an autopsy, and I don't think they would have, I shouldn't have done a thing about it. I'm saying all this," he stopped pacing around and sat down next to Asey, "because I feel pretty cut up about it."

"But—"

"I do, I feel infinitely worse about this sort of thing than what happened over in Whitefield last week. That was the other extreme. A fellow was slashed to pieces, and his girl friend had a gory razor in her hand. Told the cops she'd just dropped in for a chat, and picked up the razor to clean it off. She'd tried to clean up some of the rest of the mess, too. Clearest case of murder I ever saw. And it was suicide! Suicide, mind you! Fellow was an ex-prize fighter who went crazy with D.T.'s, fought all his fights over again against himself, with the razor! That room looked like a slaughter house. You'd have sworn that ten men had brawled there for a month. And it was suicide, and the girl told the truth. She popped in, and was dazedly cleaning up!" he made a little gesture of despair. "And here's this business here. Something I'd have called the most natural death in the world. And it's murder. There you are. You can't tell!"

It was clear to Asey that the doctor's professional pride had taken a tremendous beating.

"'I shouldn't reproach myself so much," he said. "Someone was bankin' on foolin' you, an' they nearly did. They'd of fooled me, if Gerty hadn't been there to give me moral s'port. If I'd of known Mrs. Babb b'forehand, an' about her heart, I don't think I'd of said a word."

"What d'you think of this burglar theory?" Dr. Stern looked searchingly at Asey.

"Ain't thought."

"It doesn't appeal to me, either. You know what my wife said, when I told her it was undeniably a man who killed Char?"

"Mebbe," Asey said, "she figgered as I did. That it might be a man, on account of whoever put them bottles of shampoo out did a punk job, an' forgettin' the spray, an' usin' the wrong kind of towel, an' leavin' her in a dinner dress, an' all. Sort of thing a man mightn't be so bright about. On the other hand, it might be a woman, who knew better on all counts, but wanted to leave a false trail b'hind her. That it?"

The doctor rose. "No need for me to linger here," he said. "'You're three weeks ahead of me, and I haven't scratched the surface of what you've thought. And—er—Mayo."

"Yup?"

"I take it all back. All the hayseed bumpkin, and—oh, you know! I apologize. I changed my mind the minute I saw you last night."

"It's mutual," Asey told him. "You don't really look like a stockbroker. It's just formal clothes an' that stand-up collar. Oh. One more thing. I told Hank an' the p'fessor, an' that Sparks kid—"

"Leon? Is he already mixed in this?" the doctor sighed. "I feel for you. Once last year he decided to be a doctor, and he followed me around night and day for three months. If he's decided to be a detective, you're definitely out of luck. You can't shake the boy."

"What about him?" Asey asked. "Can you b'lieve him, or is he the kind of liar Vail said? Somethin' with a name a mile long. Anyways, Leon told me somethin' I'd like to b'lieve. Would you, offhand?"

"I wouldn't know," the doctor said. "I've never known myself whether to believe him or not. But I'll tell you one thing that few people know. Even his teachers think it's a mistake. Leon has the highest intelligence quotient of any kid in Monkton. They sent him over to me to take him to the city and have him checked on. Thought there was something wrong with their tests. Same thing happened at the clinic. Way above average. Of course he's a nuisance, and his environment hasn't given him any semblance of social charm, and God knows he could be bright and still lie. But if he's entering into your calculations, you might take that I.Q. into account."

"Okay, I will. Anyhows, doc, I told all them fellers not to cry it from the housetops," Asey said, "but someone tried to pick me off last night."

He summed up again his adventures of the night before.

"You don't mean it!" The doctor's jaw sagged.

"I do. Got any thoughts on that?"

"Harper Dixon," Stern said. "I—oh, hell, I promised my wife I wouldn't stick my nose into this, but I thought of Harper right off the bat! And—oh, that clinches it! Of course! You know, often in my spare time, I've sat down and tried to figure out the proper psychological nomenclature for Harper. I've given up. At one time or another, that fellow has exhibited definite signs of every psychosis and neurosis in the books. Go after him, Mayo, and when you need testimony, let me know. It'll be an opportunity I've longed for these twenty years! Go to it. Now, I've got to tear along. I'll be back later, and if I can help, let me know. Glad to do anything, any time."

After the doctor left, the butler sidled into the sitting room and stood there expectantly.

"Want me, do you?" Asey said, thinking how much the man resembled the Reverend Bascom, back in East Pochet.

"Yes, sir. If you're not busy. I am Edward, sir. I am the butl—"

"Sure, I know. You're the one that thinks we went an' drunk up all the liquor in the house Saturday night. That right?"

"Oh, no, sir. Not at all. Just the contents of the decanters. Seven of them, sir."

"If Harper was around," Asey began.

"I greatly doubt if Mr. Harper touched them, sir. I'm sure he didn't."

"Come, come," Asey said. "You can't tell me he's any tee-totaler, Edward!"

"No, sir, but," Asey liked the way the fellow stuck to his guns, "but Mr. Harper wouldn't touch what was in those decanters, sir. It was something Mrs. Babb bought at a bargain sale in a department store in New York, sir. She—er—liked bargains. I know the decanters were full, too, because I filled them myself."

His tone indicated that he had done so against his will and against his better judgment.

"Well," Asey said, "that gives us just one thing more to look into. Now, where's Pete?"

"Waiting for you, Mr. Mayo. But first, may I ask you about something Dr. Stern said? Am I correct in understanding him to say that Mrs. Babb had been killed around eight o'clock?"

"More or less. Why?"

"Well, sir, I don't like to contradict anything the doctor may have said, for of course he knows far more than I. But I think the doctor is wrong."

"Go on," Asey said. "Go on! Why?"

"Well, sir, at nine-thirty, when I called from Whitefield, she was quite all right. I spoke with her."

9

"AT nine-thirty she was— Edward, give us the story. Unbend. Let yourself go. Quick!"

Obediently Edward told his story.

They had gone to the movies early, and had got out shortly before half-past-nine, to find that any thought of returning home was out of the question. Even in town at that time the streets were practically blocked for cars. After consulting with the other servants, Edward went into a drug store and phoned Mrs. Babb to tell her that they would spend the night with his wife's cousin until they could get through to Blight.

"The connection was bad, Mr. Mayo. It took me at least ten minutes to get the house, but Mrs. Babb answered. She said it would be all right for us to stay. That was at nine-thirty. Or a little after. I thought Dr. Stern might have made a slip of the tongue when he said it happened earlier, and I felt that you should know."

"You're sure," Asey said, "that it was Mrs. Babb who spoke?"

"Why, who else could it be, sir? There was no one else here. Mr. Pete and Mr. Harper—"

"Yup, I know. But did you actually recognize her voice, or did you just sort of take it for granted that it was her, b'cause it ought to of been her, an' you was expectin' her to answer, an' not thinkin' of anyone else bein' here?"

Edward considered. "I can't say that I thought her voice sounded at all natural, Mr. Mayo, but the connection was very bad, as I said. I don't really suppose I could swear to it that it was Mrs. Babb. But it ought to have been, sir! I shouldn't have brought the matter up if I had not thought it was Mrs. Babb."

" 'Course not," Asey said. "I know what you mean. But you see what I'm drivin' at, too, don't you? Someone answered, the connection was bad, the voice wasn't natural. It could of been someone else?"

"It could have, I suppose." Edward sounded rather annoyed by Asey's questions.

"Remember the conversation? Did she say much?"

"I explained the situation and asked if it would be all right if we stayed, and if she were all right," Edward said, "and she repeated after me, 'All right.' At least, that's all I heard. She may have said more. But the connection—"

"I know. Thanks, Edward," Asey said. "I'm glad you told me. Even if you maybe was talkin' with someone else, the fact that someone answered means consid'rable."

He sat there alone several minutes after Edward had gone. Then he went out to the hall, where the Brandts of the Blight fish market awaited him.

"We wish you'd look at the window," the Brandt son said. "The one that was unlocked. It seems the logical window. No drift there, or anything."

Asey started to say something, then changed his mind, and nodded.

"Okay, let's take a look."

They led him to the window out in a back entry which connected a kitchen and a store room.

"There. See the lock?"

"No prints around?"

"Vito went over it. Not a print. It was sort of oily, like someone had rubbed it with an oily cloth. Same way with the things upstairs."

"I see," Asey said. "Now, is Pete Dixon here?"

"He went back to town with the doctor. He said he'd be right back."

"D'you know if they's a safe in this house?" Asey's question amazed the Brandts.

"Why, yes, there is one. In the library, I think. My cousin helped put it in for Mrs. Babb's sister, Mrs. Crane."

"Let's get Edward," Asey said, "an' see about it."

Edward informed them that there was a safe in the library, but that only the family knew the combination.

"Is Harper here, then?"

"He—er—he's not been home since yesterday afternoon," Edward said rather shortly. "Not in the house. Shall I send someone to the greenhouse for him? He may be there. He spends much of his time there."

"No, thanks," Asey said. "I'll wait for Pete. Ask Miss McKeen to see me in the library, will you?"

"Got anywhere?" Gerty looked smaller and slighter than

ever, curled up in the big leather chair. "Got your mind settled on anything yet?"

"Yup," Asey said unexpectedly. "I got a stray thought I'm
dallyin' with. May make sense, an' then again it may not.
I'm r'versin' everythin'. May work out better that way."

Gerty wanted to know what he meant.

"Oh," Asey said, "when you got a lot of things massed together inside a circle, the usual an' proper way to get order is
to start in the middle or round the edges, an' make a b'ginnin'. It's dawnin' on me this mess inside this p'ticular circle
ain't even orderly enough for that. So I'm startin' from the
outside. Gerty, you had some sort of beauty kit or other with
you, didn't you, that you left b'hind in the bus the other
night?"

"Yes, my little case. They got the bus back to town this
morning, and called me from the garage to tell me they
had it."

"That woud be Tim Sparks, the brother of the kid I met
last night?"

"No, one of the other boys phoned."

"Gerty, I don't like to delve into your private life, but you'd
been havin' trouble with Sparks b'fore I come, hadn't you?"

Gerty's face turned scarlet. "Yes. I—I thought you guessed,
that night."

"Wasn't in a state you'd call sober, huh?"

"That's right. I knew you'd guessed, with the bus half in
the ditch, and the ploughs not touched, and all. I didn't
know he was in any state like that, or you can bet your
boots I wouldn't have started out with him. He minded his
own business until the others got out, and then he got play-

ful. I began to worry some when he didn't take the fork."

"I figgered that," Asey said, "when you said he missed it. Bus drivers most usually know their way blindfolded. They don't miss forks like I did."

"Well," Gerty said, "he'd heard me tell Mrs. Clarke I was going to Dixons', and he started kidding about Harper. At least, he thought he was kidding. I didn't really get upset until he pulled the bus around and got it stuck. Things— well, things got sort of complicated after that, and so when I got the chance, I beat it out the door and hid."

"Hid?" Asey said. "God A'mighty, child, where?"

"Underneath," Gerty said simply. "Under the bus. It was snowing so, he couldn't of found me if he'd been sober. After a while he lumbered off. He was yelling my name. When I couldn't hear him any more, I got back inside the bus. I hunted around and found the lights and turned 'em off, so he couldn't find his way back. When you came, I thought you was him. That's why I run away from you, and all. Honest, Asey, I could of kissed you when I recognized you. Offhand, I can't think of any one of the people around the town who might have come along that I'd have wanted to be picked up by."

"I see what you mean," Asey said. "Now. When you got back into the bus after givin' him the slip, did you notice if your case had been tampered with?"

"Asey," Gerty said fervently, "that case was the last thing I was thinking of then! Why do you want to know about that?"

"I'll get there. First, though, the road where the bus was stuck swings off the main road, don't it? An' where they meet is a couple miles down from where I met you. But would them two roads be far apart if you just cut 'cross the distance b'tween 'em?"

"Probably half a mile, at that part," Gerty said. "Further on, the road where the bus was stuck circles back to Monkton. Why—"

"Now," Asey said, "if Br'er Tim Sparks cut across that short distance b'tween the two roads, he'd be on the main road. An' if the p'fessor managed in his absent minded way to get to Dixons' along that road, it seems to me that Tim might of got there, too, even if he was a mite drunk. An' if he was chasin' you, knowin' that you was on your way to Dixons', it seems sort of likely he might of headed here. Am I right?"

"Right?" Gerty said excitedly. "Right?—listen to me! Asey, listen! In one of his playful moments when he was lunging around, he decided it was a nice time for me to give him a manicure. We had—you know, it's perfectly possible that he might of got into that red polish after I beat it! And Mrs. Babb didn't have any upstairs. In that kit of mine, there's every color under the sun. Gold and silver, too. I—Asey, d'you think that's it?"

"S'posin'," Asey said, "he stuck on the polish, an' then ploughed over here. Hm. How would he get in?"

"Well, there's that window they found unlocked. What's the matter with that?"

"Matter is," Asey told her, "that the window that they showed me in the entry was one of them I happened to notice was locked b'fore we left this place yest'day mornin'. 'Member how I come down for some coffee, an' got lost, an' you piloted me to the kitchen? I stood back to let you go through the door first, an' I r'member that window bein' locked, clear as day. It was rattlin' like sixty in the wind, but it was locked. Well, supposin' Tim come, anyways, an' got in. An' went through the d'canters to while away the time b'fore you should come."

"But what'd make him think I'd be coming, Asey?"

"Well, you was intendin' to come, an' you run away from him. He might of figgered, bein' in a kind of addled c'ndition, that you'd run to the Dixons'."

"What you mean," Gerty said, "is to Harper Dixon for protection, don't you? Well, even supposing all that—"

"How'd Sparks an' Mrs. Babb get along, or didn't they know each other?"

"Mrs. Babb," Gerty said, "probably never thought of Tim as anything more than a part of the bus, like a horn or a spare tire. But Tim hated her like poison."

"How come?"

Gerty lighted a cigarette and looked at Asey speculatively.

"I don't know, Asey, if I can make you understand. I mean, I know, but it's hard to explain. You see, Tim is one of those guys that hates anyone that's got more than he has. He thinks the world owes him a living, and he thinks it owes him not just a plain living, either. He wants something good and fancy. He likes his wealth shared, that is, he'd never share a dime with anyone else, but if he seen anyone else with a dime, he wants nine cents. I—d'you see?"

"I'm 'fraid," Asey said, "I know the type. We got a lot like that back home. The Spit an' Chatter Club. Gerty, do you s'pose that Tim, after downin' Mrs. Babb's bargain booze, might of got inspired to kill her?"

"It wouldn't take much," Gerty said, "to inspire him to do

anything. Ask me! Only it don't seem to me that even sober he'd think of drowning her. He'd use his fists. That's his way. He wouldn't know enough to dress things up like it was an accident. Even if he knew she had heart trouble, he wouldn't have brains enough to think of it, and figure out murdering her like that. Say, when they called up about my case in the bus, they didn't say a word about Tim, or where he was. Whyn't you phone and see? And listen, Asey, if that window was unlocked Sunday morning, who unlocked it?"

Asey shrugged. "Now you're askin' questions. Gerty, hop an' call up about Tim, will you?"

Gerty was grinning when she came back.

"They don't know where he is. Ain't seen him since Saturday night. Are they sore!"

"Sore, but not worried?"

"Not about Tim, Asey. They got kind of philosophical about him. He goes off every month or so for a couple of days' spree."

"Nice feller for a bus driver," Asey commented.

"He never drives or tries to when he's been drinking. That's why they keep him on. That's why I was sort of caught unawares the other night. He's really a swell driver. Asey, where do you suppose he is?"

"It don't hardly seem," Asey said, "that he could of got very far if—Edward, do you want me some more?"

Edward came over to Asey's side and spoke confidentially in his ear.

"I'd like to see you alone, sir."

"What's the trouble? Don't mind Gerty."

"It's noises, sir."

"Meanin'," Asey asked, "that you hear noises, like a ringin' in your ears, or you b'long to the league against noises, or what?"

"Noises in the wine cellar, sir."

Gerty and Asey looked at each other and whooped.

"Is it locked?" Asey demanded.

"Yes, sir. I have a key, but I thought you might care to be with me when I opened it. I spoke to the Brandts and the other officers, but," Edward sounded very hurt, "they laughed at me and asked me if I were scared."

"Asey," Gerty said, "I bet you—yes, sir! I bet you that's the answer. He was the one—hullo, Harper."

Harper strode into the library. "What's this I—"

"I said, hello, Harper!"

"Oh, my God, hello! Hello! Hello! Edward, Martha says there's someone in the wine cellar. What's all this nonsense?"

"I've just asked Mr. Mayo to investi—"

"Why should you ask Mr. Mayo, Edward? Why not call me? Where's Pete? Where's the rest of that unshaven mob of flatfeet the place is overrun with? Why—"

"You need a shave yourself," Gerty interrupted coolly. "I told you that this morning. Asey couldn't ask Pete because he's not here. And you weren't around."

"What's the matter with the coppers, then? Why—"

"They laughed at me," Edward said, "and refused."

"Well for Christ's sakes, can't you open a cellar by yourself if you have to? What're you waiting for? Come on! Come —what're you laughing about, Mayo? I suppose you think you know who's in the cellar, do you?"

"Sure," Asey said.

"What? Will you bet on it?"

"Sure," Asey said again.

"All right!" Harper was yelling at the top of his lungs. "All right! A thousand dollars! Now, who's down there?"

"Tim Sparks," Asey said. "Now, sonny boy, go see if I'm right."

Ten minutes later Harper slammed a check down on the table beside Asey in the library, and slatted out of the room without saying a word.

Asey pocketed the check. "Dunno," he said, "as I ever made a thousand dollars any easier. Dunno as it was so fair of me, either, but it kind of does my heart good to see that fellow taken down a bit. Oh, got him, Brandt? My golly, what a horrid lookin' mess he is!"

Tim wasn't a pretty sight as the two Brandts led him into the library. He wore only a filthy suit of long woolen underwear and a pair of knee high laced boots, with whose laces he had apparently been unable to make any headway. His eyes were swollen and bloodshot, and his face was matted with a heavy growth of beard.

Gerty pointed a finger at the underwear, rolled her eyes expressively toward the ceiling and giggled as though she couldn't stop. Tim winced at the sound, and began to fidget. He almost shrank in stature as they watched him.

"R'venge," Asey said, "b'longs to the Lord, Gerty, but I should say he'd passed a handful over for your use. My, my. Tim the masher, huh? An' ain't it nice, one hand all manicured with nice red polish!"

"How'd you know about him?" The state police sergeant looked on Asey with something akin to respect.

"I just guessed about that lad, an' I was goin' to ask you to hunt him up when Edward—say, Tim, do you know that I—

—oh. Hullo, Hank. Hi, Mrs. Westcott. Come in an' see what we found!"

"How perfectly foolish!" Nell said. "How perfectly foolish he looks! Asey, isn't this nice, your settling things so quickly! I said you would, and you didn't believe me. Really, what a thoroughly repulsive thing! It's so hard to believe he's human, isn't it? Just the same, he looks the way I always expected a murderer to look. Of course," she added hurriedly as Hank started to speak, "I never thought particularly about the underwear, I'm sure. It's the sort of thing you see hanging on lines in trains—"

"Nell," Hank said, "you know as well as I that no underwear hangs on lines in trains. Perhaps you mean, from trains. Anyway, you're getting awfully involved. Found the jewels, Asey?"

"Say," Tim Sparks finally found his voice, "say, what is this, huh?"

"You'll soon find out, my good man!" Nell told him. "I saw you that day in the bank, looking at those jewels! And much as I dislike the idea of going to court, and publicity, I shall none the less go and tell all about the way your eyes gleamed! When Char put the jewels in her bag—"

"Nell," Hank caught Asey's eye, "Nell, I want to show you the hallway. And the front door. The exterior has been greatly admired. Gerty, don't you want to see it, too?"

Sparks watched their departure and then turned to Asey.

"Say, what is this? What's that crazy dame talking about? What's the matter with youse guys?"

"How did you get in this house?" Asey asked.

"What's it to you? I—"

"Brandt," Asey said, "you know what I think would be fun? I want you to parade that fellow just the way he is up an' down the main streets of Blight an' Monkton. Later on, of course."

Brandt grinned.

"Now," Asey continued, "How'd you get in, Sparks? What time?"

"Ah, the door was open. The front door. I walked in. I guess I was tight. I don't know what time."

"N'en what? Sit him down, Brandt. I got a lot of things to ask him."

"Then," Sparks said sullenly, "I sat in the hall to wait for—"

"I'm sure," Asey interrupted, "you wasn't waitin' for no certain person, was you?"

"Well," Tim looked at Asey, "well, I guess not. I guess I was tight. Then I seen a bottle of whiskey, an' I drunk it."

"Did you see anyone around?"

"Nah. Wasn't no one here. I yelled when I come in. There wasn't nobody come. Then I guess I slept some. Then I heard someone come in, so I went upstairs—"

"Where, an' why?"

"Well, I didn't have no clothes on. I mean, I was like this."

"It's a habit of his," Brandt explained to Asey, "when he gets drunk. Once we found him in our front window Sunday morning. Lucky it was early. We got him out before more than a handful seen him."

"Go on, Tim," Asey said. "You went upstairs. Did you answer the phone at any time?"

"I think so. Yes, I think I did. I think someone asked me if I was all right, and I said I was. I don't know. Later on some people came in, like I said, and I put the lights out and tried to hide. I guess it was the Dixons. They put the lights on, and then I locked 'em in a room. I was scared, so I found another bottle. I don't remember much more."

"R'member unlockin' the door of the room you put the people in?"

Tim rubbed a grimy forehead with a grimier hand.

"I don't know. I think—I think I thought they'd die without air, so I think I let 'em out. I don't know. Say, what'd she mean, that dame, about murderers? Say, I didn't lock 'em all in an' leave 'em, did I?"

"How'd you get into the cellar?"

"Jesus, I don't know! I wanted to get out, but I didn't want to go into the storm, an' I seen a key on a stick as I went down cellar—"

"That's true," one of the troopers said. "He had it down there. It's a spring lock, too."

"So you unlocked the door, an' went in, Tim, an' slammed the door b'hind you. Huh. No signs of these missin' jewels an' their case, is there?"

"What's going on?" Tim demanded.

"Tell him," Asey said. "I hear a car comin'. Maybe Pete can help—"

Pete was overjoyed at the news that Sparks had been found in the cellar.

"Asey, I—oh, believe me, that rat is going to get all that's coming to him!"

"You got to r'member they's some drawbacks," Asey said. "Like there ain't no sign of Mrs. Babb's jewel case, an' all."

"Oh, he's hidden it!"

"Just for fun, if you've got the key to that library safe with you—have you? Then for fun, twist the safe open, an' unlock it, an' let's see if maybe she didn't put 'em in there. Or did you look?"

"Why, no. Char could have, of course; she had a key and knew the combination and all. But she never used it for anything. She hated being bothered about locking things up."

"She," Asey said, "an' Ernest. Well, let's look."

Rather reluctantly, Pete led the way to the safe, behind a picture in the library.

"I don't think this will net you anything, really," he said as he spun the dials. "I'm about the only person who uses it. Harper keeps his stuff at the bank. I—my God!"

He pulled out a jewel case and passed it to Asey.

"The thing's full, or feels it. Open it, Asey. The key's in the lock." Pete sounded dumbfounded. "What do you make of that?"

As far he as could tell from a brief examination, nothing was missing.

"Say," Tim Sparks spoke up, "can I go along, huh? I'll pay for the damage. I—"

"Pay for the damage?" Pete looked at him. "Pay! You certainly will pay! Just because you didn't steal the jewels is no reason to think you didn't kill Char. Is it, Asey? She must have put 'em there herself."

"Kill?" Tim's jaws parted. "Kill? She—Mrs. Babb's been killed? She—kill—she—"

"Oh, stop parroting!" Pete said. "You ought to know. You did it."

Asey managed to stop them before they actually did each other any great physical damage.

"Pete," he said, "you ought to know better. An' b'sides, I think you're maybe wrong. You—"

"Wrong, nothing! I know he killed her. I demand that he be arrested—"

"You can get him for enterin'," Asey said, "an' he admits to petty larceny. He'll be 'rested an' kept safe, all right. But b'fore any of you start tellin' the papers he's a murderer, you want to be a mite more sure, like. Brandt, will you and the sergeant come down to the cellar with me?"

Both men agreed with Asey, after a careful examination of the wine cellar, that Tim Sparks had undoubtedly been there since Saturday night.

"Slept on his pile of clothes, next the empties," Brandt said. "Say, he had his boots on. Didn't you notice any wet prints when you came Saturday with the other people?"

"We was too wet ourselves to notice," Asey said. "It was around eleven, an' most of his wetness ought to of dried out. Later when we got unlocked an' went upstairs, Harper was with us, an' he was all snow laden, so we didn't notice then, either. But I'm willin' to swear Sparks didn't kill Mrs. Babb. We got the time element to figger, an' lots of other things, but he ain't been out of here since Sat'day night till just now, an' I think whoever killed Mrs. Babb, also did some shootin' at me last night." He told them about it. "So I'd say, hold onto Sparks, but don't give him any credit."

"The time would clinch it," Brandt said. "That is, if you could prove—"

"I can find out about the time he left his bus," Asey told him. "I'll look into it now. B'fore I go, though, there's one thing I want to ask Pete."

Pete Dixon frowned at Asey's question.

"I—well, I hadn't thought of that side. But I do know about her will. I helped both Char and Aunt Gene with their business affairs, though of course both of them were entirely capable of looking after things themselves. Three-fourths of her estate, or thereabouts, comes to me. Harper and the servants and odds and ends of people—relatives and friends,—have the rest. I hadn't thought of that side. But if you're making any deductions about inheritance, I guess I'm the one you should label."

"Thanks," Asey said. "I'll be back shortly."

There was a puzzled look on his face as he went out to where Hank Thorn waited with the beach wagon. Of course Pete should know, but Steve Crump had told him that the entire estate, except for the odds and ends, went to Mrs. Babb's nephew Harper.

10

"I'VE taken Nell and Gerty home very much against their will," Hank said. "They're screaming with terrific rage at the thought of missing something. Tell me, Asey, what about brother Sparks?"

"What," Asey answered with another question, "do you think?"

"Frankly, if I were writing the story," Hank said in all seriousness, "I'd never pick Tim Sparks for a murderer. No color. No personality. No brains. Sparks is a low comedy element, sort of, if ask me. Of course it's entirely possible I'm doing the fellow a grave injustice. Perhaps he's cram full of color. Maybe he's a fine potential murderer at heart. Only if I'd written this, he'd not be the master criminal."

"In that case," Asey said, "you prac'tcly wrote it."

"Really?" Hank sounded pleased. "That goes to show you

that—really, no one's going to tell me again that my stories are far fetched. Far fetched my eye! Asey, if things really happen this way, I can double my income within six months."

"Couldn't just figger out the last chapter now, could you?" Asey inquired drily. "It'd contribute largely to the ben'fit of all c'ncerned, as my uncle Gil used to say when he went out tryin' to c'lect road taxes."

"Things have to happen first before I'm any help," Hank said. "I can't guess endings. But I can tell you after things have happened if they'd make a good story or not."

"Huh," Asey said. "If we slip up anywheres, just you sing out, an' we'll b'gin all over again. Hank, you crazy coot! I do b'lieve you think this is all happenin' for your special ben'fit!"

"Now you sound like Nell," Hank complained. "She's always telling me I have no feelings because I make impersonal comments on events and the characters concerned. I—oh, I'd better not get started. Anyway, it's inevitable that Tim was involved with some of the things that happened to us on Saturday night, but he simply hasn't the wits to kill anyone as cleverly as Char was killed. Of course you'll never be able to convince my sister of that, though."

"I think she's a lot easier to convince than you give her credit for bein'," Asey remarked.

"Maybe, but she places an inordinate amount of faith in the way people look, and Tim looks like a murderer to her. You know, she always votes by the looks of the candidates, and she refuses to vote for anyone without a mustache or a beard."

"Ain't she sort of curtailed?"

"I should be, myself, but Nell claims that all politicians are bald, bulgy and clean shaven, with an aura of Turkish baths. But statesmen have beards, and mustaches, and all—"

"Like McGuffey's readers, an' their pictures?"

"Just so. Asey," Hank started the beach wagon down the drive, "where can I take you?"

"To your house. I want Gerty." He ducked back as the car passed by the reporters. "Say, I don't understand them fellers givin' so little trouble. They're usually in your hair."

"I wondered, too, and I found out that dear Harper gave one a black eye and a bloody nose, and pretty well mutilated the others when they attempted to come any nearer the house. He had a horse whip."

All of which, Asey thought, would inspire the reporters to write a great deal more, and more unpleasantly, about Harper Dixon, than they would have otherwise.

The beach wagon bounded along the curving road to the Westcotts'. At the foot of the hill on which Robin had staged his runaway, Asey spotted something that made him literally sit up and take notice. It was a sleek, stream lined Porter roadster, the twin of his own back home in Wellfleet.

"Slow up!" Asey ordered Hank. "Stop!"

He sprang out of the car and strode over to the girl who prodded futilely under the hood with a screw driver.

"Carbureter," he quoted Bill Porter's telegram, "carbureter pip. Yup. A bully piece of machinery. Betsey Porter, what in Tophet are you doin' here?"

Betsey hugged him.

"Asey, you old dear! I felt it in my bones! I knew it. I knew that I'd find you here!"

"What," Asey disentangled himself, "d'you think you're doin' here?"

"Darling, I came to find you, and do please see what's the matter in there!" She pointed vaguely toward the engine. "It's missing, or something. Mr. Thorn, I've met you, even if you don't remember me. You were autographing books and saying 'Yes, Yes, how Kind' to women in a department store. Asey, when did you come?"

"Sat'day."

"I knew. You didn't even get that long cable of Bill's, did you, with the tag end about 'Betsey's bodice'? My private message?"

Asey shook his head. Bill's cable, three-quarters untranslated, reposed in the pocket of his car somewhere in Jamaica.

"I got it, all right, but I didn't read it."

"You got it? How could you, possibly, if you got here Saturday?"

"You underestimate him," Thorn said. "He turned up in the teeth of a gale, dressed in white linen. He flew. He—"

"What about 'Betsey's bodice'?" Asey interrupted.

"Well, I had a feeling in my bones that you'd find out about that bet anyway, and come popping up, even if Bill didn't tell you. We'd not heard from you in weeks, so I stuck in a lot of silly questions at the end of that report, and said for you to answer at once. When you didn't, I cabled you, and then I cabled the hotel, and they said you'd left. So then I wired Bill in Pittsburgh—he went back to fiddle with that steel place,—and told him I was going to Placid or Frontenac or somewhere, and then the storm came, and—well, here I am! Have you found out about that foolish grocery order? And whoever told you about the bet?"

"What *is* all this about grocery orders?" Hank demanded. "It keeps cropping up."

Asey stepped back from the car. "Wait'll I fix this, an' then we'll do some clearin' up."

In ten minutes he wiped his hands on Betsey's inadequate handkerchief and pointed to the car.

"Upholstery's soft, anyways. Sit down, an' I'll go through the whole dum business. What's time, after all?"

"Well, I never!" Betsey said at the conclusion of his long recital. "I—"

" 'Fore you take to oh-in' an' ah-in'," Asey said, "catch me up on what really happened that night of the game at the Hybrid Club. I been wantin' to know, but I wasn't goin' to call on Bill."

Betsey obediently gave him Bill's version. "And," she added, drawing two letters from her pocketbook, "stare at these. One is Bill's check to Harper. I was supposed to mail it, but even before I knew you'd left Jamaica, I decided to present it in person. The whole thing was too crazy. And this one here is what came for Bill just after he left. It's postmarked Blight, and I suppose it's from Harper. I've been pining to open it, but of course I haven't. I think there's a check clipped inside, for I can feel the clip. I've done about everything but x-ray it. I had some idea of telling Harper he was a fool. I've already planted a similar thought in Bill's mind, about himself. I was going to try—well, you know."

"Betsey Porter, dove of peace," Asey commented.

She stuck her tongue out at him.

"Someone ought to do something about that feud. Of course it's always Harper who gets the blame, but it doesn't reflect Bill in any brilliant light. Hearing about it, you would never consider Bill a very bright boy. It's bad for business. Bill's just as childish and silly as Harper, and I'm sick and tired of both of them carrying on. I want things settled. I don't care if they've both paid up, and if Harper dismisses it as a drunken inspiration. I want that grocery order settled, and I want Harper and Bill settled."

"Don't ask much, do you?" Asey said. "I—"

"It's immense," Hank said dreamily. "Immense. I wish I'd thought of something like that."

"What?" Betsey stared at him.

"Why, that bet, and the grocery order. There's something so completely innocuous and commonplace about a grocery order. But stick it into fifty thousand dollars' worth of bets, and it looms. Why, it's superb! You've got something. You—"

"Don't mind him," Asey told Betsey. "It's just genius, burnin' away. He's plannin' on supportin' his old age with this affair. Bets, exactly how do you think you'd go about pryin' details of that order off'n Harper?"

"Ask him."

"Yup. I tried that, too."

"You drive me there," Betsey said, "and let me talk to him. Go on. I dare you."

"Gerty tried to converse with Harper," Asey reminded her. "She got socked."

Betsey laughed. "He won't sock me. You know there's something I've never dared tell Bill, but while Harper was at General Braden's, years ago, and I was at Miss Maud's, at school—Harper once kissed me under the mistletoe at a Christmas party. He gave me a bell button off his best uniform, too. I kept it for years. He even wrote me poetry."

"If you'd saved that," Asey said, "maybe you got some chance of blackmailin' him. Otherwise, I don't think you'll get far with that guy, even with your nice sent'mental mem'-ries. But—"

"No buts. Take me along to him. After all, what can he do? If he kicks and bites, I can kick and bite back, can't I? Besides, he won't."

She battered down every argument that both Asey and Hank could think of against her interviewing Harper.

"For heaven's sakes," she said at last, "do be reasonable! You've gone and promised to find all these things out, Asey, and how will you ever know about this old grocery order if you don't take steps? Come on. After all, you taught me jiu-jitsu yourself. Let me go at him point blank. Why beat about the bush? He knows you want to find out, and you know he knows. Let me have a shot at him."

Asey sighed. "Have it your own way!"

"I intend to."

"Very well, but if you get into any trouble, I r'fuse to hold myself r'sponsible for that fire eatin' husband of yours. First off, I want to see Gerty. You an' Hank go in the Porter, an' I'll tag b'hind in the bouncer. I'm havin' to bounce to save my good name from bein' tarnished with the c'mercial in-t'rests of them ole money-changers, the Porter fam'ly. Golly, wouldn't the ole Cap'n of hopped if anyone called him a money-changer! Git, you two."

Betsey laughed, and the roadster darted away. Asey watched it over the top of the hill, grinned, and climbed in behind the wheel of the beach wagon.

Although he knew perfectly well there was no car behind him, he automatically glanced in the rear view mirror before starting up. Then he paused and leaned on the wheel, and thought.

The canvas curtain in the back had been snugly tied in place when they left the Dixon house. But now it was flapping.

Asey got out of the car and went around back. Yes, someone had certainly undone all the snaps.

Who on earth would be likely to try hiding in the beach wagon?

"Leon," Asey said, "come out from under them rugs an' that seat! Hear me? Come out!"

Slowly the figure of young Leon Sparks emerged from under the pile of robes.

"Get down," Asey said. "Come on, hop down!"

Leon jumped down and stood, lank and unabashed, in front of Asey.

"How long you been there? When'd you get in that car?"

"Just now."

"Been listenin' to our conv'sation in the roadster b'fore that, huh?"

"Gee, ain't it excitin'?" Leon's eyes sparkled. "Say, just like Thorn said, it's like a book, ain't it?"

"So," Asey observed, "you been in the car—listen, kid, how long you been lurkin' in that jitney?"

"Since about six this morning," Leon said. "I was in the town car most of the night, and then I heard a maid tell Frank to use that, so I climbed into this. Gee, I was glad when you decided to use this. If you'd of gone in the big car, I wouldn't of known nothing."

"Words," Asey said truthfully, "fail me."

"Say, ain't it excitin'? Say, don't you think Tim killed her, really? I don't. He ain't got the guts. He just talks big. He often says he'll smash me, but he never did. Once he tried, when

I was a kid, but I hit back, and he ain't never touched me since. Say, who do you think it was that shot you last night? What's the bet about, anyway? Do you think it was Harper shot you?"

Asey sighed. His first impulse was to send the boy packing, but he immediately perceived the folly of any such move. Leon had heard all Betsey's story, and all his own, all the facts of the bet, all Thorn's theories, all his own theories, and considerable personal touches. To let him loose, with all those reporters lurking around, was out of the question.

"Was you under that back seat when Gerty and Mrs. Westcott drove over to Dixons' and back?"

"Yeah. Gee, Gerty's soft on Harper, ain't she? She—"

Leon rambled on, but Asey barely paid any attention to him at all. Leon had to be won over and shown the wisdom of holding his tongue. That alone was a herculean task. Leon could not be allowed to circulate freely and at will until he understood that silence was golden. On the other hand, it might almost be simpler for a while to keep Leon on tap. If Leon was a liar, any promise he might make about keeping quiet wouldn't count. It all boiled down to a single problem: Leon couldn't be allowed to talk. But he undeniably would.

"Much," Asey said wearily, "as I hate the thought, Leon, it looks like you had to go on my pay roll. Would you like to go on it, kid?"

Leon almost quivered with pleasure. "Gee, say, Mr. Mayo, you don't have to hate the thought. I know you must feel that way on account of Tim, but honest, I can help you, and all that business about Tim, that won't influence me none. And I don't want to go on your pay roll, neither. Say, it's a privilege to help a fellow like you. And there probably isn't no one in Blight or

Monkton that knows this place around here like I do. Say, I know every inch of it. I know all about it. What'll I do first?"

Asey carefully restrained his joy. "Well," he said gravely, "there's a lot of hard things to be done, Leon. I—uh—" he sounded, he thought irrelevantly to himself, like Ernest Vail discoursing on his own vowel split, "I—uh—don't quite know if you—"

"Say, don't you worry none about me! You just tell me what to do, and I'll do it! Say, you know what?"

"What?" Asey said obediently.

"I thought you was going to send me off. Everyone does. I was going to tell those reporters everything, if they'd pay me. I didn't think you'd ever let me help. Say, you just tell me what you want done!"

"Well," Asey said, "do you know anythin' about detectin'?" He racked his brains to think of some distant mission that Leon might undertake. But if the boy knew this vicinity, it might almost be better to have him around.

"Well, I read books about detectin'," Leon said. "I know how you solve things, too. I read about your ways in the paper. You always say 'Common Sense.' Well, I got some common sense."

"Leon, did you really see Harper around last night?"

"Sure."

"See anybody else?"

"I seen somebody with a rifle."

"Come, come, Leon," Asey said, "don't let's b'gin with no flights of fancy. I don't b'lieve you seen a solitary soul with a gun. I think you heard me say I'd been shot at, an' then made that part up. Ain't that so?"

"Well," Leon hesitated. "No. No and yes. Early yesterday

afternoon when I first came out, I seen someone on skis across the valley yonder. I thought it might be one of the Sunday bunch, so I started for 'em to see if they was—"

"Lost. I know."

"That's right. But before I got started, whoever it was went down the far slope, an' jumped the fence there, an' went out of sight, lickety split."

"Where'd the gun come in?"

"Well it seemed to me they had three poles," Leon said. "I didn't think about it much. Some of the bunch that comes here, they carry four, two for spares. Some don't have none. They're all crazy, that winter sports crowd. So I didn't think of it, but when it turned out you was shot at, I got to wondering if maybe whoever it was I seen couldn't of been the person waiting to shoot you. Maybe the third pole was a gun."

Asey nodded. Perhaps Leon was lying, but on the whole his story was sketchy enough to have a ring of truth. It was probably what had happened, someone lurking around to shoot him, over by that cabin. Skis were a touch he hadn't thought about, but they were an excellent idea on the part of this possible lurker. And if Leon were lying, wouldn't he go whole hog, and describe the gun and the person?

"Kind of a gun was it?" Asey asked. "Who was the person?"

"I don't know much about guns," Leon said, "and anyways, I couldn't see. I don't know who it was, either. The sun was going down, and it was glarey. Someone in a dark suit, dark pants, dark jacket and cap. I know most of the people around here a long way off, but I couldn't tell. It seemed a tall sort of person."

"Leon," Asey said, "I got somethin' for you to do. First, you want to r'member that you mustn't let anyone know you're helpin' me. You might get shot at." He didn't say by whom. "You mustn't talk to them r'porters. 'Cause if they found out you was Tim's brother, they'd make a fuss an' then the cops might grab you. An' I can't have that happen when I need you so."

Leon nodded. "Why, I wouldn't say a word!"

"Not to anyone. Except me. Don't you tell no one what you found out, either. Now, I want you to wander around here, keepin' under cover, an' I want you to see if you can find any traces of that person you seen with the gun. Tracks, or anythin'. Think where you'd of gone if you was that person waitin' there, an' you seen someone comin' toward you, as you come towards them. Figger where you'd of stayed an' watched, till the person that was you, really, had gone. Get the idea, do you? An' of course if you could find me a 30–06, that'd be like the gun in that cabin last night, I'd like it fine. Think you can do that?"

"Sure. Say, that's nothin'!"

"Don't kid yourself," Asey said. "It's goin' to be hard. Play around with that idea, an' then come to the Westcotts', an' tell me everythin'. This evenin' I'll have somethin' different for you. Okay?"

"Gee, yes, thanks!"

"Say, wait a sec b'fore you set out. Want snowshoes, or skis, or somethin'?"

"I keep a pair hid up here," Leon said. "I keep one pair home, an' one here. I got sort of a little lean-to, like, way over beyond. I can get to that all right."

"When," Asey asked, "was you home last, by the way? How'd you get to Westcotts'?"

"Oh, I bummed a ride back last night with one of the Brandts, and this morning I come over on the plough, early. I brought my lunch," he added hastily. "I ate it while I was listening to you and Thorn and Betsey. Swell looking, ain't she? Say, is she married to this Bill? I couldn't tell, the names she called him. First it was fool, and then it was darling."

"I'm sorry," Asey said, "she's married, Leon. I'm 'fraid you ain't got a chance."

"There's always divorce," Leon returned airily, and set off through the deep snow.

Asey chuckled, and got into the beach wagon. Maybe, if he could keep Leon busy enough, and if the labor were sweetened with an occasional bank note, maybe Leon wouldn't talk. He might possibly even be an asset.

"Anyways," Asey murmured, "he's p'sistant."

He found Hank and his sister and Gerty and Betsey almost on the verge of setting out after him.

"The Asey Mayo Rescue Project Number Two," Hank informed him, "was in the burgeoning state."

"Deary me," Asey said, "I do hope you ain't gone an' got them poor St. Bernards roused up again. Gerty, what time did Tim leave the bus?"

"I been thinking of that. It was about—well, quarter to eight, or eight. No earlier. May Adamson was sore because the bus was so late, because she missed some radio program she wanted to hear. The girl was being hypnotized, or unhypnotized, or something, that night, and May almost counted the minutes all the way from town. We left her at her door about seven-fifteen, and she'd just missed it. She was sore as a boil. I think Tim left about half an hour later, though it seemed," she added honestly, "about ten years. He couldn't have got to Dixons' before eight, even if someone give him a lift. He's out of this, isn't he?"

Asey nodded. "I s'pose I ought to go back there an'—"

"Have tea first," Nell said. "We're starved, and we've been waiting, and I've no doubt some food will make you think better. Really, you may be right about this Tim Sparks, but it does seem to me like discarding such a perfectly splendid murderer!"

"I ought to get along, honest—"

"Nonsense," Betsey said, "and besides, I've thought of something that's burning me from within. Asey, you said that Bill sent you three telegrams on the night of the big game, didn't you?"

"That's right. Three."

"But he told me, Asey, that he sent two. One about the cars, or something, and one about the game. I went into it thoroughly, because I thought he might have sneaked off some message to you. He swore on bended knee that he hadn't. He—"

"He did," Asey said, "an' I'll c'nfess I was glad to get that last one cleared up when Root told me about things. I thought Bill was tellin' me to go to blazes for sendin' him the message I promised you I'd send. The one about not fightin' Harper. As a matter of fact, I was kind of sore about bein' told off. That's mostly why I ain't written—"

"Asey Mayo!" Betsey stood up and went over to him. "Asey, what did it say? Oh, dear! He—Asey, are you sure it was from Bill? He swore he didn't send any word to you at all! What did it say?"

From his wallet, Asey took a limp piece of paper and passed it to her.

" 'GLEASE GO TO—' "

"'Please,'" Asey said. "Not 'glease.' 'Low for errors in transmission."

"'PLEASE GO TO BLIGHT. X.'" Betsey stared at him. "No wonder you—" she read through the message again, and then smiled triumphantly. "Asey, you lamb, in your place I'd have shot Bill Porter. But Asey, Bill didn't send this. I know he didn't."

11

BETSEY perched on the arm of Asey's chair and thrust the cable under his nose.

"Look! Asey, you got this the day after the game, didn't you?"

"Uh-huh. All three to once. We ain't got a phone, so they was mailed out from Kingston, an' my messenger brought it up."

"Asey, listen. Bill was in the writing room, waiting to make his speech at the banquet when Harper came in. The speech was scheduled for ten-thirty. I'm positive of that, because I'd tried to make Bill say he'd take the midnight home. But Harper came in, and it was after eleven before they had their encounter. It was nearly midnight before those bets were made and settled, and all. But look at the time this message was sent. Asey, look!"

"Ten-ten! Betsey Porter!"

"Don't you see," Betsey said excitedly, "it was sent even before Harper and Bill met, or before those bets were made! Thank goodness, Bill told the truth! I knew he did, of course, but this proves it. He didn't send you this. But Asey, who did?"

"P'raps that ole fuddy-duddy Root," Asey began, "could cast some light—say, don't he take care of the cables an' wires at his ole desk there in the lounge? Mightn't he know somethin'—"

"He knows everything. Nothing goes on in that club, particularly about Bill, that he doesn't know about. The man's a walking encyclopaedia. Asey, did you save the other messages Bill sent? What a pity. But the car one would have been in the morning, because he talked with David then. The game one would have been after the game. They must have been at different times, or he'd have combined them. I'll bet, though, that old Root sent all three at once. Probably there was a mixup. Asey, how can we get in touch with him? We must be able to, somehow! What's the name of his boat, and where was he going?"

Asey shrugged. "He told me, but I wasn't payin' much attention. They'd know at the club. I'll call an' find out, an' get the ship's itin'rary. First, though, I'll call the Dixons an' tell them fellers about the time Tim left the bus."

"I want to see Harper," Betsey said. "Don't forget—"

"T'morrow'll do. Let's straighten this out now."

Pete answered the telephone at the Dixon house. His voice sounded as though he were weary and distraught.

"Oh, it's such a mess," he said in answer to Asey's question. "It's hideous. They've got their experts here, and they've fine tooth combed the place. Can't find any prints in Char's room but her own, and the maid's. They've got lots of Tim's, on the stair case rail and the landing. Apparently he was in the grabbing and holding on state. They found one or two on the powder room door. But Tim didn't go into her room, they say. They can follow him all over the house, except there. He shut the door on you people, and all. The expert found'em there where the other men couldn't. Well, I suppose if he left the bus then, he's innocent, but I just don't see how he can be!"

"Just for fun," Asey said, "you didn't happen to know where I was this winter, did you?"

"What? No. Nell, or someone said you'd come up from Nassau, or Bermuda, I think. Why?"

"Wondered. Is Harper there?"

"I don't know," Pete said sadly. "He was. He stormed around the library looking for a book on insect pests, and the professor was there looking up something else, and they had a fight. Threw volumes of morocco bound Shakspere at each other's heads, and ruined father's Whitman collection entirely. The place is a mess. Harper stormed out, and Vail's there now, crying on Sue's shoulder. Asey, haven't you any leads at all?"

"I told you," Asey said, "your state police were the ones to tackle your problems. They got the equipment. You put your trust in them, right now. I'm sort of strayin' around, at this point."

"They may have the equipment," Pete said with bitterness, "but a fat lot of good it seems to do them! Asey, you must have some ideas!"

"Loosely speakin'," Asey said, "I have. But don't try to pin me down. They're kind of nebulous thoughts. I'll be seein' you."

"Wait," Pete said. "Can't you come over here and settle things? I haven't told you about the Brandts. They're sore at the detectives, and the sergeant and Edward have come to blows, and those reporters have got in. They're over the place like locusts, and—"

"It don't sound to me," Asey said, "like any place where I could do any concentratin'. Nothin' tendin' to aid tranquil brain work."

"It's a mad house! Can't you do anything?"

"Tell Vito and the others that you'll call the gov'nor," Asey said, "if they don't get order. Scream about your polit'cal friends, an' start callin' up senators. Call the reporters' bosses, whether you know'em or not. Ain't they some big shots in the Hybrid Club? Well, call'em. Call that s'preme court feller, an' tell him your rights as an individual is bein' trampled on, an' he's got to stop the reg'mentation. He will. He always does. Make a lot of noise an' bluster, an' they'll come to heel. Be spirited."

Pete's reply was very spirited.

"Well," Asey said with a chuckle, "get a hoss whip, then. You can get rid of'em. I'll see you later, maybe. 'Bye."

"Is he having trouble?" Hank asked as Asey hung up the receiver.

Asey summed up Pete's information. "Sounds," he concluded, "like he was havin' his hands full. An' with Ernest an' Harper fightin', too. Huh. I'd like to of seen that. Wonder why Vail's weepin' on Sue's shoulder?"

"He told me once," Nell observed, "that it gave him intense physical pain to see a book maltreated. He must have been pretty mad to throw books around. Oh, dear, this is all so terribly foolish, isn't it? Are you going to phone about that man, now?"

The name of Mr. Root's ship, and his itinerary, were supplied by the Hybrid Club staff without a second's hesitation. Clearly both had been impressed on their minds.

"I know her." Asey referred to the ship. "One of the big liners they hire out for cruises. She'll have a radiophone. Uh— I'll add it onto my bill, Mrs. Westcott."

"I wish," Nell said, "you'd stop worrying about phone bills. I'm not used to it. Only, don't please ask him if it's raining where he is, and what he had for lunch. That's what Hank's friend wanted to know when he called his Hollywood girl, the time she went to Honolulu."

It was nearly ten o'clock before Asey succeeded in talking with Mr. Root.

"So excited," Asey reported later, "that you could almost feel him hoppin' around. He says those three wires all come in at dif'rent times that day, got mislaid, an' so was sent at one time. He didn't see Bill, or anyone else, give in the last one about Blight, but he r'members it well. Straggly, careless writin', an' he thought Bill'd been drinkin' when he sent it."

"Wouldn't he know who paid for it?" Nell asked.

"I asked that, an' he said he charged it to Bill. Said a lot of messages on game day just got written an' left on the desk, but he most always managed to know who to charge."

"I bet he does, the old busy-body!" Betsey said. "He knows every member of that club down to third cousins and in-laws twice removed. Asey, this doesn't get us anywhere, except we know that Bill didn't send it. D'you suppose Harper did?"

"After the scene he made here yesterday when Pete asked Asey to help?" Hank said. "Fat chance! Asey, there are so many unexplained things. Like this message, and the grocery order— truly, I'm beginning to brood over that order! And who shot you, and how did Char's case get into the safe, and what about that unlocked window? It's crazy."

"I think," Asey said, "we can assume Mrs. Babb put the case away in the safe. Probably it's all we'll ever know. I don't understand about the window. Looks like someone in the house was tossin' red herrin' around."

"It seems to me," Nell said, "that the strange message and the order are queer, but they don't have anything to do with poor Charlotte Babb! After all, she's been killed, and nothing's been done about it!"

"I wouldn't say that," Hank remarked. "We know she was killed around eight o'clock, and we know Tim didn't kill her. The servants are out of it. Harper and Pete left the house at the same time, and they check each other. They're out. So—"

"Why are you so sure about Harper?" Nell interrupted. "He looks like a murderer to me, sort of. He's so dark."

Hank sighed. "That's not the point. The point is, we've eliminated certain things."

"What about Ernest Vail, have you eliminated him? He was over at Dixons earlier, and he was wandering around at large when Asey was shot."

"But he came to the house after Char had been killed."

"You've only his word for it," Nell said. "And even if the gun at Sue's cabin was rusty, it doesn't mean he couldn't have another, does it? Really, Hank, I think you're unreasonable! Every time someone enters into this who appears to have some connection with the case, you promptly start in excusing them, and apologizing, and alibiing, and trying to make them out such honest, innocent lambs!"

"Nell, I was just trying to show you the other side of the—"

"Let's say no more about it," Nell said. "I still think Tim Sparks is the one to arrest and hold on to. He looks like a murderer, and I'm sure he is."

While she and Hank entered into one of their long winded arguments, Rochelle brought in Ernest Vail.

His eyes were red behind his glasses, and his face was daubed with little spots of iodine.

"P'fessor," Asey said, "you look unhappy."

"I am," the professor said fervently. "I am. Most. This has been a most upsetting experience, really. I'm still very much upset."

"I hear you been brawlin' with Harper," Asey remarked. "How come? What happened?"

"Why, I went over there and asked if I might make use of their library, and Pete most graciously assented. While I was reading, Harper came in and started to pull books from the shelves and throw them on the floor! He was hunting for a book on plant pests, he said. He accused me of stealing it! I remonstrated with him for treating the books that way, and he began to throw them at me! I tried to ward them off without injuring myself or the books, and really, it was a disgraceful scene! All that wonderful collection of his father's! Why, it will take someone weeks to repair those books properly! Irreplaceable damage. Wanton. Vicious. I lost control of myself completely."

The professor's cheeks grew redder as he spoke.

"But," he continued more mildly, "that is not what I came here about. My cousin Sue Vail, Asey, told me that yesterday afternoon she set out for the cabin where we were last night, but it was so cold that she turned back. Twice, she said, she caught sight of a figure on skis. She thought nothing of it at the time, for on Sundays there are many winter sport addicts around out here. But after hearing of your unfortunate experience of being shot at, she remembered that this person she saw appeared very anxious to keep out of sight. Hugged the trees, so to speak. She asked me to tell you about it."

"Well, well," Asey said, "so Leon does tell the truth sometimes. She didn't know who it was?"

"She had no idea, except that the person was tall. I don't know that the fact will be of any value, but I thought you should know. Er—good evening."

"Wait, Ernest," Nell said. "Why don't you spend the night here? You've got such a long walk back, and it's so cold, and you've had such a—uh—distressing day. Spend the night here, and—"

"And relax," Hank finished up. "Come on, Vail."

"No, no," Ernest said. "Really. Thank you, no. I've much to do. I'm behind in my work as it is. I—er—should like to borrow a book, though. A novel I began yesterday."

"Did we corrupt you entirely?" Nell asked. "Of course you may borrow anything you want. What's that tome under your arm? It has a familiar look."

"It is a treatise of Schwellenstadt's," Ernest said, "dealing with the more obvious aspects of—why, dear me! It isn't either! It's—how amazing! It seems to be a thing called 'Culinary Herbs, their Uses and Cultivation'! What a pity. Now I shall have to go back to Dixons' for Schwellenstadt. I—oh, dear me!"

Without even saying good night, the professor abruptly departed.

"How nervous and irritable," Nell said, "the academic mind can get! And—"

"And he's left the herbal behind," Betsey picked it up. "I'll run after him—"

"Don't you do anything of the sort!" Nell said. "It's mine. I lent it to Charlotte Babb two years ago, and I've been trying to get it back ever since. I thought it looked familiar. Just you—"

"Oh, but his notes are in it, too!" Betsey said. "See, a whole sheaf of them! Asey, dash after the man and give'em to him, or he'll have to tramp all the way back here again! Here. I'll go. They're probably awfully important to him."

Grabbing up her coat, Betsey flung it around her shoulders and ran out doors and down the driveway after the professor, who accepted the pages gratefully.

"Thank you, Gerty. I'm afraid you'll think I'm very absent minded, like a professor in a cartoon—oh, it isn't Gerty, is it?"

"I'm Betsey Porter. No one thought to introduce us. These are your notes, aren't they?"

"Yes, indeed. Yes. After all that has gone on today, I seem to be unable to concentrate as I should. Thank you. Thank you so much!" he cleared his throat. "Er—thank you. You have been so kind—"

"That's all right." Betsey was a little embarrassed by Ernest's profuse thanks. "It's never fun to lose notes. Good night."

As she started up the walk, Leon Sparks stepped out from behind the shadow of the trees.

"Hi, Mrs. Porter. How do you like Blight, from what you've seen of it? Nice place, huh?"

"Wh—oh. You must be Leon." She remembered Asey's story of the boy. "Why, I guess Blight is all right. Do you want Asey?"

"Yup. I got some things for him to look at. Is he here?"

"Come in. He's wondered where you were."

Leon followed her into the living room.

"I always wanted to know what the inside of this place looked like," he announced, staring casually around. "Quite a nice place you got here, huh?"

"We," Nell returned crisply, "like it."

"If it was mine," Leon said, "I'd have papered walls instead of this wood. Don't you like paper? I do. You like paper, Mrs. Porter?"

"Some times, and in some places," Betsey said. "But I like pine panelling, too. We have some at home."

Leon surveyed the walls again. "Well," he said, "I suppose I'll like it better after I get used to it. I—what did you say, Mr. Thorn?"

"I said, God forbid," Hank told him. "Asey, you do something, quick!"

"What you find?" Asey asked. "Got anywhere? Better take off your coat, an' things."

Leon removed his heavy leather jacket, three sweaters and two scarves, and sat down comfortably before the fire.

"What do you pay for maple logs?" he inquired. "I know a man in Whitefield that—"

"What did you say you found?" Asey interrupted. Mrs. Westcott and Hank and the others had promised him faithfully that they would not alienate Leon's affections, but he foresaw difficulties.

"Well, I found these." Leon got up and presented him with three match flaps, identical with the two Asey had found the previous night, and the one which Thorn had tossed away in the cabin.

"Mine," Hank said. "I told you I used thousands of matches last night."

"I told him to find things," Asey said, "an' he found'em, Hank. Let him go on."

"An' this." Leon pulled a plaid cap from his hip pocket. "That's Vail's. I know it. I seen him wear it. Ain't it the limit?"

"Guess that's the one he claimed to of lost last night," Asey said. "I'm glad you found that. Proves that maybe Ernest ain't been foolin' me. Anythin' else?"

From a pocket of his leather jacket, Leon produced a small package wrapped in oiled paper.

"Cigarette butts," he said. "Covered with lipstick. Four of'em, chucked away in a dry place near the top of the hill by the cabin. Must of been put there since the storm. A rock sticks out, and it's dry around one side. Seems like someone sat there."

Asey looked at the butts. "Common enough brand. Gerty, can you tell me anything about this lipstick?"

Gerty sniffed professionally. "Not much smell left, Asey. Let me scrape this piece off, and I might be able to tell. It's a greasy cold creamish kind. I sell a lot of it around here winters. Yeah, Asey. I know it. It ain't got a brand name. They make'em up, and then stick the name of the store or shop on'em. Or you can get'em plain with a gadget to put initials on with. That's what I do. I've sold a lot, because of those initials. Mrs. West-cott's got one. Mrs. Babb had. I got one myself."

"Let's see," Betsey said. "It's a sort of raspberry taste, isn't it? Let me get mine from my bag. I think mine's like it, too."

Gerty said that it was. "And you paid two-fifty for that? I— well, the price tag's still stuck on the bottom. Two-fifty?"

"Is that too much?"

"I sell'em," Gerty said, "for eighty-nine cents to people in Monkton, and a dollar to people in Blight. I make plenty on'em, and I buy in small lots, too."

"I resent that," Nell said. "I resent that intensely. Gerty, I want eleven cents back at once!"

"I'll credit you," Gerty said. "Gee, I forgot you was from Blight. I always think of you swells out here as being from another planet," she added.

"We're not," Nell said. "And some of us are quite nice, too. Asey, what do you make of Leon's collection?"

"I d'duce," Asey told her, "that Hank hunted me far an' wide, as he said, an' that some woman—any woman, as far as I can make out from Gerty's detectin',—sat on a rock an' smoked cig'rettes, an' that Ernest had two caps like he claimed, an' that's about all. Was the rock in a nice shootin' p'sition, Leon?"

"Yeah. I'd picked it," Leon said. "You'd be out of sight from the road, but you could see clear, and you'd hear people coming to you on any side, because of all the rocks around that ain't snow covered. Footsteps. It's a swell place."

"Any foot prints around?"

"The snow's blown over so it's smooth as silk. Only reason those butts didn't blow away was because they was on a dry spot around the rock, and the crust is eight or nine inches above it, where it melted. What," Leon concluded, "do I do now?"

Hank grinned and looked at Asey. "Think quick, cap'n," he advised. "Think quick!"

"Eaten?" Asey asked hopefully. "Maybe Rochelle'd scare up some food—"

"Oh, I bummed a ride home, and ma got me some supper. She put me up a lunch. I'm all set till tomorrow."

"What about school?" Nell asked. "Don't you have homework, and school, and things?"

"Vacation, this week." Leon looked around the room. "Say, I think I like this pine panelling, Mrs. Porter, after all. It grows on you. Say, Asey, what do you think about Sue Vail? Do you know Sue Vail, Mrs. Porter?"

"She was in the lower school at Miss Maud's," Betsey said, "when I was a senior. I forgot she was engaged to Pete Dixon. I think of her as a fat little girl with pigtails in a middy blouse that always seemed too small. She was always getting the most sumptuous boxes from Pierce's. What do you mean, what does Asey think about her?"

"She's a whiz on skis," Leon said. "She can shoot, too. She always uses a lot of lipstick, too. Say, why couldn't it of been her?"

"Because," Hank answered, "the person who killed Mrs. Babb, Leon, presumably shot Asey, too. Grant that Sue can ski and shoot, the fact remains that she was at home throwing a stupendous dinner party at the time Mrs. Babb was killed."

"How do you know?" Leon demanded. "She's got a cook, and people to do all the work. She wouldn't be busy getting supper, would she? She could of—"

"I happen to know she was at home around that time," Hank said, "because I phoned her—I hear a car coming, Nell. Want to see anyone?"

"Anyone but Harper," Nell said. "Or those horrid reporters. Odd time for callers."

In a few minutes Hank ushered in Sue Vail.

Betsey, who hadn't seen her for years, opened her eyes wide. In place of the fat little girl in a middy blouse was a slim, stunning young woman with blue black hair, and a manner usually associated with Miss Maud's school.

"Nell, dear," Sue said, "isn't this whole thing awful? Betsey! What are you doing here? Hullo, Gerty. Everybody. And you're Asey? Asey, Pete says that Harper is on the rampage, and can't you do something? Harper's driven the reporters out of the house, and then he began on the police, and he's simply in a state. Not drunk as much as crazed. Pete wants to know if you'll help corral him. I've done my best, but I simply can't cope with things, and Pete is done up, completely! He hasn't slept for days, and he's simply all in. Will you help?"

"Why, sure," Asey said. "I'll do what I can. Only I ain't no restrainin' influence on Harper, nor soothin' either. Harper don't care for me one bit. He says so, right out."

"But you can twist him around your little finger," Sue said. "Pete said so. The police can't do anything, and poor Pete is too exhausted even to kid him out of things. Will you—"

"Where is he now?" Asey asked.

"When I left, he was chasing one of the Brandts over the house—"

"Wait," Asey said. "Listen! I heard a shot!"

"You're catching Hank's imagination," Nell said. "I'll admit it's contagious—"

"Come on, Asey!" Hank pulled at his arm. "I heard one, too. I—"

"No, you don't go out, either of you!" Betsey grabbed at Asey's other arm. "If there's any shooting, you stay right here—"

"Will you," Asey said, "listen? Listen, all of you!"

"Another!" Hank said. "And—hear that? Someone's cracked up in a car, outside—"

12

LEON grabbed his jacket and streaked out of the room at top speed.

"Come on!" Hank tugged at Asey's arm. "A crash—hear it? Car crash, after that last shot! Hurry! Come on!"

"Hurry nothing!" Betsey said, keeping a firm grip on Asey's other arm. "No hurrying out there till I know it's not some trap meant for Asey. I—"

"Mrs. Porter," Hank said pleadingly, "let go of him! It's a crash! Someone may be hurt. Dead. Dying! Come on, Asey! Hurry!"

He tugged one way and Betsey tugged the other.

"You go, Hank," Nell said. "You—"

"Look," Asey interrupted, "the ham in this san'wich is kind of takin' a beatin'. Leggo me, you two. There. Now, we'll all go. We—"

"Betsey's right," Nell said. "You've been shot at once, and there's no reason in exposing you to any more shots. Hank, you—"

"I 'preciate all this," Asey said, "but we'll all go. We—"

"Asey Mayo!" Betsey, the cool imperturbable Betsey, was crying like a child. "Asey, if you get killed—"

"Come, come." Asey tried to soothe her. "I ain't been killed yet, an' I don't intend to be. If you'll all just come along, there ain't a chance in the world of my gettin' hurt by no one. B'sides, it was prob'ly only backfires we heard. If it's shootin', well, they can't hardly attempt no massacre. Where'd that kid Leon go?"

Leon came bounding back in the room.

"It's only Harper Dixon." He looked disappointed. "He—"

"Harper? Oh!" Gerty ran out.

"Is he hurt?" Asey demanded.

"He looks kind of pinned under things, but he says he ain't hurt but for his arm. It's broken."

"Hank, call Pete Dixon," Asey said. "Did you say that Dr. Stern was over there, Miss Vail?"

"Yes, he was. I'll phone Pete. This will be the last straw for him, poor boy! I'll take care of it."

"Okay. Come on, all of you. Betsey, grab a coat for Gerty. She'll catch her death of cold out there, without no wrap on."

They trooped down the gravel driveway to the main road. At the entrance to the drive lay the remains of a car. Asey thought that he had rarely seen such a complete wreck.

"An' yet he's alive, is he? Huh." Asey strode over to Gerty, who was helping Harper disentangle himself from the debris.

"He's alive, all right," Gerty said. "His arm's broken though, he thinks. Help me here, Asey."

There was no doubt, Asey decided as he leaned over to help Harper, but what the fellow had been drinking. Probably this was another of his usual crack-ups, of which Gerty had spoken.

"Can you get up?" Asey asked.

"Of course. I don't walk on my hands, you know."

Harper got to his feet, and steadied himself with a hand on Gerty's shoulder. His left arm hung limply by his side.

"Hurt?"

"Hurt? Of course it hurts. It hurts like hell. Damn thing's been broken three times before. Gerty, go call Stern and tell him to come over and patch the thing up."

"I've already had him called," Asey said. "Just what happened, did you lose control?"

"No," Harper plucked the cigarette Gerty had lighted for herself out of her fingers, "no. I've joined your select group, Mayo. I've been shot at."

"You?" Nell said. "You? *You*'ve been shot at?"

"Why not? You've yearned to shoot me yourself, haven't you? It's a natural impulse of people I know, wanting to shoot me. Only this time someone actually did. Will you invite me in, Nell, to wait for the doctor, or mayn't I darken your doors?"

"Of course," Hank said. "Come on."

"D'you mean," Asey asked slowly, "that you were shot, or shot at? Where were you hit? Was the car hit?"

"No, wasn't it a pity?" Harper asked.

"N'en," Asey said, "why the crash? What happened?"

"What do you think, Mayo?"

"Well, if you wasn't shot, an' the car wasn't hit, what made you lose control?"

"Oh, for God's sakes!" Harper flicked his cigarette into a snow bank. "I drove it against Nell's stone wall on purpose! Can't you do anything but ask stupid questions? Can't you see? Haven't you eyes in your—"

"What direction did the shot come from?"

"When," the sarcasm in Harper's tone made Nell Westcott writhe, "when I drive a car, Mayo, of course I invariably keep my eye peeled for snipers. I keep one ear cocked for the sound of shots. Oh, always. Always! And—why shan't you die if it isn't Betsey Porter I see! Well, Betsey! I told your husband some months ago I'd no doubt that you were the brains behind the homespun sleuth. After all, put you and Bill and Sherlock together, and you're a mental colossus. Did he send a hurry call for you, Betsey?"

"I came on my own account," Betsey said, "to—"

"Ah, yes. Just ran up to Blight to see the snow covered hills. Ah, yes indeed. I thought Placid was more your line. Really, faced with a choice of Placid or Blight, I'd take Placid, just for the name—"

Asey watched Betsey's face under the street light as Harper rambled on in that same grating tone, deftly insulting the Porters and Bill and Asey, and anything he could think of to insult in passing. Some of it stung. Asey knew that by the entire lack of expression on Betsey's face. It hurt, but she would probably die before letting Harper guess.

Suddenly she grinned.

"And to think," she said sweetly, "you used to kiss me under the mistletoe, Harper! And d'you remember the poetry, too? Perhaps that's the trouble with you, Harper. You're just a thwarted poet with indigestion. You do seem a bit liverish."

Gerty giggled. "Harper," she said, "you'd better say uncle, and go in. She's got you sewed in a sack and zipped up tight. Come on inside."

To everyone's surprise, Harper went without another word.

"How perfectly astounding!" Nell said. "Really, I'm not given to profanity, but I call that a god damned miracle! Betsey, did he really? Write poetry, I mean? My dear, you've given me a weapon I've yearned for. Oh, my. Let's go in at once, while I gloat over the possibilities!"

"The female of the species," Asey remarked as she went off, "is more deadly than the male."

"Isn't it," Hank agreed, "the truth! I don't understand it. Harper has brushed aside the cold steel of a woman's tongue on more than one occasion. But she got him. If he doesn't come to very soon, Nell will have her revenge. The fellow'll be a slashed and ribbony mess. I've got to go in and listen. Come on, Sue!"

Asey, with Leon by his side, remained by the wreck of the car and surveyed it thoughtfully.

"Fake, huh?" Leon said.

"What's that?" Asey was startled to hear his own thought put into words.

"Fake, ain't it? Say, I bet it was. He shot twice, himself, an' then crashed. He forgot the stone wall was under the snow bank, though. I guess by the smell he'd had just about enough to forget it."

"An' why would he do it?" Asey asked. "R'member he's takin' a chance of hurtin' himself, bad."

"Aw, you know," Leon said wisely. "You tell me!"

"Nope," Asey said. "I want to see how good a d'tective you are."

"Well, you been shot at, ain't you? And he was around when you was. If *he* gets shot at, then you'll figger it wasn't him that shot you, but somebody else."

"That," Asey said approvingly, "is using the ole I.Q."

"Huh?"

"The ole grey matter. Like a job, Leon, while I peer 'mong the bolts an' nuts? Well, you pace off seventy-five feet. Nope, he was a pitcher, wan't he? Well, pace off from here to the next light. N'en take this flash of mine, an' hunt."

"What for?"

"Well, I'd like you to find a gun," Asey said. "An' while you do that, I'm goin' to set under this light here, an' figger."

In about ten minutes, Leon called out.

"Hey, Asey. Say, here's a gun. It ain't more'n twenty feet from the car. Look. Here it is!"

Asey examined the revolver that Leon brandished.

"Ain't that nice," he said. "Ain't that nice. Two shots fired. Well, well. Stick it back where you found it, Leon."

"Huh? Say, what for? Why?"

"To see," Asey said, "if Harper remembers that."

"I get it," Leon said. "Say, ain't you the cagey one, huh? If he remembers it an' comes after it, it'll mean he's afraid you'll find it an' do some thinkin', huh? An' if he don't think of it, maybe it don't mean a thing. Say, here's a car. I bet it's Pete an' the doc. Say, did Harper write her poetry, honest? Betsey, I mean. Did Harper write her poetry? Does she like poetry?"

"That's a problem," Asey went forward to meet Dr. Stern and Pete Dixon, "you'll have to take up with her."

"Is he badly hurt?" Pete demanded.

"Just his arm. The left."

Stern sighed. "Again? I wish he'd break the right, just to

break the monotony. Hop on the running board and we'll take you up to the house."

"Just a sec." Asey bent over and whispered to Leon. "Got that? Okay."

The doctor looked at Harper's arm with less sympathy than Asey had ever seen a member of the medical profession display.

"Filthy mess," he said. "I'll run you over to the hospital and have Bremer fix it up."

"You'll do nothing of the kind," Harper retorted. "You'll fix it here, yourself, and right now."

"I won't," Stern said flatly.

"You will. My God, you know the arm, don't you? You've set it plenty of times before, haven't you? Well, go ahead and do it again. Got an orange crate, Nell? Tell Hank to get Aesculapius here some splints."

"Harper," Stern said, "that's a mess, that arm. I'd want x-rays and—"

"Are you a doctor, or aren't you? Go ahead and set this arm, then!"

"I might ruin it." The doctor sounded as though he would rather enjoy doing just that.

"Whose arm is it? I say, go ahead!"

"I need a nurse."

"Well, let Gerty wave ether cones, or hold adhesive tape, or whatever. She's used to nasty sights, like women in the raw."

"Harper," Pete said, "I rather think you might take some-one's advice, once in a while. I—"

"Peter," Harper mimicked his tone, "I rather think *you* might take my advice, and go to Hell. Go on home and look after the mess there. If you can."

Pete shrugged and beckoned to Sue Vail.

"That's right," Harper said, "beat it, all of you. Except Gerty. You stick around too, Sherlock. Maybe I'll mutter secrets."

"Oh, Lord," Stern said, "Harper, you're the damndest nuisance I ever knew. Nell, got a room we can spoil with this hulking brute? Come on, Harper, then. Let me get you over with. Can't see why you can't be reasonable for once in your life!"

Two hours later, Harper's arm was in splints, bound to his side.

Dr. Stern yawned. "Nice job, if I did do it. Next time, Harper, break your neck. Gerty, any time you want a new occupation, let me know. Where'll you go, Harper? Home?"

"I'm staying right here," Harper said. "I've been shot at once. I'm not going to poke my head outdoors again tonight."

"Do as you please," Stern said. "Only get an x-ray of that arm when it pleases you to wander to my office, or to the hospital. And see if you can keep quiet a few days. Coming, Asey? 'Night, Gerty. Don't pamper him. He's all right."

Asey followed the doctor downstairs where Hank Thorn, in pyjamas, waited for them.

"Nell and Betsey've gone to bed. What came over Harper? What's he insist on staying here for? What's he up to?"

"Ask us somethin' easy," Asey said. "Seen Leon?"

"Nell said he'd gone. Asey, I'm stuck. I never wrote anything like this!"

Asey laughed. "You will, Hank, you will! G'night. I'm goin' to bed."

Up in his room, he sat by the darkened window and peered out down the drive. In a few minutes he saw Leon slip up toward the house. Quickly and quietly he went down to the front door.

He undid the chain and stepped out.

"Gerty." Leon whispered. "She's just found the gun. She come from the back drive. See. She knew where it was. Almost went right to it. See, she's sneakin' back—"

Asey intercepted her.

"Chilly night for a walk, ain't it?"

"Oh. Oh, Asey!"

"Why'd he want the gun?" Asey asked. There was no sense, he thought, in mincing words with Gerty.

"How did you know?"

"Come indoors," Asey said, "an' let's talk it over. Leon, are you frozen to death, waitin'? Where'd you stay till the doc went?"

"In the barn. I ain't cold. Say, what now?"

"Bed. Quick. Hop up to my room. Second door at the head of the stairs. Scat!"

He turned to Gerty. "Now, what'd he want the gun for, Gerty?"

"He remembered that two shots had been fired," she said, "he thought you might find it and—"

"Jump to c'nclusions? I already jumped. What's Harper up to?"

"He told you the truth, Asey. Someone shot at him."

"At him, maybe, but they didn't hit him. Why'd he deliberately smash up that car?"

"He didn't. He lost control of it."

"Why'd he want to stay here tonight? What's he up to?"

"He told you. He's afraid."

Asey laughed shortly. "Just scared to pieces. Yup. Gerty, what's this magic power he holds over you?"

"If you must know," Gerty said quietly, "he owns half my business. So what?"

"There ain't no answer to that," Asey said. "Good night."

He didn't know whether to feel pleased or ashamed at the sound of Gerty's sobs as he went upstairs to his room.

Before he opened the door, Gerty was beside him.

"You don't seem to—to even consider," her words ran almost together in her haste to get them out, "that that fool professor's been around—outdoors—when you were shot at, and when Harper was tonight. And he was at the Dixons' Saturday night too! You're a swell detective, you are! You—oh!"

She turned and fled down the hall. Slowly, Asey pushed open his door and went into his room. He cut short Leon's flood of questions, and walked over to a chair by the window.

"An' to think," he said to himself, "I came here to solve a gro'cry order. Two pounds of salt fish, an' a can of beans an' brownbread. Huh!"

Asey arose early the next morning, and was surprised to find Betsey, Nell and Hank already eating breakfast in the dining room.

"We couldn't sleep," Nell explained. "I've been awake half the night, and I'm so confused I've already tried to butter my coffee and pour the roll on my oatmeal. Asey, they've gone. Did you know? Gerty and Harper. Rochelle says Harper phoned for a car, and Gerty went with him. Hours ago. At the crack of dawn. She left a message for you, via Rochelle. She said she had three permanents today, but to call her if you wanted her for anything."

"Did Harper leave any billy-doos?"

"No," Hank said. "He tipped the household staff just right and left, and what d'you think the lout did? Left a five-dollar bill with his card for Nell. Can you beat it?"

"Nice feller," Asey said. "Charmin', almost. Well, Betsey, you still think that d'rect questionin's goin' to get you anywhere with that gro'cry order business?"

Betsey looked at him. "I got him last night, didn't I?"

"You did," Nell said, "but it'll never work again!"

"Maybe it won't. But if it's the last thing I ever do, I'm going to find out about that order! Whether you do or not, Asey. Little Harper presented me with a few cracks last night that got under my skin. I'll grant that Bill Porter's no monument of brains, but he's no fool. And—"

"An' the likes of Harper can't say so?"

She nodded. "You may wander from that grocery order, Asey, but I'm not going to. I see now why he gets Bill's goat so easily. It's those little tack hammer cracks of his. They don't mean much singly, but their cumulative effect is terrific! Harper must have the hide of an elephant, himself!"

Asey agreed. "When you can dish it out the way he does, you got to take a certain p'centage back, anyways. He—"

"Just a moment, Asey," Nell said. "What d'you want, Ra— I mean, Rochelle? What's happened now?"

"It's Miss Vail at the door, Mrs. Westcott. She says she wants Mr. Mayo right away quick. I asked if she'd come in, but she said she wouldn't bother. But she wants him, right off."

"Tell her I'm comin'," Asey began.

"Tell her," Nell said, "he'll be out as soon as he's finished his breakfast. That's quite all right, Asey. I know Sue Vail and her right-away-quicks. If it were anything of vital importance, she'd be in here on top of the toast right this moment. If she won't bother to come in, let her wait."

Betsey didn't say anything, but Asey knew she felt in complete accord with Mrs. Westcott. She had been casually amiable to Sue Vail the previous night, but Asey missed the enthusiasm Betsey usually displayed toward people she liked.

He finished his breakfast without haste, and went out to where Sue Vail waited in a car by the front door. Pete Dixon was with her. Pete, Asey thought, looked as though he had been soaked for days in a wash tub and then ground through a laundry mangle.

"Asey," Pete said wearily, "this isn't any of my doing. Sue made me come over. She thinks Harper will—I mean, she thinks I ought to tell you some things before they come to light and perhaps put me in an unpleasant situation. She—oh, Sue, you tell him!"

"I've been thinking about things all night," Sue said, "and what with that episode of Harper, it seemed to me that Pete should at least settle his side of this Dixon problem you have on your hands, Asey. To begin with, Pete inherits most of Char's money."

"So Pete told me."

"Well, that gives him a motive, doesn't it? Technically? In all the murder cases I ever read, inheritances always loomed frightfully. Last night, Pete was out hunting Harper at the time Harper smashed up. I—well, you know and I know he was just out hunting Harper, but—well, d'you know what I'm trying to say?"

Asey smiled. "Meanin' that the same thought might occur to Harper, an' that he might bring out the point that Pete was huntin' him?"

"Exactly. And now, this is going to be hard, because it sounds so incriminating. But after—oh, Pete, I wish you—I wish we hadn't started this!"

"She's trying to say," Pete said, "that Saturday night after I started out for her house, I went back into our house again. Believe it or not, I'd forgotten a cigarette case. Isn't that banal? It was on the hall table. Perhaps you've noticed that I smoke those brown paper Cuban messes. Horrible taste, I know. Anyway, most people can go off without cigarettes and feel more or less certain that their hostesses will have every kind under the sun, including theirs. But even Sue doesn't and won't stock up with mine. So I dashed back and got the case."

"Whyn't you bring this up before?" Asey asked.

"On my word of honor, I never thought of it."

"Why didn't Harper say somethin'?"

"Perhaps he didn't notice. He'd started off on the far path by the time I turned back. Anyway, if he did, and thinks I'm holding out on the information, you know he'll produce it, himself, whenever he thinks the most inopportune moment has arrived."

"Yup," Asey said, "on the whole I think you might d'pend on that. Anythin' else?"

"Well, that jewel case was in my safe. Oh, Asey, it's—don't you see how diabolical everything is?"

"For every*thing*," Sue said, "read every*one,* and then change that to—"

"Stop, Sue," Pete said. "Asey, there you are. What're we going to do? Ought I to give myself up, or something, before Harp—I mean, before anyone starts things?"

"Pete," Asey said, "where was you Sunday aft'noon?"

"Sunday? I didn't stir from the house. The Brandts and Dr. Stern—but why? What's that got to do with Saturday? That's when Char was killed. Asey, what'll I do?"

"Go home," Asey said, "an' go to bed. An' stop worryin'.

This ain't the sort of thing you can try to understand at one swig. You got to sip it easy, like boilin' hot coffee, a teaspoon at a time. You've dropped ten pounds in two days, by the looks of you. An' don't let that brother of yours upset you none. I'll handle him, or Betsey Porter will. You go get some rest. Forget all this nonsense."

Sue Vail leaned out of the car and kissed him swiftly.

"Asey," she said, "you're a dear. You're as swell as Polly Rich wrote."

"Polly Rich? Why, she was a youngster on my boat, goin' down to Jamaica," Asey said.

"Yes. She wrote me about you, and she still carries on about you at the drop of a hat. Remember, Pete, the letter I got from Polly the day of the big game? She said Asey'd found a bracelet of hers that someone stole, and I'd just lost an emerald ring the day before, and it was breaking my heart—"

Pete laughed.

"First time you've cracked a smile," Sue said, "for weeks, it seems. Yes, Asey, I was so wretched about that ring, I said I'd ask you to go to Blight, if I thought you could do as well by me."

"You—what's that?" Asey said.

"I said, I'd ask you to go to Blight," Sue repeated, "if I thought you could find my ring. A friend of Bill Porter's, Jerry Penn, he was all for cabling you. Jerry was in a mood when he wanted to cable everyone."

Pete laughed again. "He actually did, later on. They had an awful time with him, at the club. He sent messages to Minnie the Moocher, and the King of Sweden, and Shirley Temple. Poor old Root went mad, trying to separate them from the ordinary wires and telegrams and all. The ones Jerry signed with crazy names were easy, but those addressed to more or less logical people, and signed with more or less legitimate names all went out. He caused some awful rows, Asey. It was a riot. Look, thanks a lot for—well, for everything. I guess I've been brooding too much. But you've relieved my mind."

"You," Asey said, "have also relieved mine. Thanks. Good bye."

At least, he thought to himself as he returned to the house, that telegram about going to Blight was cleared up, once and for all. It was one of Jerry Penn's maudlin messages that had slipped by old fuddy-duddy Root.

13

NEITHER Nell Westcott nor her brother made any effort to conceal their disappointment when Asey asked only Betsey Porter to accompany him to the Dixon house.

"I got," Asey tried to smooth the situation over, "to have someone home to org'nize rescue exp'ditions, ain't I? Think of them poor St. Bernards. They wouldn't feel to home less they was rousted up an' almost put into action at least once a day."

"You're mean," Nell said. "Asey, do take pity on me! I shall chew my fingernails to shreds, sitting here waiting for news. Hank and I will fight. He'll probably decide to rearrange the living room. That's what he always does when he feels the least bit restless. While he was writing that last serial, I tied red ribbons on my favorite chair, so I could find it without a long hunt."

"I ain't moved," Asey told her with a grin. "Don't you give us a thought. We'll be all right."

He had announced his intention of going to the Dixons', so Betsey called out a warning to him later as he ignored the Dixon house and kept her roadster headed toward the town of Monkton.

"Asey! Asey, you've passed it! Oh, didn't you intend to stop there? What about Harper? Don't think you're going to gyp me out of my interview with him about that grocery order!"

"You won't be. Only I want to see Gerty first. Bets, is she sweet on that fellow?"

Betsey considered.

"I don't know," she said at last. "Of course, she rushed out when Leon said Harper was the crash—where is Leon today, anyway? He fascinates me."

"I hope he's hunting," Asey said. "I sent him off to grub some more. It's the sort of thing I ain't got the patience to do myself, an' he might find somethin'. He's awful leechy, like Hank says. B'sides, I enjoy Leon better in small doses. He's kind of exhaustin'. Go on about Gerty."

"Well, she raced out after Harper, and she seems to stand up for him whether she actually says anything or not. She has a protective attitude about him. But she's got such a poker face when she wants to put it on that you couldn't really say for sure if she was in love with him or not. Perhaps she's just an underdog champion. I don't know. But Harper is pretty fond of her."

"Think so? He treats her like a piece of old horse hair furniture."

"Oh, that's not unusual. Bill treated me that way for years. Don't you remember? He used to be perfectly horrid for weeks on end. He claims now that he was testing out my disposition. It's the Porter in him. Always testing out something, even if it's only axle grease."

"I could wish," Asey remarked, "that he had wasted just a mite more of his testin' on this new model. Well, well, this must be Monkton. Tidy little place. Looks like an Easter card. I wonder where—"

"Asey, haven't you been here before?"

"Only in a blizzard, an' that don't hardly count. Any signs of Gerty's hangout?"

"Over there," Betsey said. "See? Next the colonial fronted chain store. Does itself well, Monkton does. That's a nice looking little shop of hers, Asey. Not messed up with ads and bottles of hair tonic and false curls, like so many of them. Very chaste sign, too. Just 'Gerty.' No Madame Gertrude, or Itsy Bitsy Beauty Shoppey, or anything. She—oh, there she is, Asey. Pull over!"

Asey swung the Porter to the opposite curb.

"Hullo." Gerty waved at them and unlocked the door she had just shut. "I was going to bum a ride and find you, Asey. Come in, instead."

They went into the neat little shop.

"I see," Asey commented, "you still got my picture up with the King an' Gary. I'd kind of got a feelin' I'd be on the trash heap by now."

Gerty offered Betsey a cigarette, lighted one herself, and sat down on a footstool.

"Asey," she said, "I'm sorry about last night. I found out a lot of things later that made me wish—well, the whole point is, I've changed my mind about Harper. Now mind you, I still don't think he could have killed Mrs. Babb; I'm sure he had nothing to do with that. But I think he's gone crazy. And if he doesn't come to his senses, he's going to land in a lot of hot water. I told him so. I told him to come and tell you. He said he might, but after he left I called up Mrs. Derby and cancelled her appointment, and decided to find you and tell you, just in case he didn't. It's the sort of thing you'll find out sooner or later, or someone will. If you add it on to the rest of the crazy things, it's just too bad for him. Too bad!"

"This," Asey said, "seems to be the time for gen'ral c'nfessin'. What's the story?"

"First," Gerty said, "I want to explain what I said last night, about him owning half my business. When the bank here busted a couple of years ago, I was licked. He found out about it and offered to help. I didn't want him to, but I didn't want to lose my business either, just as I was getting some place. That's all there is to that. And don't," she added firmly, "don't you think any different!"

"He won't," Betsey assured her.

"Well, that's why I want this business of Harper cleared up quietly. If he gets into the papers any more, and gets really in trouble, they'll find out about his owning half this place, and me and my business won't be worth," Gerty snapped her fingers, "that. Monkton's a small town, if you know what I mean. And wouldn't the Blighters like to know an item like that about Harper, and me too! So that's why I want things settled."

Asey sat back and wondered what was coming.

"You see," Gerty continued, "Harper went back to the Dixon house Saturday night after he left with Pete."

"Forgot his cig'rette case?" Asey inquired.

Gerty stared at him. "You don't believe—well, I knew you'd

raise an eyebrow. He forgot a present he had for Sue that he'd
left on the chair in the hall. It was a peace offering. He'd had
an awful fight with her that week. Anyway, he went back and
got it, and went on his way. You can see it didn't take him long,
because he and Pete both reached Sue's at the same time. Harper thinks he may have been the one who left the door on the
latch. There. That's the story."

Asey pulled a pipe from his pocket, filled it and lighted it, and
puffed a while in silence.

"Where was Harper all day Sunday?"

"Wandering around, I guess. I don't know. In the greenhouse, probably. He plays around with flowers all the time."

"What's this business of the grocery order?" Asey asked.

"That," Gerty said honestly, "I don't know. I don't understand it."

"Where's Harper now? Home? Well, call him up, Gerty,
and tell him if he'll explain that order satisfactorily, I'll put
him in the washed-of-his-sins class with the others that are
cleared up."

Gerty went into a booth at the rear of the shop.

"What an interminable conversation," Betsey murmured
after ten minutes. "It must have been a long order!"

Gerty talked for ten minutes more, and then came back to
them.

"I don't understand," she said. "I don't see—Asey, he says
there wasn't any grocery order at all! Or isn't. He swears it.
He says he was drunk, and that's all there is to it. I never heard
him so mad. He says he's paid Bill Porter, and that's that.
'That,'" she mimicked Harper's voice, "'is what you may
blithely tell Mayo as the last word.'"

"Huh." Asey grinned at Betsey's obvious disappointment. "Well, got anythin' else to say, Gerty?"

She shook her head. "No. It seems to me every time I try to be of some use in this, I just make a mess of it. But honest, Asey, no matter how it looks, Harper was scared stiff last night. He was still scared this morning. He's scared now. I don't know what about. Whether it's your knowing he went back to the house, or what. Of course," she admitted, "he's making a lot of noise and being nasty, but that's just on the outside. I never seen him scared of anything before. He is now."

"P'raps," Asey said, "it's Betsey's poetry he's fearin'. Well, Gerty, Harper seems to be tellin' the truth when he says that's that. Anyway, this's this. Let us know if you pry any more out of him."

"You don't get me yet," Gerty insisted. "He's told you all he knows, and all that's happened that he's connected with. He did go back to the house, but he didn't go upstairs. He was drunk when he made all that fuss about the order. Someone did shoot at him last night, no matter what you think. I—oh, well. No use convincing you if you won't be convinced. You don't believe me."

"Do you, Asey?" Betsey asked later as they sped away in the roadster. "Do you believe her?"

"Dunno," Asey said. "I'd b'lieve her more'n I would if I'd found out about Harper myself. Yes, I b'lieve Gerty all right, but I kind of got my doubts about Harper."

He turned the car off the main street and onto the wide concrete turnpike that led to Whitefield.

"Where now?" Betsey asked.

"I just want to drive," Asey said, "an' give myself a sort of false feelin' of gettin' somewhere. Y'know, Betsey, a very little

Blight goes an awful long ways. I want to do some phonin', too."

"Harper went back," Betsey said. "Pete went back. And I suppose they both have motives if you consider the money and inheritance angle."

"But Harper could of shot at me Sunday," Asey said, "an' Pete couldn't of."

"But Pete," Betsey pointed out, "could have shot Harper last night. I mean, if you're bound to consider every vague possibility."

"He could," Asey agreed, "only I wonder if Harper didn't shoot his own gun off, an' then smash up on purpose. Takin' a long chance, maybe, but it's the sort of thing a guy like him would do if he thought it might kind of allay suspicion."

"Asey, what about the professor?" Betsey said. "Now he was at the Dixon house Saturday. He was roaming around on Sunday. He was roaming around last night. Of course he doesn't seem to have any motive, but you never can tell. I mean, he's so absent minded, he might just have—"

"Have held Mrs. Babb's head into a bowl of water until she drowned, an' then dressed up the scene to look like it was an accident, all in an absent minded an' off-hand manner? Maybe, only it ain't sensible."

"His very personality, or lack of it," Betsey said, "does seem to rule him out."

"Yet," Asey said, "he told me he was a swimmin' fool, an' a rifle expert—Bets, know anyone who knows him back in Cambridge? We might look into him an' see how much of him is put on, an' how much is real."

"Corcoran," Betsey said. "Carl Corcoran. He's a cousin of Aunt Prue's. He knows everyone there."

"I'll look into Vail," Asey said, "an' I want to call Steve Crump again. He promised me a lot of information that don't seem to of been forthcomin'."

They drove in silence for almost an hour. At last Asey swung the car off the road by a tiny gasoline station near a lake.

"At this point," he said, "we'll give man an' car a light lunch, an' survey the scenery. Nice to know there's water here somewheres, even if it's covered with ice an' snow. I shouldn't mind Blight so much if there was a bit of water you could look at except what dripped out of a faucet. Let's get out. Bets, does it seem to you somethin' is rumblin' inside that rumble seat?"

"What? Asey, what—"

He strode around to the back of the car and climbed into the open rumble seat.

"Leon, get out! Leon Sparks! You—get—out!"

Leon unwound himself from the blankets on the floor and nonchalantly jumped out.

"I thought I told you to hunt!" Asey said.

"I was," Leon told him. "I—"

"Yup. I s'pose whatever you was huntin' got up on two legs an' walked into the back of this car, huh?"

"It did," Leon said.

"What? Leon, I thought you an' me had a kind of agreement to stick as near the truth as poss'ble."

"Say," Leon became indignant, "say, I'm tellin' you the truth! Say, Mrs. Porter, tell him I'm not lyin'!"

"Well, how come you—say, get to the bottom of this," Asey was beginning to lose patience. "By golly, I wish somethin' could be got to the bottom of! What do you mean, what was you huntin' that took you into this rumble?"

"I got up," Leon said, "even earlier'n you, an' Rachel there, she got me breakfast—say, was she sore at Harper! She asked if he rested comfortable, and he said the bed wasn't tucked in right at the foot. She could of slew him. She—"

"Crawl back to the point. If any."

"Aw, I got breakfast, an' then I went out to the barn—I mean, garage, to get my snowshoes, and it was then I seen this fellow sneaking around the corner of the barn. He had a package under his arm."

"Whyn't you call me?" Asey demanded.

"How could I? You was in bed asleep, and by the time I'd got you, he'd been gone. First I thought it was Frank, anyway. Anyhow I sneaked up on him, and he went into the garage, and then I stumbled against a bucket, and it banged against the cement, where the snow was cleared away, so I ran in because I knew this fellow'd heard it too. But when I got in the garage, he'd already beaten it out the back door. But I could see when he run out, he didn't have no package. At least, I couldn't see none."

"Whyn't you follow?"

"Say, it was dark out then, and he was a mile away before I got to the back door. Besides," Leon added practically, "how'd I know he wouldn't shoot me? Anyway, I started in looking for the bomb."

"The—the what?" Asey said.

"Well, what else would have been in the package?" Leon said. "In books, a package like that is always a bomb."

Asey and Betsey looked at each other hopelessly.

"So," Leon continued, "I looked through all that place to see if I could find anything, an' then when it got lighter, I put on my snowshoes and set out after that fellow's tracks. Well, he'd left his snowshoes against a tree just in back of the garage, and say, he legged it plenty, let me tell you!"

"Did you track him down?" Asey asked. "Who was it?"

"I followed him as far as the road at the end of Dixons' land, an' then he had a car waiting, I guess. No more prints, but plenty of car tracks, an'—"

"Did you follow them?" Asey demanded. "Where'd the car go?"

Leon shrugged. "I don't know."

Asey looked ready to cry. "Oh, Leon, whyn't you follow them tracks? You could of told—wasn't there chains on the tires? Whyn't you follow—"

"Why how could I?" Leon was, by the sound of his voice, completely exasperated. "The plough was about ten feet away when I got to the road, an' before I had any time to think, wheee went the plough over everything!"

"I feel," Betsey said, "the way I used to after the regular Saturday afternoon installment of Pearl White in 'The Iron Claw.' Leon, as a hanger of people on precipices, you have practically no equals!"

"What then, Leon?" Asey asked.

"Well, I went back to the garage, and I got to worrying about the cars. You see, there's your Porter in there, an' this Porter of Mrs. Porter's, an' Mrs. Westcott's big sedan, and the beach wagon you had yesterday, an' Hank's convertible they brought over last evening from Vail's road. Gee, you ought to see that car—top torn, gee it's a mess! Anyway, I thought the fellow might have left the bomb in the car, see? So I climbed into Mrs. Porter's first. I—well, her rumble was open, see, and it would be easy to stick somethin' in. So I climbed inside. And just about then, Frank come in an' come over to the car, see? Frank don't like me, an' he told me to stay away from the cars yesterday, so I got down to the floor, and waited for him to go, but he didn't." Leon took a long breath and continued, "He brought the car out for you two instead, see? I couldn't hardly say nothin' then, so I just stayed. I thought maybe I might hear the bomb ticking, and I could save you."

His naïve conclusion charmed Betsey, but Asey felt that he had heard about enough from Leon.

"This yarn of yours," he said, "makes the story the p'fessor told about your seein' some man with a bucket—"

"It was a green and white striped bucket," Leon interrupted, "and the man—"

"Leon," Asey began, "you—"

"Come, come, Asey," Betsey said, "don't scold. He had my welfare at heart, and his intentions were sterling. He shan't be scolded. Leon, dash in and order hot dogs for us. Two for me and two for Asey, and however many you want. You should be able to down a dozen if you've been bumping around that rumble all morning. Have the man start them, and we'll be right in."

Leon raced away, visibly delighted at the chance of serving Betsey.

"What," Asey inquired, "what do you *do* with someone like that, for the love of heaven?"

"Ever occur to you that he might be telling you the truth, Asey? I mean, it's so hard for anyone to lie all the time."

"It's 'curred to me, all right," Asey said, "an' the very thought makes me hope the kid *is* lyin'. On account of what if that kid is bein' truthful, we're home in bed snoozin', an' this is fiction entirely."

Betsey laughed. "Anyway, I think he's a splendid child. He's so irrepressible. His imagination fascinates me."

"Then," Asey told her gently, "just you take this genius in hand for the d'ration of the war. I won't be r'sponsible for him no longer. C'nsider him your own special property. Maybe he can help solve your gro'cry order. Come long an' eat. B'tween you an' me, a hot dog'll taste good after all the highfalutin food to Mrs. Westcott's. Not that it ain't good, but I ain't used to such fanciness. I keep thinkin' of the unemployed."

Inside the gas station, Leon demolished six hot dogs in record time, and lingered over a seventh.

"I guess," he said slowly, "I can't make away with a dozen for you, Mrs. Porter, but say, if I went into trainin', I could, easy. I went into trainin' for the pie eatin' contest at the county fair last year, an'—"

"Don't tell me," Asey said. "Let me guess. You won. Betsey, amuse it while I make my phone calls to Steve Crump an' your friend Carl Corcoran."

He came out of the phone booth with a furrow in his forehead and fire in his eyes.

"Come on," he said, "let's go. We got things to do."

"Did Steve—"

"I didn't get hold of him. They told me at his office that he was plannin' on comin' here later on in the day. But I got hold of Corcoran's son, an' he got hold of someone else, an' I found out some very int'restin' an' profitable information. Hustle."

He packed Betsey and Leon into the roadster and drove back to Blight at a speed which charmed Leon and caused Betsey surreptitiously to hang onto the side of the car. There was no use, she knew, in trying to ask any questions of Asey in one of his granite jaw moods. Even Leon miraculously grasped that. He didn't even open his mouth all the way back.

As they paused for a traffic light on Monkton's main street, Betsey noticed the professor walking along the sidewalk.

"There's Ernest," she said. "See his green felt book bag. Wouldn't you know he'd carry a green felt book bag? I think he's going into the public library—"

"Leon," Asey said, "go nab him b'fore he gets lost among the vowels and bring him over to the car."

Disregarding traffic, Leon dove out across the street.

"I'll bet you money," Betsey said, "if he's got library books in that bag, they're over due. Asey, do something—neither of those two is paying the slightest bit of attention to traffic! That truck—oh, dear—oh. What d'you want Ernest for—"

"Ah, Asey." The professor smiled wanly. "Mrs. Porter. Somewhat more seasonable weather, don't you think? Er— Asey. I have some books to return to the public library, which unfortunately appear to have been due several weeks ago. I wonder if you would be good enough to wait until I settle the matter, and then possibly you might accompany me to my—er—cabin?"

"What for?" The professor, Asey noticed, was haggard and nervous, and he had nicked himself in half a dozen places while shaving that morning, too. "Why?"

"Well," Vail said, "as a matter of fact, Asey, I rather would like to make a full and complete confession."

14

"ANOTHER, huh?" Asey said. "Leon, go with him while he pays his fines, an' then bring him back. Bring him back alive while you're at it, too."

"What's it mean?" Betsey demanded.

"Well," Asey said, "I found out that he lied to me about one thing, an' bein' as how it was the first lie I found out yet in this, I was aimin' to rile him some. I didn't expect no c'nfessions. My golly. First Pete an' Sue, they come an' involve Pete. Then Gerty, she involved Harper. Now the p'fessor is pinin' away to a frazzle to involve himself. Betsey, this ain't natural."

"Do we have to take him all the way to his cabin," Betsey asked, "before we know what's up? I don't think I can stand it."

"Let him do it in his own way," Asey told her. "After all,

we got to be c'nsid'rate. This is his c'nfession, an' I s'pose he's got the right to stage it as he chooses."

But on the road back to Blight, Asey brought the car to a stop.

"Ernest," he said, "what's the story? I can't bear to watch you another minute. If you get any redder or whiter or tremblier, you'll have me jittery. What's the story?"

The professor gulped.

"Asey," Betsey grasped the situation, "suppose I take Leon and go for a brief walk? I've been so cramped up, sitting in the car for so long. I'd love an opportunity to stretch my legs, and I'm sure Leon would, too."

Her tone indicated that she was being a martyr to Ernest's delicate sensibilities, and that she was entirely aware of the fact.

"Er—thank you," Ernest said. "Thank you. Thank you so much. I—really, that's—I mean to say, I'm very grateful to you."

"Blow the horn," Betsey said, "when you're ready to pick us up again, will you, Asey? Thanks. Leon, I know you want to walk with me, don't you? Come along. Quickly. I'll race you—"

"Now isn't that thoughtful of her?" Vail said. "She is a very thoughtful young woman. Very. Last night she was most helpful, returning my notes to me. I should never have thought of looking for them in an herbal, I'm sure, though I do sometimes find them in odd places."

"Ernest," Asey said, "git to the mutton."

"Well, really, I hardly know how to begin!"

"Not knowin' where to begin," Asey said, "ain't no uncommon failin', an' it's simple to cope with. Just haul off an' b'gin at the b'ginnin'. No better place."

"The other evening, I told you—that is, I gave you to understand—or perhaps, I should say, I made several statements concerning my—or, putting it another way, I deceived you intentionally, yet—"

"Are you by any chance tryin' to say, Ernest, that for all the number of sidelines you told me about, the only ones that's so is the stamp collectin' an' the chess club?"

"Yes." Ernest, relieved, sat back against the leather cushion. "That's it exactly. I—why goodness me, Asey, how did you know?"

"It come out in the course of investigatin'," Asey informed him. "Why did you fib so?"

"It—er—was so clear," Vail said, "that you thought me rather a fool, you know. I wanted to raise myself in your estimation, if I could. Knowing you were from Cape Cod, I inserted that bit about the swimming. And because you were a detective, I said I was a rifle expert. I was sorry as soon as I had made the statements. It was very childish of me, indeed. But I'm not large and tall and physically strong, like Harper, or clever like Hank Thorn, or good all around like Pete, or—or thoughtful like Mrs. Porter, or—or—" he stopped and made a little gesture of despair. "I'm not much, at all. Just a small preoccupied man. A comic strip professor. A—"

"Come, come," Asey said, "that's no way to carry on about yourself. Go on."

"Go on—you mean, get out and walk? You think so— I'm sorry. I really feel—" Vail started to get out of the car, but Asey grabbed him.

"Ernest! You'll have me weepin' in a minute, you will, if you don't stop bein' plaintive! Come *back* here, an' go on with the rest of the story."

"Why, that's all, really. It has bothered me so, that I felt the only way to be at peace with myself was to tell you at once. I do not lie, and I am not accustomed to lie about myself. As I got to know you, however, and noticed the regard others felt for you, I felt that I must confess at once, and clear it all up. I know many people attempt to appear better than they actually are, but I should not have made any such stupid effort."

"Is that all?" Asey asked. Somehow the professor continued to make him feel thwarted.

"Why, yes."

Asey touched the horn button and played a tune on Betsey's fancy side horns. In the rear view mirror he could see Betsey and Leon dashing for the car.

"Of course," Ernest said, "there was all that which happened last night. If I thought you had forgiven my falsehoods, I should ask you to investigate that for me. I—"

"All of what, last night?"

"My cabin. Quite ransacked, it was. Isn't that strange? I thought so."

"What?" Asey yelled. "Your—wait." He leaned his head over the side of the car and called to Betsey. "Hey, you an' Leon crawl into the rumble an' hang on. Tight. Yup. Now, Ernest, is the road clear to your place?"

"I think it must be. You see, I thought of calling in the police, at first, but of course they're very busy, and on matters vastly more important. Quite."

"Ernest, is the road open?"

"Oh, yes. Yes. The oil truck got there. That was the root,—rather, the crux of the situation, you see. The oil. I find that oil very troublesome, myself."

"Go on," Asey said, as Vail showed signs of stopping. "C'n-

tinue. Don't stop. Keep right on. Tell you what. You b'gin
from when you left Westcotts' last night. That's somethin'
tang'ble you can get your teeth into. You left, an' Betsey run
after you with your notes. N'en?"

Then, it seemed, the professor walked back to the Dixon
house to get the book which he had left there.

"The one I thought I had with me," he explained. "The one
that turned out to be an herbal."

He had not intended to look at the book—the right book,—
until he reached his own home. But after clearing up some of
the disorder in the library that had resulted from his fracas with
Harper, he had sat down, and in spite of himself he again became absorbed in the volume.

When Pete and Sue returned from the Westcott house, long
after Harper's crash, Ernest was still there, scribbling notes
on the backs of envelopes.

It occurred to him when he saw Sue Vail that he had originally set out for her house to order oil. He remembered that oil
was his sole motive in leaving his cabin. His oil supply had
given out.

"And everything runs by it," Vail said. "Everything. Heat,
light, water, refrigerator—everyone seems to think it is so con-
venient, but I find it rather a nuisance. No sooner does one remember to get oil and have it brought, than one has to begin
to order oil all over again."

He told Sue Vail of his original purpose in setting out, and
how he had absently taken the path to the Dixons'; once there,
his only thought was of the library.

"She insisted, Asey, that there was no possibility of getting
any oil, even from her supply, to me at that time of night,"

Ernest continued, "and she insisted that I spend the night at her own house. So I did. I disliked the idea, for it is always so noisy there."

"Noisy?" Asey said. "Seems to me it ought to be pretty quiet. It's far from the road, an' this ain't a noisy place to begin with. Nothin' sounds around here but one auto horn a day, an' a lot of wind through pine trees."

"But several of Sue's dinner guests of Saturday," Vail said, "seem still to be there. They've just stayed on. It's rather a spur of the minute house party, I gather. There are five people there, from the city. Sue doesn't pay any attention to them, but they appear to be quite at home. I was given to understand by the cook—admirable woman, Katy,—that they have been drinking to excess for some time. They are over in Sue's guest house ordinarily, and no one minds them much except of course the servants. But last night they apparently forgot to go home. They stayed in the main house, and as I say, they were very noisy. I requested them to be more quiet, and even Sue did, but they paid no heed. I have wondered, Asey, if possibly the ransacking of my cabin was not perhaps due to them? They might have retaliated at what they considered my unauthorized intervention."

"Did it seem like a drunken ransackin'?" Asey asked.

"It didn't seem to be inspired by any particular motive," Vail returned. "I went home as soon as it was daylight, and there the place was, all in upheaval. And those people were still being noisy, and at no time did their noise cease. It seems to me that had they been responsible, there should have been some let up in their—er—din. Here you are, Asey."

The professor's cabin was not unlike the one to which Asey

had gone Sunday night. It consisted of a large living room with built-in bunks at one end, and a kitchen. Above the living room was a large open attic.

"For extra guests," Vail said. "I've cleaned up some, but don't you really call this going too far?"

Two walls of the living room were covered by built-in book cases which presumably had been filled to over-flowing with books. Now most of the volumes were flung helter-skelter on the floor.

Mixed with them were bed clothes from the disarranged bunks, and everywhere Asey looked were sheets of manila paper, hundreds and hundreds of them, many torn and crumpled.

"My notes," Ernest said sadly. "Practically a year's work. Really, when I saw things, I almost didn't dare to set to work figuring the damage. I—I cried."

"I should think you would have!" Betsey said indignantly. "Asey, isn't this beastly!"

"I saw those library books thrown near the door," Ernest said. "I'd quite forgotten them. I thought possibly if I went away and—er—cooled off, I might be able to attack the mess."

"Is anythin' missin'?" Asey asked.

"Not that I can discover from a cursory examination. Have you seen the kitchen? That is very discouraging."

Betsey looked for a few minutes in silence at the shambles there. Foodstuffs, pans and dishes had been pulled from the shelves and drawers and piled in the middle of the floor. Over everything had been emptied a bag of flour and pounds of sugar.

"It's unspeakable," Betsey said, "but at least it's something I can cope with. Leon, what d'you say, shall we clean this up for the professor?"

"Say," Leon said, "it won't take ten minutes. Sure."

"That's fine. I wouldn't dare touch the papers. Asey, go help him with 'em. And Asey, see anything funny about those glasses on the floor there, and the tumblers?"

Asey nodded. "I seen it on several other things. Not a trace of a print. In fact, it's a cinch someone wore gloves." He picked up one of the glasses and examined it. "Yup. Well, well. Ernest, let's dig in."

It took them an hour to get together all the notes and manuscript. Quietly and efficiently the professor sorted and filed, and smoothed out the crumpled sheets. Working with a paste pot and a pair of shears, Leon and Betsey pasted together the torn pages, or mounted them on clean sheets.

Finally Vail sighed with relief. "It's all here. I don't know how to thank you! It's all here, and no damage has been done, really, for it's all got to be typed later."

"I'm glad for you," Asey said. "Now, while I take Betsey out for a breath of fresh air, you an' Leon scurry through everythin' we ain't touched, an' see if anythin's gone. Leon, you could pile some books for him, too."

Out doors, Betsey looked questioningly at Asey.

"What about Ernest? What caused this? Why?"

Asey shrugged.

"Don't you know? Asey, why'd you drag me out here, if not to tell me things?"

"Thought you needed a breather," Asey said, "after all this unaccustomed house work. I—why, where you goin'?"

"Back to pile books," Betsey said. "Unaccustomed house work, my eye!"

Grinning, Asey scraped the snow off a settee near the house, and sat down and filled his pipe.

When anyone did as thorough a ransacking job as that, without a lot of actual breakage, it meant that they were hunting one specific thing. It wasn't just messing things up for the sake of messing things up. And not a speck of a fingerprint, either.

But what did they want from Ernest Vail?

Certainly no one wanted a lot of spidery looking notes about vowel shifts. Even, he thought, if Vail had managed to dig up a lot of vital statistics on vowel shifts that no one had ever dug up before, even if the stuff were of great value to someone, the type of person requiring such information would never go in for ransacking in that manner.

Someone wanted something. But what?

He puffed at his pipe. There was an alternative, of course. But it was amost too remote to consider in this case.

A car drew up beside Betsey's roadster, and Harper Dixon extricated himself from the front seat.

"Wait for me, Edward," he said. "I won't be long. Ah, Sherlock. Did Gerty tender you my apologies?"

He was breezy and genial, rather the way he had been Saturday night.

"Gerty relayed your yarn," Asey said. "What's the idea? Bein' Hyde for a change?"

Harper laughed. "Asey, I knew that Pete had come back to the house, and Pete knew I came back, and both of us were suffering thereby. Only as you've doubtless noticed, we suffer in different ways. I've made up with Pete, and Pete's made up with me, and after I've made up with you, I'm going in and make up with old Ernest, the pride of the shifting vowel."

"For what?" Asey asked. "Playin' hob with his papers an' cabin?"

Harper smiled his sardonic smile. "Has Ernest got it in the neck, too? How unfortunate. No, that's not one of my jobs, and you can prove it. I was at Nell's all last night, and Edward's been with me all day. No, I'm making up with Ernest over the book hurling scene. Ernest is a fine soul, doubtless a hero to dogs and children, but he annoyed me last night."

Asey didn't say anything.

"Well," Harper remarked, "this is just going to prove what I told Gerty, that no good would come of any reformation on my part. I've thought of reforming on several occasions, but it doesn't work. There you sit, thinking as hard as anything what a horrid soul I am. I—what's the phrase? I come clean. That's it. I come clean, and you think all the harder how—really, Sherlock, I expected better things from you! This ain't the old Cape spirit. This ain't—"

"Look," Asey said, "if you didn't take nothin' from Ernest's place, what'd you plant there?"

Harper looked at him for a second and then walked to the cabin's front door and entered.

Slowly, Asey followed.

It was possible that he was doing Harper a grave injustice. But certainly something must have happened to change him so completely. Something to his advantage. This mess in the cabin had been to someone's advantage. It was a pity that he couldn't make connections.

"—and I apologize," Harper was saying to Ernest. "I'm sorry. I'm sorry, too, that your place has been disturbed. I—"

"Don't I come in on this?" Betsey inquired acidly. "Aren't you apologizing to me?"

"My dear girl, I'm sure I don't know what for, but if it makes you any happier, I apologize. There, having scattered my little dew drops, I shall—"

"Wait," Betsey said. "Leon, get my pocketbook, will you? It's out in the kitchen. Harper, did you send Bill a check?"

"I did."

Betsey pulled two envelopes from her bag. "Is this it? In this letter to Bill?"

"It is."

"Fine. Now, here's Bill's to you. You can do with it what you want, but here goes yours."

Briskly, she tore Harper's letter and check in two and tossed the pieces into the professor's fireplace.

Harper smiled, and followed suit.

"Well?" Betsey said. "Well? Can't you— Harper Dixon, now that's all over, what's this nonsense about this grocery order?"

"You," Harper observed, "have already admitted that it's all over. So long."

"Er—don't go," the professor said. "Er—now that we are friends again, so to speak, won't you stay and have a cup of tea?"

Knowing that Betsey was not in the least pleased by the invitation, Harper characteristically accepted.

"Didn't you tell me, or Sue, or someone," he asked, sitting carefully down on a couch, "that you hoped to go to England this summer?"

"Yes." Ernest sighed. "I hoped to, but of course it's an expensive trip. Unfortunately my—er—nest egg for the journey was wiped out by an operation last summer. And of course my research has been expensive, although to the layman it might not appear so. It—"

"Leon," Betsey said, "let's see to the tea."

Asey followed her out into the kitchen and wisely shut the door.

"That—that fellow!" Betsey said. "What a chameleon like thing he is! He's getting poor Ernest all worked up over that trip, and he's taking Ernest in like—"

"Like a pea an' shell artist," Asey agreed. "Yup. There is somethin' kind of now-you-see-it-now-you-don't about him, ain't there? Betsey, what's he so worked up about? He's almost pleasant!"

Betsey nodded. "Oh, I hate that type of person! Why, the professor was glowing like anything, and now Harper comes along and makes him negative! I always thought Pete Dixon was a negative person, too, but I suppose it's due to his close association with Harper. He just monopolizes things, doesn't he, whether he's pleasant or nasty!"

"I should say," Asey observed, "that no one within a radius of ten miles of Harper had much of a chance to d'velop proper. He r'minds me of that elm Matty Mayo used to have in her front yard. You wouldn't want to see a finer elm, but it blighted everythin' on her place. Betsey, I want to find out what's come over Harper to change him so an' make him so dum chipper. Brew your tea an' bring it in. I'm kind of expectin' somethin' here. If nobody took nothin', an' it don't look like they did, then —well, hustle the tea up. Tea! My, wouldn't Dr. Stern snicker to think of Harper Dixon settin' down an' drinkin' aft'noon tea!"

Harper not only drank his tea, but requested a second cup.

"I've got my pipe," he said as he fumbled in his pocket. "Betsey, will you yank it out? I haven't got hands enough. And may I borrow some tobacco, Ernest? I forgot my pouch."

"Certainly. Certainly. Of course you may! Of course. Yes, indeed!" The professor was in an expansive mood after Harper's suave attentiveness. "Of course, dear fellow! It's right there in the tin, Betsey, on the table next to you. That's it!"

Betsey picked up the tin as though it were a hot coal.

"Cover's stuck," she said, not trying very hard to open it. "Asey, officiate, please."

Asey smiled, and twisted off the lid.

The expression on his face never changed as he strolled across the floor toward Harper.

"Nice t'bacco." His voice had taken on that purring note which Betsey knew so well. Apparently whatever he had expected either had happened already, or was about to happen. "Very nice t'bacco. Costly. I—"

"Oh, no indeed," Ernest protested. "It's not expensive. It's quite common—"

"Let's have your pipe," Asey said to Harper, "or can you manage to fill it with one hand? P'raps, on the whole, you better."

He placed the tin on Harper's knee.

"I suppose I shall have—where did that come from?" Harper pointed with the stem of his pipe toward the tobacco tin. "Ernest, where did that come from?"

The professor hurried over and peered into the tin.

"Why," he said, "isn't that amazing? I wonder how long that's been there! I haven't touched that tin in several weeks. I smoke on very rare occasions, you know. I—"

"The hell with you and your smoking habits!" Harper was on his feet, bellowing at the top of his lungs. "How'd my Aunt Charlotte's pearls get into your tobacco tin?"

15

THE living room at the Dixon house two hours later reminded Asey of his cousin Benjy Cobbman's funeral, years ago in Pochet. That was the most mournful occasion he could recall on the spur of the moment.

Pete Dixon sat on the edge of his chair, his chin propped in his hands. For almost an hour he had stared unblinkingly at the under pattern of the rug. Across from him Professor Vail sat stiffly in a straight backed chair, his hands folded in his lap. Every now and then he twiddled his thumbs, methodically reversing the motion at intervals.

Betsey Porter and the ubiquitous Leon played double solitaire at a table far too small for anything but the bowl of flowers that belonged on it. The only noise in the room for the last forty minutes had been the scuffle of Leon's shoes as he scrambled after cards that slid off to the floor.

The game was new to Leon, and it delighted him. Probably, Asey thought, the boy had won the pie eating contest at the state fair with that exact same brand of enthusiastic persistence. Betsey was playing away doggedly, putting down each card as though she were laying a cornerstone.

To the relief of everyone, Harper was upstairs in bed. During the uncontrolled fifteen minutes which had followed the finding of Charlotte Babb's pearls in Ernest Vail's tobacco tin, while he yelled and screamed and stormed at the professor, Harper had lurched against a pile of books, and fallen on his injured arm. Wincing with the pain that for once effectively silenced him, he had allowed Edward and Betsey to bring him home. He even welcomed Dr. Stern's appearance.

"Aren't they ever going to get those fingerprints on the pearls settled?" Pete demanded, as though it were an entirely new idea, and not a question he had already asked a dozen times before. "Can't they get to it? What's that idiot of an expert fingerprinter here for? Been here the whole blessed day, and he can't find anything in the whole house! It does seem that he might function at this point!"

"Give 'em all time," Asey said. "You can't go over a house this size, particularly when you don't much know what you're goin' after, without takin' some time at it. They—"

"That's just it! They know what they're after in the matter of the pearls, don't they? Asey, who took them out of my safe?"

" 'Member," Asey said, "you ain't sure they was in that jewel box. You didn't check the items in it—"

"How could I? I didn't know what she had out, and what was in the vault. I'd need the inventory, anyway. I—and you've got to admit that case was full when we saw it! And there were pearls in it!"

Asey nodded. There was no use in reminding Pete that by his own admittance, Mrs. Babb owned no less than six different strings of pearls of varying size and value.

Finally Mackinson, the newest expert to arrive on the job, came downstairs with Dr. Stern.

"Only Harper's prints," the doctor said, "where he picked 'em out of the tin, apparently. And Char's own. Can you beat that? Can you tie—"

"I do want to make it clear to Mr. Mackinson," Ernest had contained himself as long as he could, "that Harper Dixon's accusing me of stealing those pearls, and murdering his aunt for them in order to finance my studies and research—that's all the most absurd—I mean to say, it's impossible and untrue, and—it's a lie! Are you," his voice quavered, "going to arrest me?"

Mackinson shook his head.

"May I—er—go?"

"Yes, only don't wander from town. I'm going to send one of my men home with you."

"To—to watch over me? Am I under surveillance?"

Mackinson smiled at Asey. "He's to watch over you, professor, but for your own good. Somebody doesn't seem to like you one bit. Mayo, I'd like to see you."

Asey followed him out into the hall.

"How you comin'?" he asked.

"It's a mess," Mackinson said. "Vito and the others said so, but none of us believed them. We've gone over everything in that room and that bathroom, we've gone over her clothes—

everything. We can't find a trace of anyone. It's unholy. If Stern and Dr. O'Neil didn't swear she was murdered, I'd say suicide. Look, there are her prints. Prints of the maid who cleaned the room. But the maid was away. There's that window that was opened. The lock's been cleaned off. There's only one thing the other fellows slipped up on. That's the glass stoppers of the bottles on the wash bowl. I'm taking them back with me, but I don't expect to get anything. If I do, it'll probably be a fake. That's the way I feel about all this. Asey, haven't you any ideas? Come on upstairs."

Asey looked around Mrs. Babb's room.

"Wa-el," he said at last, "someone tiptoed in here while she was settin' in there manicurin' her nails by that little table. I dunno how they did it, but from what Stern says, someone just filled the wash bowl, swung her around, dunked her head down an' held it there. Stern couldn't find any marks where she'd struggled with anybody. Afterwards, the person went out. Only he took care of prints first. There you are. Didn't leave no collar buttons, nor cig'rette butts, nor anythin' else. Didn't even have no watch on to stop c'nvenient like, she didn't. Taken it off b'forehand. 'Twas on her dressin' table. Seems to me the only clews you got is what has happened, rather than things strewn around, or not strewn around. What's happened, an' what's still happenin', to judge from the p'fessor's cabin."

"See if I've got the story complete," Mackinson said. "When you folks came Saturday night, Sparks was rollicking around, and he played with the lights and locked you in, and then unlocked you. So far, so good. He came in the front door. Then you found Mrs. Babb. Then things began to happen, didn't they?"

"More or less. That window was a fake, it's bein' unlocked an' all. I dunno about the jewel case an' the safe. Even if it wasn't her custom, she might of put it inside."

"I understand from the Dixons," Mackinson said, "that Pete went up and talked with her before they left, and that she was alive when they left. Harper says so. Pete saw her last, but Harper called out to her before he left, and she answered. But both of the boys came back. And Vail came back. And do you know what? I don't think any one of them did it."

Asey nodded. "I'm sort of kind of agreed with you on that. For example, whoever killed her has to of been in several places at several spec'fied times, like. They got to of been able to be here b'tween seven-thirty an' eight. Both the Dixons an' Vail was. They got to have had a chance to monkey with that window. The Dixons had, but Vail didn't go downstairs after I seen it locked. At least, not out there. They've got to of been able to shoot at me Sunday aft'noon. Vail an' Harper could of. If you believe that Harper's smash-up wasn't a fake, then Vail or Pete, either of 'em, might of engineered it. For last night's goin's on at Vails', Harper is out. He was at West-cotts'. Your own men can prove that Pete was here. I don't think there's a chance that Vail done it himself. I'm sure that string of pearls was planted on him."

Mackinson sighed. "Not one of the three could have been responsible for everything. The servants—if only they could enter into it! But we've checked on them, and every last one was at the movies, as they said. Tim Sparks has had Reilly with him every minute since he left here. Asey, it simply must be someone with access to this house. Someone around here. What d'you think of this Suzanne Vail? It may sound crazy, but Pete Dixon said she knew about the safe combination, and she's pretty much taken for granted here."

"I dunno why," Asey said, "but the same thing entered my head. Only she was at Westcotts' the time Harper says someone shot at him last night. An' she was givin' a dinner party the night Mrs. Babb was killed. I think it was Thorn that said he called her up around eight—say!" he stopped short and whistled. "Say, I never thought of that! The doc said—well, no matter. That's an item I'll look into. It's somethin' that never—well, well! I don't know about Sue Vail, but I don't think she's mixed up in it. Mrs. Westcott said she an' Mrs. Babb got along fine. No money motive, no other motive, seemin'ly."

"Do you believe Harper Dixon?"

Asey shrugged his shoulders. "I think he's one of them people that wants the spotlight, an' don't care how they get it. Ex'bitionist or somethin'. There's words for it. He keeps croppin' up, but somehow it don't seem to me he'd make such a dum fool of himself if he killed her. I don't see how either he or Pete could of, anyway. Want me, Edward?"

"The telephone, sir. Calling from Mrs. Westcott's."

"Okay," Asey said. "Tell her to wait a sec. Yes, I sort of agree with you, Mackinson. They all look good, but they don't seem to fill the bill."

"Just one thing more. This girl—this hairdresser from the village. She—"

"She's out of it," Asey said. "I can vouch for her, myself."

"Sure?"

"Pos'tive. Why?"

"We looked into her," Mackinson said, "like we looked into everyone. Even you."

"Me?"

"Uh-huh. Harper Dixon got hold of Vito and told him you were a fake, and the real Asey Mayo was in Jamaica. Took us some time to follow you here with your planes and special trains and all. I tell you, we been busy. You may not think so, but in a quiet way, we got a lot done. About this McKeen girl. Her father was on the New York force."

"She said so."

"And kicked off it, did she tell you that?" Mackinson asked. "They called it gross negligence, because he had a good record, but he helped a murderer escape, and they just didn't prove he was mixed up in it himself. They didn't dare touch him, because he knew too much about other things, but he seems to have been a slick customer. Maybe the girl didn't have anything to do with this, but it's one of those details you might take into consideration. Okay. I won't keep you. If you get anything, let us know. Or if we can do anything for you, I'll be glad to see to it."

"Thanks," Asey said. "I got somethin' brewin' in my mind, an' if anythin' comes of it, I'll need you. Thanks."

He went downstairs, and as he crossed to the phone, he saw Betsey still stoically playing double solitaire with Leon, whose enthusiasm had not in the least diminished.

"H'lo. Oh." He was surprised to find Gerty on the wire.

"Asey, don't mention my name. I said it was Westcotts' calling, on purpose. Asey, something awfully queer's going on up here. Can you come, quick? Don't bring anyone with you, or attract any attention. Leave your car around the corner and stroll by the store. It ain't lighted, but I'll unlock the door for you. I can't explain, but will you hurry? Don't let anyone know."

"Be right with you," Asey said, and hung up.

He stared at the telephone a moment after replacing the receiver, and then he grinned.

Gerty's voice had held the proper mixture of fright, anguish and urgency, but it might be well to do a little checking and preparing before he went out on any wild goose chases.

Quietly he slipped up to the rear of the second floor and the bleak bedroom where Harper lay.

Dr. Stern met him at the door. "Shh. I've just got him asleep. God, what a mess he's made of that arm! I told him to keep quiet, and stay in bed. I told him he—but what's the use? He's pulled a tendon, and I hope it hurts as much as he says."

"You goin' to stay here?" Asey asked.

"For a while. Going?"

Asey nodded, and went into the library, where Pete was talking to one of the state police.

"We're making out a time schedule," Pete said wearily. "When things happened, and why. It's going to take months. I never understood how hard it was to define 'a couple of minutes.'"

"Where's Mackinson?" Asey asked.

"Out in the kitchen."

"So Gerty wants you, does she?" Mackinson asked after Asey told his story. "Hm."

"One hm," Asey remarked, "two huhs an' a handful of well-well-wells. Did you send someone with the p'fessor? Good. Then he an' Pete an' Harper is settled. Just for fun, you use this phone extension an' call Sue Vail, will you? Think of somethin' to ask her."

Obligingly Mackinson called the Vail house and asked if Sue had seen her cousin Ernest.

"Not today," he reported as he hung up. "She's there, all

right, but suppose I send someone over anyway? I think you'd better have a guard, too."

"I'll take one man," Asey said, "an' I'm takin' Leon. He knows his way around. Sort of a seein' eye arrangement. Well, in case this was on the level, I'd best get goin'. Tell you what, have someone take Betsey Porter back to Westcotts' for me, an' have 'em linger there till I get back. Okay?"

"I still think you—"

"I'll get along," Asey said. "Now, grab Leon an' bring him out here with my coat an' hat. If I have to let Betsey in on this, she'll want to come with me, an' she can be awful persuasive. I'm takin' her car."

Before Betsey found someone to inquire of Asey's whereabouts, he and Leon were half way to town with one of the police cars vainly trying to keep the Porter tail light in view.

"Say," Leon said, "this is exciting, isn't it? What's going on, Asey?"

"Dunno, but I'll tell you this. Don't you let your imagination get the better of you, whatever happens. Do what I say, an' no more."

He left the car on a side street, and with Leon beside him, walked along the icy sidewalk toward Gerty's little store.

The main street was almost deserted and the none too brilliant street lights glared down on the banks of snow piled so high along the curbing that Leon could barely see over them.

A bitter wind whipped in their faces, and Asey restrained his impulse to pull the brim of Hank's hat down further on his forehead. He wanted to see.

"Say," Leon's voice was shrill. "Say, it's kind of scarey here tonight, ain't it? Say, it's just like that gangster picture where Spot Moran got bumped off. You know, he was walking down between snow banks, just like this, and pank-rattle-rattle went the Tommy guns, sprayin' death an' destruction—"

"Leon," Asey said firmly, "will you shut up!"

"Well, it *was* like this, you know. It—"

"Leon, do you want to go back to the car?"

Leon subsided.

Asey paused at the darkened exterior of Gerty's shop.

An outside light went on, then flashed off.

"When Dick Tracy," Leon began, "tried to get old man—"

Asey put one mittened hand over Leon's mouth and held it there.

The door of the shop opened.

"Thank God," Gerty said. "Come in, quick! Who's—oh. Only Leon. Come in."

"What's the trouble, Gerty?" Asey's voice was taut. "Why not have a little light around here? What's the matter? This is like—like Dick Tracy, or something," he finished lamely.

"I thought you'd never come!" Gerty said. "Asey, this is awful. I don't know where to begin. I—I can't explain. I—oh, dear!"

"Get to the point," Asey said. "This ain't no time for hysterics, whatever's goin' on. Why'd you call me? Hustle. Snap out of it!"

"Well, after you and Betsey left, I began to feel uneasy. Like someone was watching the store. I'd cancelled one appointment and had another later, but I was so scared, I didn't dare go out. You see, it's the windows in back. That's why I haven't the lights on. They—"

"But," Asey remembered the booths in the rear of the store, "them windows is high up, Gerty. No one could look in from the ground 'less they had a step ladder, even allowin' for the snow piles."

"I know, but if they were in the windows of the building in back, they could. I'm sure I seen someone peeking down. I didn't dare look much, I was so scared."

"Whyn't you call me earlier," Asey asked, "if you been so frightened?" His eyes were accustomed to the dimness inside the store now. As far as he could see, he and Leon and Gerty were the only ones there.

"I finally left and got some lunch," Gerty said, "and come back for a late appointment. Mrs. McGlee. Just as she was leaving, there was a fire down the street, and I put on my coat and went to see it. There've been a couple of fires in that old block, and I wanted to see how bad it was, and if they could put it out and all. I didn't want to lose my stuff here. And I didn't lock the front door. I don't often, particularly if I'm in sight of the door, as I was then, and I had my pocketbook and my money with me, in the pocket of my coat—"

"And when you got back," Asey interrupted impatiently, "what then? What'd happened?"

"Well, nothing. That is, nothing I seen right off. I met Angie Lyons at the fire, and she wanted a manicure, and so she came back with me, and I did her, and talked a while with her, and then I started to close up. I got a little cash register, see? I always leave it wide open at night, like Harper told me to. It didn't have any money in it, like I said, I had the money in my pocketbook—"

"I know, I know, it was in the pocket of your coat! Gerty, can't you get to the point?"

"Well, Angie gave me thirty-five cents, so I didn't have to

make change, and I didn't even ring it up till I started to go home. Then I rang it up, and I left the drawer open, and then I looked into the drawer and what do you suppose I found?"

"A knife!" Leon said instantly. "A bloody knife! Say, was it a bloody knife, Gerty? Was it—" Asey's hand went over his mouth again.

"I found," Gerty said, "three rings, and two bracelets. Three rings and two bracelets! Two diamond rings, one emerald, and two diamond and sapphire bracelets!"

"Makin'," Asey said, "three rings an' two bracelets in all? Your 'rithmetic seems all right, but the way you list it is kind of confusin'."

"Three rings and two bracelets! And—who do you suppose they belonged to?"

"My Indian control, little White Feather," Asey observed, "ain't clickin' from the spirit world today, Gerty. Who'd they b'long to?"

"Charlotte Babb!"

"Well," Asey said, "you been a long time gettin' there, an' for a while I kind of had doubts. Now the story's over, s'pose we put the lights on. I don't care much for this gloom."

"No, no, you mustn't!"

"Why not?"

"Because," Gerty said, "don't you understand? Someone is up in that building behind, waiting for me to go out!"

"It's the influence of Leon," Asey remarked, sitting down on a stool. "Don't know how it happens, but that boy's imag'nation is as catchin' as pink eye. What makes you think that, Gerty?"

"Because I crept into the booth and looked, and I'm sure

there's someone. I—I thought they might be waiting for me to go out, with these rings and things, and then call a cop and have me arrested for having Mrs. Babb's jewelry on me. Or something. I sat here, and sat, and stood it as long as I could, and then I called you."

"Now, Gerty," Asey said, "let's get down to facts. Have you actually seen anyone in that window in the buildin' b'hind, or do you just think you did?"

"The position of the curtain's changed," Gerty said. "I don't see why it should, either. The place is vacant. And if someone just wanted to look out of a window of a vacant building, why'd they pick the only one that looks on my place, huh? There's a dozen other vacant buildings in this town that I know of, since the factory closed. I tell you, someone's there, and I don't know why, unless it's to harm me. I think it's got something to do with these three rings and two bracelets. And to make that part worse, Asey, they're ones I know for sure was Mrs. Babb's, because I always admired 'em, and joked with her about leavin' 'em to me in her will!"

"Huh," Asey said. "An' huh again. Leon, you leap back to the car, an' tell that copper to get—say, are there any local traffic cops, Gerty, or anythin' like that?"

"Probably you'll find him," Gerty said, "in the pool room. Leon—"

"I know where he'll be," Leon said. "I—"

"Get him, an' then pick up that state cop, an' tell 'em to prowl through that buildin'. Is there a back entrance, Gerty? Well, I'll look after that. Leon, you come back here, straight back, after you got them cops goin'. I'll need you. Now, beat it."

As Leon slipped out the door of Gerty's shop, Asey got to his feet.

"Which booth's best for lookin' purposes?" he asked. "An' do you have a back door?"

"A back door," Gerty said, "and I'd be ready for my grave right now! It was bad enough, wondering what was coming through those windows. Asey, you think this is funny! You come look. Step on that stool, and pull the curtain aside. I used to have the windows painted white, but I had 'em scraped after the store there was empty. More light. Now, look—hey, are you unlocking that? You can't! They're nailed! You can't lift—Asey—what—?"

"Gimme somethin' heavy," Asey ordered. "Quick!"

Without knowing quite what she was doing, Gerty reached out on the dressing table, grabbed a small electric hand drier, and gave it to him.

"Stand away!"

Three times Asey swung at the large lower pane, and then almost, Gerty thought, before the sound of tinkling glass had died away, Asey somehow wriggled through the jagged hole, and disappeared.

16

THE person whom Asey had seen sneaking out of the back door of the vacant building had more than an ample head start.

By the time Asey picked himself out of the glass covered snow bank on which he landed, the fellow was streaking up the back alley that lay between the row of main street shops and the buildings on the next street.

"By golly," Asey said with determination, "I'll give you a run for your money, mister!"

Still gripping the drier, he started off in pursuit.

A narrow path had been cleared in the alley, a narrow uneven path with a coating of ice. A false step, as Asey promptly discovered, meant a headlong tumble.

He got up and dashed on again. No use trying to make his own path, for the snow was too deep. The whole business served him right. He should have taken the gun Mackinson had urged on him. A couple of shots at that lad, and he'd have something tangible in all this mess. But he'd refused the gun. Of course, Hank's water pistol was in his pocket, but this wasn't any situation to be coped with by water pistol bluffing.

He paused for a moment. The man was out of sight, but he couldn't possibly have reached the end of the block. There was a gleaming expanse of sheer ice ahead. Yes, that was it. The fellow had skidded on that, and slid up an alley way to the left.

Asey turned, and was heartened to see the man ahead of him, trying to scramble over a high alley gate.

He popped over the top just as Asey reached out a hand to grab at the fellow's foot.

Asey dropped the drier and clambered up. There was barbed wire under the little ridge of snow. It tore at his hands and scraped one knee.

A window above him opened and the contents of a pitcher of water caught him full in the face.

"That'll teach you," a woman's voice shrilled, "teach you ruffians to leave private property alone, that will!"

He brushed the water out of his eyes, jumped down and raced for the sidewalk.

As he expected, there was no sign of the man.

"Foxy, huh?" Asey was panting. "Okay. I'll wait. You couldn't of turned either corner, an' I bet you don't try climbin' any more gates, not after them barbs!"

Two passersby glanced at him curiously. One murmured something uncomplimentary about the woman in the shadow of whose house he stood, and the other guffawed.

A girl hurried by in the opposite direction. The heels of her overshoes tap-tapped on the ice. Then a door banged and the street was quiet again.

Asey waited.

With luck, Leon would come back to the store as he had been directed. With luck, Gerty would tell him everything and together they might have wit enough to go after the cops. They should be coming along this street, anyway, to get to the vacant building. He realized suddenly that the street on which he stood angled off from the other. That was no help.

He grinned as he heard police whistles sound somewhere behind him. They were warm, but he wouldn't make any noise to lead them nearer for a few more minutes. Maybe the old gate climber could be foxed into thinking that Asey had given up, or was playing the tunes on the whistles, back on the other street.

Suddenly, across the street from him, a man appeared. Like a ghost, Asey thought, looming up in the corner of a moving picture. Slowly, very slowly—almost casually,—he started to walk towards the end of the block.

Asey grinned and sauntered out on the sidewalk.

The man walked a little faster. Asey quickened his pace.

The man began to run. Asey followed suit.

What ensued was, as he told Betsey later, etched on his brain for all time.

All afternoon the mercury had been steadily dropping, and now with the icy wind that swept down from the hills, most of the handful of pedestrians they met were proceeding at a brisk dog trot. To them there was nothing at all unusual in the sight of two men running for dear life.

"One fat feller," Asey told Betsey, "even yelled out he wished he could zip along as fast as that! Huh!"

He followed his man in and out of a narrow twisting cobweb of alleys, over back fences, through back yards high with snow.

They worked away from the small section of brick and brownstone houses to more suburban surroundings.

"An' romped," Asey said bitterly, "over more lilac bushes an' poplar trees than I'd thought pos'ble. Then he got smart. He got over on the wrong side of the railroad tracks. That was where he got me."

The drab rows of frame tenements, all looking alike, lighted with feebly flickering gas lights instead of electricity as the better section had been—that was the beginning of the end.

The snow didn't seem to have drifted as much there, and the fellow leaped over walls and broken fences like a man possessed. Then he darted across a street, and Asey, following, found himself in the open yard of an abandoned factory. A tannery, by the lingering smell. The windows were all methodically broken. Asey guessed rightly that it had been a strike fracas. The whole place loomed black and sinister.

Asey surveyed it a moment, and then admitted defeat.

He wasn't going to tackle those buildings, or the mess of debris in the yards. Not in a thousand years he wasn't.

As he stood there, a brick sailed through the air, perilously near his head.

"Home grounds," Asey thought as he ducked around a corner. "He's darin' me to come on. He wouldn't do that if he wasn't certain sure he was safe an' snug."

Grinning, he made his way along the building to a gap in the wall, and marched out into the street with a boldness he was far from feeling.

He hadn't the vaguest idea in the world where he was, and no stars showed in the cloudy sky to guide him. Either direction looked equally promising. It appeared a speck more inhabited toward the right, so he turned right. It would be the fellow's chance to harry him, now, if he had the least bit of sense.

Half way up one of the tenement blocks, a car was stuck on a snow bank, its wheels spinning, and its driver cursing loudly in fluid Italian.

The sound of a human voice was cheering, and besides, someone trying to start off in a car meant someone going somewhere. He could, Asey felt, do with a lift.

He stopped and asked if he could help.

The man in the car accepted him and his assistance without question. After a few minutes of shovelling, and the judicious placing of two stringy pieces of burlap, the car started off.

"Goin' to town, huh? You want to ride?"

"Well, I'd like to. Got room?" Asey asked superfluously. There was ample room.

"Get in," the man said briefly. "Where you go?"

"Anywhere on Main Street. The main street." Asey didn't even know its proper name. "Near the li'bry, if it's not out of your way. Cold night to be out drivin'," he added.

"Yeah. I get the doc," the man said. "My sister's sick."

"Too bad. Goin' for Doc Stern?" Asey asked.

The man laughed. "He's the rich folks doc. I think my sister kick the bucket. You know." He took both hands from the wheel and made an expressive gesture. "Die."

Asey grabbed at the wheel before the car swung into a drift. "I'm sorry. What's the matter?"

"Flu, maybe."

Three blocks later he stopped the car.

"What—" Asey began.

"Main Street. There's the librar'." He pointed.

"Thanks," Asey said. "Thanks a lot. I thought I was farther away than this. I hope your sister gets better."

"She kick the bucket," said the man. "So long."

Asey stared after the car as it lurched away, and involuntarily shivered.

Somehow the grimness of that fatalistic attitude heightened the futility and drabness of his own silly chase. He wished he had thought to ask the man's name. He might at least have sent Stern to the woman. Stern mightn't have been a bit of help, but Asey would have felt better, a little less down in the mouth about the situation.

As he stepped up on the sidewalk, three boys bumped against him; not until they collapsed into an uncontrollable fit of giggling did he realize that they were girls in ski suits. Their laughter grated on him, and he strode along the street without addressing a word to them.

Half way up the block, he stopped short.

He had been a fool. A complete and utter fool. What he had needed was a brisk little back alley chase to clear the cobwebs out of his brain. He—oh, he'd been too stupid to live!

He hurried on, not even hearing the giggles of the three girls, who had caught up with him.

Outside Gerty's he paused, looked in, and shook with laughter.

The place was fairly teeming with people. Mackinson, with a worried look on his face, talked with Sue Vail. Betsey and Gerty, both white around the gills, watched Mrs. Westcott as she bickered with Hank. The doctor sat on a pale green chair and chewed at a cigar. A trio of assorted police completed the picture. And of course there was Leon, hopping up and down in his excitement.

One more, Asey thought, and the place would burst like a balloon.

Mackinson said something to Hank, and started out the door, waving the rest of them to stay where they were.

Asey slid beside him. "Got a dime for a cup of coff—"

"No! I—"

"Selfish." Asey fell into step. "Pig. An' don't yell an' scream till we get out of earshot of that place. I don't want to waste no time on a rescue scene."

"Asey, are you all right? Good. What happened?"

"I," Asey told him, "been playin' hare an' hounds with an awful slick hare. He won."

"What a time we had!" Mackinson said. "What a time! That Mrs. Westcott, she's been calling for—"

"I know," Asey said. "St. Bernards."

"Naw. Bloodhounds. Can you beat it?"

" 'Fore I go home," Asey observed, "I'm goin' to wander off on a hillside an' let her give the canine pals a treat. Mack, a thought has come to me—prac'tcly a rev'lation. In fact, like old Theobald Spratt kept sayin' the last time he got forced to sign the pledge, I see lights! Look, you pop inside an' tell Stern to amble out in a business like way, will you? I want him. An' kind of on the side, how long has Sue Vail been in the shop?"

"Oh, a long while. Asey, are you on to something?"

"I'll let you know about this light of mine," Asey said, "as soon as it starts glowin'. Right now it's at the theory stage. Kind of a sane theory I hadn't caught on to b'fore."

"Okay. I'll get Stern."

"Finegle about. I don't want that bunch on my neck yet a while."

Mackinson went back to the store, and after some ten minutes, returned with the doctor.

"Here you are," he said. "The women are furious. They think that he ought to be kept there to receive your mangled body. Anything I can do? And, by the way, a Mr. Crump's at the Westcott house. They wanted him to come over here, at least Mrs. Westcott and Gerty did, but he said he knew you and he refused to be worried in the least."

Asey grinned. "Well, if the doc's willin', we'll amble back to Westcotts', then. Keep that bunch worryin' around for an hour or so more, will you, b'fore you s'gest that you bet I'm home in bed? Fine. An' did Gerty pass over some jewelry to you?"

"Yes, and what do you make of that?"

"More plantin', I think. I dunno. Be seein' you."

"Well," Stern said, "honestly, Asey, this—this is crazy. All of it."

"You're tellin' me?" Asey led him to where Betsey's roadster was parked. "You're tellin' me? Why, I seen more of this town of Monkton t'night than most native Monkeys see in a life time. Mind takin' this car, or is yours here?"

"Mine's around somewhere," Stern said. "Don't worry about it. I don't often get a chance to ride in Porters. What's going on?"

"Did you ever have someone say somethin'," Asey asked, "an' have it kind of ring a bell within you, like? That's what happened to me t'night. It set me thinkin'. Doc, what about Aunt Eugenia? Mrs. Crane, I mean. The Dixon aunt that died a year or so ago."

"What about her?" the doctor's eyes narrowed. "Well, what d'you mean, what about her? She was an angular New Englander with a conscience, the most methodical soul I ever knew. She came to town at ten-thirty four days a week, and my wife used to set the hall clock when the car went by. Like that. All the servants at the Dixons' are hers. That is, trained by her. Edward's been doing the same thing at the same time every minute of the day for thirty years. Clockwork. A grand old war horse, Genia Crane was."

"What did she die of?"

"Bronchiectasis," the doctor said promptly.

"It's a new one on me," Asey said. "Is it somethin' you get, or catch, or what?"

"In days gone by, most cases of bronchiectasis used to be called chronic bronchitis," Stern explained. "She had a terrific case of pneumonia about two years ago, and that brought it on. I had a fight on my hands, trying to treat her. She said she had the family heart trouble, and whatever bronchiectasis was, she didn't have it, and she knew she didn't have it, and she never heard of anyone who did have it. It's a condition in which the bronchial tubes are dilated beyond their normal size. You get a bad case of pneumonia, or flu, usually—though of course once in a blue moon you'll get a congenital bronchiectasis, too. Anyway, you get an infection of the bronchial wall that causes particularly a destruction of the muscle and elastic tissues. The —d'you follow?"

"More," Asey said, "or less. Go on."

"Well, the weakened bronchus becomes permanently dilated. Bad business. Genia Crane wouldn't let me send her to a hospital, and she wouldn't allow an operation. When a firm determined woman like that makes up her mind to anything, God and all the snapping turtles in the world couldn't make her change it. I warned her—my God, I explained till I was blue in the face. Harper and Pete and Char all did their best. But Genia had her mind made up on the heart trouble, and there we were. Might as well try to argue with a stone wall."

"Now let's get this." Asey slowed down. "I ain't so hot on terms, here, but she's got bronchitis, like. An' the bronchial tubes is dilated. That is, they're enlarged, or expanded, huh? So if she died of the bron—well, this trouble, then—well, what I'm drivin' at is, this what-you-macallit is a disease of the air passages, ain't it?"

"Well, yes. You might—"

"An' death would r'sult from the cloggin' of the air passages? Uh-huh. Then you could call it asphyxiation, couldn't you? I mean, the air's cut off."

"You wouldn't," Stern said, "but you could."

"Uh-huh. Now." Asey stopped the car. "Drownin' is asphyxiation too, ain't it? Water keeps the air from comin' into the lungs?"

"Yes, but Asey, are you trying to suggest that Genia Crane—Asey, are you—oh, but that's absurd! What on earth makes you think—it's crazy, I tell you! She had bronchiectasis, and she absolutely would not be properly treated for it, and she died of bronchiectasis. No doubt of that at all!"

"Mrs. Babb," Asey said, "had high blood pressure an' a bad heart. Offhand it looked like she died of heart trouble, didn't it, doc? But she was drowned."

Stern leaned back and stared at Asey. "What in the name of God made you think of this?"

Asey told him about the Italian who had picked him up and taken him to Main Street.

"He was so sort of r'signed an' casual about his sister's kickin' the bucket. An' I'd been thinkin' since Sat'day what in the world Mrs. Crane's groc'ry order had to do with the price of beans, an' how it might be c'nected up with the rest. An' if it *was* c'nected up. Gerty said that Mrs. Crane died a year an' a half ago, or so, an' Mrs. Westcott said the same thing, an' both of 'em was so casual about it. I mean, she just died, an' they was sorry, an' that was all. An' when this feller talked about kickin' the bucket, I kind of thought—you know how—"

"Asey! I—"

"Wait. You know how you think of things that don't c'nect, seemin'ly, sometimes. Well, I got to thinkin' 'bout ole Cap'n Bangs, the feller I first went to sea under. He had an awful temper, an' he used to march along the deck kickin' out at things when he was mad. Man or beast, he didn't care a rap," Asey said feelingly. "He started to kick out at me one day, an' it was only my first v'yage, an' I didn't intend to be kicked by no one. I stuck out a nice oak bucket in time for him to toe that instead of me, an' he busted three toes. So when anyone talks about bucket kickin', I'm inclined to be r'minded of that, real vivid. I—"

"But look here," Stern interrupted, "that's all very well, but how can you connect any such thing with—"

"Gimme time. This takes a sight longer to tell than it took me to think it. I'd been thinkin' of Mrs. Crane an' that order. When that feller spoke about kickin' the bucket, I thought of ole Bangs. You know, he was drowned right in Wellfleet Harbor, in two feet of water, he was. Been to sea forty years, an' couldn't swim a stroke. In—"

"In other words," Stern said ironically, "your next association was drowning."

"Just so." Asey wasn't moved by his sarcastic tone. "Just so. Mrs. Babb was drowned. But her death nearly fooled you.

I was just wonderin' if Mrs. Crane's death, that was all so casual an' natural, might pos'bly have been a drownin', too."

Dr. Stern snorted.

"Well," Asey said, "there's some reason behind that order. Harper may be tellin' the truth when he says there ain't. Maybe he was drunk, like he says. But drunk or sober, this come out. It ain't nothin' casual. You don't get so casual over fifty thousand dollars' worth of bets."

"Possibly not," Stern said, "possibly not. But you'll never know about Genia Crane, Asey. Her body was cremated and its ashes are now reposing in an expensive urn, suitably engraved, in the local cemetery."

Asey tried another tack.

"Look, will you grant me that there is a pos'bility that she might have been drowned?"

"It's possible," Stern said, "that she was killed by a bolt of lightning, or a death ray from Fu-Manchu, or someone leaping up behind her and saying 'Boo.' In fact, the 'Boo' is the most possible of the three. Of course it's possible. Practically anything is possible, but it's not probable."

"Pos'bility an' prob'bility," Asey said, "sometimes is closer together than most folks think. A week ago, you thought I was a hick hayseed, a jack of all trades. A kind of publicity mistake. For all I know, you may still. If anyone asked you if you thought you'd be meetin' me an' knowin' me this week, what'd you of said? It was pos'ble, but it wan't prob'ble. If anyone asked you last week what you thought of Mrs. Babb's bein' murdered this week, you'd of said the same thing."

"Yes, but—"

"There," Asey interrupted. "That's just it. That 'yes-but.' Take it another way. S'pose you go down street an' meet someone you ain't seen since he yanked you out of a shell hole in no man's land. You go home an' say to your wife, well, well, most amazin' thing. Met ole So-an'-so. Hadn't seen him in twenty years. Hadn't even heard tell of him.—Now, don't you realize, doc, the amazin' thing ain't that you just met him. The amazin' thing is that you didn't meet him b'fore, or hear of him b'fore. The things that don't happen," Asey was warming up, "is the amazin' ones. The—"

"Oh, I'll grant you all that," Stern said, "but you couldn't convince me that Genia Crane was murdered."

"How long," Asey said, "after she died did you see her? Think back, will you?"

"It was a Thursday afternoon. I remember that. The servants were out. I don't know where the boys were, but they weren't at home. Char found her, down on the living room couch, and called me."

"No nurse?"

"Yes, she had a nurse, but we had to pretend she was just a companion. Genia wouldn't let her wear a uniform. She'd gone to the city for the day. She—Asey, the look on your face is too—don't look so damn cocky! It was a coincidence that she died on a Thursday, when the place was practically deserted. I'm sure she didn't plan it that way!"

"Maybe someone else did."

"But Charlotte was around the house. Out in the far garden, or somewhere in the vicinity! Genia had a bell to ring if she wanted help. Besides, she could get around all right. She wasn't bedridden, or anything. She had—"

"Go on about when you found her," Asey said.

"Why, I came directly Char phoned me. I knew, Char knew, everybody knew what had happened! You see, she had a good side and a bad side, and she was lying there on the bad side. She always had trouble when she—she—my God!" the doctor stopped short. "My God, Asey Mayo! I've just remembered! Her—her—no. No, that's not possible!"

"Her hair," Asey suggested in his purring voice, "was damp, maybe?"

"Are you psychic? Are—how did you know?"

"People don't vary their methods," Asey said, "much. So her hair was damp, huh? How'd you rationalize that at the time?"

"No rationalization about it!" the doctor was thoroughly angry at Asey's insinuation. "It was a part of the situation. Just you listen to this, Asey Mayo, and maybe you'll change your mind about a few things! Genia Crane had had a shampoo that afternoon. And do you know who gave her that shampoo? Your little friend Gerty McKeen! That's who!"

17

ASEY started to back the car toward town.

"Where are you going?" Stern demanded.

"Backin' to that lane clearin', so's I can turn around an' go for Gerty. You can dash in an' yank her out of the store. I still don't feel ready for one of Nell Westcott's mustard poultices, an' sure as shootin', she'll want me to go to bed with a dozen plastered all over me, soon's she sees me."

"Don't you think it might be well for you to let them all know that you're safe?"

"Mrs. Westcott," Asey said, "will worry more after she knows than she's worryin' now. If Betsey's broodin', she's more of a fool than I think."

He put his foot down on the accelerator, and Dr. Stern, who had never been warned about Asey's apparently absent minded speeding, clung to the door and held his breath. He managed to refrain from commenting until Asey deposited him on Main Street near Gerty's store.

"You very nearly," he remarked, "had a concrete illustration of a bronchiectasis right before your very eyes. Talk about dilated tubes! Why, I chewed my right auricle to a pulp, back at the cross roads! I don't know about my lungs, but my heart will never be the same again!"

Asey chuckled. "Git Gerty, an' be careful you don't bring the whole mob."

Gerty was genuinely relieved at finding Asey intact.

"My God," she said, "what a day, what a day! Say, I got grey hairs since noon. Nests of 'em. I don't know why I'm back on the carpet, Asey, but I'm glad to see you just the same. You couldn't blow me to a cup of coffee, could you? I don't seem to have eaten for six months."

"Now you speak of it," Asey said, "neither've I. Got a lunch room around?"

"There's a quick and dirty on the next street."

Over nicked white mugs of coffee, and thickly cut sandwiches containing the thinnest and palest slices of ham which Asey had ever seen, Gerty was questioned.

"Turn your mind back to Eugenia Crane," Asey said. "You shampooed her hair the day she died, didn't you? Now, was her hair dry when you left?"

"Of course!" Gerty's professional pride was hurt.

"Could you look into your books, or somethin', an' find out what time you—uh—done her?"

"Don't need to. I know. She always had a two o'clock appointment, no matter what it was for. She always laid down after lunch, and if she was done then, she felt she hadn't wasted time, see? She couldn't ever understand how Mrs. Babb would drop into the shop all hours of the day, and spend so much time there. She said wasting time was criminal."

"Now," Asey turned to the doctor, who had taken one look at the nicked mug and then proceeded to sip his coffee from a paper spoon, "can you r'member what time Mrs. Babb called you that day, or what time you got there?"

"I've been thinking. My wife was giving a hen party, and there was a mob around. Must have been around five."

"An' let's see, Gerty. What time would you of left? Two-thirty?"

"Three. Long hair, she had," Gerty explained. "I dried it with one of those little driers like you smashed the window with tonight."

"An' you can prove she was alive when you went at three?"

Gerty smiled. "By the grace of God, I can. Mrs. Westcott came in as I left. She had a big bunch of chrysanthemums for Mrs. Crane. I had to hurry back for a three-thirty."

"Went in the bus, huh?"

"In my own. That was before the bank flopped. I had a car then."

"I presume," the doctor said sarcastically, "that you can even remember your three-thirty, too, can't you?"

"It was your own daughter," Gerty told him. "It was just after she was kicked out of that finishing school in New York. Remember? She came for a facial, a hair cut, a shampoo, a wave, and eyebrows. She said that after two solid days of that tongue of yours, she needed to relax. She told me to charge it, and I did, and I sent the bill to you six times," Gerty obviously was enjoying her recital, "and you didn't pay it, and finally I bullied that blonde in your office that you had then to make out a check for the amount without my name on it, and you signed it when you signed a lot of others, and that was the only way I got my money."

Asey chuckled at the doctor's discomfiture. "She's got you done up brown," he said.

"Well, what of all this?" Stern asked. "We can't prove anything."

"Maybe not," Asey said, "but it's nice to give Gerty a chance to pull out of it, ain't it? Gerty, can I take you home?"

"Mrs. Westcott asked me to stay there tonight," Gerty said. "I wouldn't of, but I'm still sort of scared."

"Come 'long with me, then. Shall we drop you, doc?"

"Take me over to my car. Asey, I'm stumped. I can't believe you're right about this, but—"

"Sleep on it," Asey said.

He whisked Gerty to the Westcott house after leaving the doctor where he had parked his car.

Stephen Crump, the Porters' lawyer and the general legal adviser for most of the Hybrid Club members, was waiting for him.

"They told me a lot of nonsense about your leaping through a window after someone and disappearing into thin air," he said as he greeted Asey, "but I ignored it. Asey, I'm going to be brief, because Ralph has got to take me back tonight. I'd not intended to dash off, but young Steve just phoned me, and they want me tomorrow morning. Asey, this Dixon business is damned odd. So odd I'm going to tell you, though I've no right. Harper and Pete have called me, but I wanted to look into everything first. After I looked, I decided to see you first. Now look. You didn't ask me about Eugenia Crane—"

"But anythin' you might say," Asey told him, "will be gratefully r'ceived. Delve right into Genia. Quick."

"Genia Crane," Stephen Crump said, "was a very determined woman. She—"

"I kind of gathered that," Asey said.

"You may have gathered it, but you don't know how determined. Furthermore, she was the most orderly individual I ever knew. Beats old Lucius, my bookkeeper. Now Char Babb was inclined to be scatter brained, but Genia was a hard headed business woman, like her father. She made a will years ago. I had it in my safe, but don't ask me the contents, for I never knew them. She drew it up herself, and had it properly witnessed. I never for a moment would question any document Genia Crane drew up, by the way. Now, about a month before she died, she phoned me and ordered me to destroy that will at once. I did so. She asked me to come out the next week-end and draw up another. I couldn't get out then, and the next week she was sick, and cancelled the invitation herself, and the upshot of it all was—"

"I can guess," Asey said. "She died intestate."

"Exactly. Her estate went to Char. Now Char was very decent about it. Gave the servants what she thought Genia would have left, and added some for good measure, and she took care of some distant relatives who were broke, as distant relatives always are. In fact, she was a damn sight more generous to 'em than Genia would have been. Genia felt that if you were poor, it was your fault for not being bright enough to make money. She did, always."

"Hetty Greenish?" Asey suggested.

"In a way, very."

"What about Harper an' Pete? Did Mrs. Babb do anythin' about them?"

Crump shook his head. "No. She said they had more than

enough as it was, and they ought to have something to look forward to, or words to that effect."

"Pete said that most of Mrs. Babb's money went to him."

"Pete's mistaken," Crump said. "She changed her will last fall. It's Harper who gets the lion's share now, and I'm inclined to think that he knows it. But here's the point, Asey. Genia plans to change her will, and she dies. Char changes hers, and dies. And here is something I didn't know till yesterday. She called at the office last week, and spoke with young Steve, and said she hadn't time then, but she was coming in this week, and wanted to change her will again. She made an appointment for Monday. Yesterday. And like Genia, she dies before the change is made. What do you make of all that?"

Asey was on the point of telling him that it sounded like a recipe for goulash when Betsey, Hank and Mrs. Westcott arrived.

"One word," Nell Westcott looked at him reproachfully, "one word, and you couldn't stop me talking for months, Asey. How mean of you! How—"

"What," Asey interrupted her, "is that horrid noise I hear outside?"

"It's the bloodhound," Hank said. "She's going to keep him in the barn for the duration of your stay. She mulled over the idea of keeping a St. Bernard or two—the Phyfe-Jordans finally got the poor beasts here,—but we persuaded her with difficulty against it. But she would have the bloodhound. Simply couldn't dissuade her."

"Where," Asey tried to stave off Mrs. Westcott as long as possible, "is Leon?"

Gerty, who had come downstairs, heard the question and laughed.

"I saw him pop into the rumble of Mrs. Porter's roadster while we were in the quick and dirty. I didn't tell you, because I was sort of sore at you just then. I guess you'll find that he's around."

"Maybe he's in bed," Asey said, hoping that the hint might be taken by the rest. "Guess he's had a hard day, like all of us."

"Hard," Betsey said, "is right. I've lost weight over you today, Asey, you old fox! And if I never play solitaire again in my life, I'll be quite happy. I have never played so much double solitaire in my life. In that shop this evening, I—"

"Aw, say," Leon appeared in the doorway gripping two packs of cards, "aw say, Mrs. Porter, we didn't finish that last two games out of three! We got—"

Betsey looked at him, emitted a shrill screech, and fled upstairs.

"I kind of feel like doing the same thing," Gerty said, "even if I ain't been playing cards like she has. Good night!"

Stephen Crump arose. "I'll be going myself," he said, "we've got three hours of driving ahead of us, unless they've done some more ploughing beyond Leicester. Asey, I've told you all I know. Maybe you can make something out of it. Maybe not. Let me know if you need me. I'll probably be over to see the Dixons later tomorrow."

Only Mrs. Westcott remained downstairs when Asey returned from seeing Crump off.

"No," she answered the question he hadn't asked, "no, I'm not. I'm not going to bed. Not if I drop on my feet. I'm not going to be tricked out of missing any more. No matter how purry you get. And if you want to know what I think, I think it's about time you took off those wet, messy clothes, and had a nice hot bath, and—"

"An' maybe a mustard plaster?" Asey inquired.

"Well, a hot water bottle, anyway. And Frank should give you a nice rub. My brother says he's very good. He used to work in a Turkish bath or something before he became a groom and a chauffeur, and although I personally can't vouch for him except with horses, I should think he'd be most efficient."

"Wa-el," Asey drawled, "I ain't never had no one go at me with a curry comb, but it's an int'restin' prop'sition, as the ole lady said when they offered her a thousand dollars to test a life preserver."

Mrs. Westcott picked two magazines and a book from the table and settled back in her chair.

"If," she said, "you went upstairs, and let Frank give you a nice rub down, and all, I might be persuaded to tell you what I remembered about this grocery order business that's worrying you and Betsey so."

"You—you what?"

"I really don't see why it should worry you," Mrs. Westcott continued blandly, "because they were the clearest, most logical orders in the world. I mean, I write down things like 'p.d.r.fss,' question mark, and 'h.m.v, ask H,' and things like that. It takes so much time to figure them out. Could you?"

"No." Asey said. "Could—I mean, can anyone?"

"Oh, p.d.r.fss, that means piece de resistance, Friday, Saturday, Sunday," Nell explained. "And h.m.v, ask H., is how many vegetables, ask Hank what he wants. But Genia's orders weren't like that, written on the backs of envelopes. She wrote them in that neat, fine script of hers, on index cards, and if she had two, she clipped them together."

"Er—what," Asey said, "did you say you remembered about that order, now?"

"I didn't say," Nell told him. "But I might—mind you, I *might,* I don't say that I would, but I *might,*—if you went upstairs and let Frank—"

"Oh, m'God," Asey said, "call Frank, an' tell him to bring in his curry combs an' the mange cure, an' all the rest. Just one thing b'fore I go, to set my mind a little bit to rest. The last time you seen Mrs. Crane, the day you brought her them chrysanthemums, the day she died, d'you remember anythin' about her hair?"

"Merciful heavens, how *did* you find out about those chrysanthemums? I—oh, I know—I met Gerty as she was leaving, and she may have remembered. They were really lovely chrysanthemums, you know. I won two firsts with the same kind at the flower show the next week. They were—"

"Her hair," Asey said. "How did it look?"

"Awfully well," Nell told him. "I said as much, and she was so pleased. Gerty'd done it—well, soft around her face, you know, with just a touch of wave. Just a touch. And Genia was so inclined to be severe about her hair. She—"

"Was it dry?" Asey asked.

"Dry? Of course it was dry! What a perfectly foolish question to ask, Asey! Was it dry! Gerty's awfully careful about that. Oh, always. Many's the time I've begged her to let me out of the drier, or baker, or whatever it is, and she just is simply adamant. She said to me last week, Mrs. Westcott, she said, do you want me to let you go out and get your death of pneumonia? Because, she said, you certainly will if I let you go now. And I said, I'll certainly dry up what brains I have if you let me bake here another minute, do put me on low heat, and—"

"Will you," Asey was completely defeated, "ask Frank to come up, please? Thank you, ma'am."

Nell Westcott smiled to herself as he left. There were, as she always said, more ways of killing a cat than choking it to death with sour cream. The late Stafford Westcott had been another man who hated to change wet clothes and take proper care of himself. She knew the type.

Before Frank finished with Asey, Hank Thorn wandered in to Asey's room with a dressing gown and a pair of pyjamas slung over his arm.

"I'm sorry they're silk," he indicated the pyjamas, "but I picked you out the quietest clean pair I own. All this excitement has played hob with the laundry. Asey, isn't it your turn to cope with Leon? I taught him Idiot's Delight, in self-defense, and he's playing it all over my bed. Betsey taught him to back flip his shuffle, and it makes it sound like ten snare drums. There's no use talking, he's a teachable lad. But what'll I do with him, lock him in a closet, or what? And what're you looking at those pyjamas like that for? They're very swell. A girl I know gave'em to me. Nell said—"

"I'll bet they both did," Asey said. "Hank, look at that neck! What do you think I am, a kulak? An' I got to go down an' face your sister in'em! Hank, what's she know about this gro'cry order business?"

"Did she say she did?"

"Did she? She inveigled me into comin' up here an' bein' kneaded in the hope of findin' out somethin'."

"She never murmured a word about it to me," Hank remarked. "I do hope it's not a snare and a delusion. She can be very snarey and delusiony when she sets her mind on getting things done. And don't you really feel better?"

"I could win the Kentucky Derby," Asey said, at which Frank snickered.

"Will you wait a second," Hank asked as Asey started downstairs. "There's something I'd like to—by the way, how many confessions have you listened to today?"

"I've lost count. Sue an' Pete, an' Harper an' Gerty, an'—oh, most everyone. What's on your mind, the call you made from the Dixon house at quarter to eight on Sat'day night, when you an' your sister dropped in there?"

Fortunately there was a chair where Hank happened to sit.

"Asey Mayo, how did you know?"

"Well, the doc called the Dixon house then, an' the line was busy, an' you said you called Sue, an' I just asked Frank what time you left here, an' he said just after seven-thirty. An' I asked Rochelle if you called b'fore you left here, an' she said you an' Mrs. Westcott argued about it, but you didn't phone. You must of called from somewheres, an' the Dixons' is the only place you could of, en route. One way an' another, I sort of figgered it out. Whyn't you mention it?"

"We drew up in front of the Dixons' and blew the horn," Hank said, "and then I got out, and I knocked, and then opened the door. I felt sure none of the family were home, and I didn't care about the servants, so I went to the hall phone and asked if the dinner were still on. I didn't want to go much. Sue said yes, so I came out again, and on we went. There wasn't any reason to tell you when we met you that night, and afterwards, after we found Char—well, it didn't seem very wise to tell you then. I haven't said a word about it to Nell. I don't think she's thought of it since. I knew she thought someone let me in. I didn't bother to explain. I wasn't inside the house two minutes. Do you believe me, Asey, or am I under suspicion, or something?"

"Where were you," Asey asked, "when Mrs. Crane died? Were you here with your sister then?"

Hank thought. "She died a year ago last autumn, didn't she? Let's see. What was I doing—oh, I know. Of course. I was in Mexico, with a friend of Bill Porter's, by the way. Jerry Penn. He lives over near Whitefield. Jerry was discovering Mexico about then, and he wanted to write a book about it, but nothing ever came of it. Why do you—by George, do you mean there's some connection between Genia's death and Char's?"

"Would it," Asey inquired, "make a nice story?"

"A corker! Say, if that's so, Asey, you can rule out the Dixon boys. Did you know that? They were both away when Genia died, I'm sure. Nell went over there that very afternoon, and knew about everything. In fact, Nell was the last person to see her—" he stopped. "Asey, if I were writing this, and someone said that about Nell, and it had already been discovered that—that is, well—that someone who was Nell's brother had been at the house that night—oh, I'm all involved. But I'd make quite a point of it, you know!"

"I bet you would," Asey said, "but we ain't goin' to waste no paragraphs on it here. You can't tie up with the rest."

"That," Hank said, "is ruining a good chapter break, that is. You ought to play Nell and me along, and end on something exciting—"

"Like," Asey suggested, "a crash without?"

"Or footsteps. They're always good. Slinking footsteps, falling—"

"Falling forninst him," Asey helped out. "That was the way I felt in that tannery yard tonight. The—"

"The tannery?" Hank said. "Our tannery? That is, our tannery that was? Nell's husband owned that. She sold out in twenty-six. Think of that, will you? Think of there being someone who sold out, and got paid in full before twenty-nine? And believe it or not, she invested the money with an utterly strange broker whose looks she liked, and he pulled her out of the market the week before the crash. But really, I'm almost rather hurt, Asey, that you should dismiss me, and Nell too, all so casually!"

"Cheer up," Asey said. "I may be foxin'. You can't never tell. I may be leadin' you on to the jaws of fate. Let's go see your sister—"

He broke off as a terrific crash sounded downstairs, followed by a scream from Nell Westcott, and her urgent call for Asey.

Hank nodded with satisfaction. "That," he said, "is picking the old story up. A crash within, a woman's scream, and a cry for help. Yes, that's *good!*"

18

"I DO b'lieve," Asey muttered in exasperation as he raced out into the hallway, "I do b'lieve, Hank, you'd stop to figger out dr'matic effects on your death bed, an' linger on long enough to stick 'em in a yarn! Hustle—"

Hank pounded down the stairs after him, damning the cord of his dressing gown, which nearly tripped him twice.

Nell Westcott was in the living room, sitting calmly in the chair where Asey had left her. At her feet were the shattered remains of a blown glass vase.

"For God's sakes, Nell!" Hank demanded breathlessly, "What's the matter? What happened? What were you yelling about? What are you staring dreamily into space about now? For God's sakes, what's wrong?"

"Please, Hank," she reproved him, "don't *swear* so at me! It's—"

"What's the matter, Nell!" Hank was commanding an answer, not requesting it.

"It simply isn't human," Nell said. "I never knew I—"

"Eleanor Westcott!" Hank thundered. "Stop beating around bushes, and get to the point!"

"Why, it was the horehound beer. Horehound beer—"

"I bet," Asey murmured, "there was a hound or two mixed up in it somewheres!"

"Nell," Hank said, "what do you mean, it was the horehound beer?"

"Why, Char had some, and you thought it was so nice, and so different. You said so. It takes a pound of horehound, and some ginger and coriander seed and block juice and sugar and—"

"Oho." Asey stepped forward. Beyond the broken vase lay the book on culinary herbs and their uses and preparation, which the professor had brought over from the Dixons' the previous night.

"Is it somethin' in here?" Asey inquired. "Is it this that struck you all of a heap, like?"

"That thing!" Hank snorted. "Well, really, Nell, I admit Char's horehound beer had a nifty kick to it, but there's no need for you to dissolve at the sound of the recipe!"

"But you don't understand!" Nell said. "You don't understand a bit, either of you! I never saw such stupid men! Sometimes I think there is no limit to the stupidity and obtuseness of men. Even the brightest of you has—oh, dear, don't you see? I found it! It was stuck in that page, right next the recipe for horehound beer!"

"What was stuck?" Hank grabbed her by the shoulders and shook her. "Nell, come to!"

"Why, Genia's grocery order! See?"

She picked up a neat white index card from her lap.

Asey and Hank looked at each other.

"Some things," Asey said, plucking the card from her hand, "is b'yond words. This—"

"That won't do you the faintest bit of good," Nell said. "Really. I was so excited when I found it that I knocked over the vase that dear Margaret Sumner sent my last birthday. I yelled for you, Asey, before I read it. I recognized it the minute I laid eyes on it as one of Genia's. That neat writing, and all. Oh, Betsey, did I disturb you, too? I'm so sorry. But I found your order."

"You—don't you tell me it was in that herbal! I looked at it! Myself!"

"My dear, it was, and it's no earthly good at all. The order, I mean. It's just an order!"

"Let's see." Betsey leaned over Asey's shoulder and read it aloud. "Oh, dear, isn't that dull! It's not even an exciting order, is it? Two pecks potatoes. Lettuce. Carrots. Tomatoes. Broccoli. Green beans. Gallon of molasses. Two bottles cooking sherry. V.O.F. cheese. What's that, Asey?"

"Very Old Factory," Asey returned. "Fancy store. I used to buy whole cheeses for ole Cap'n Porter b'fore we set out in the yacht. I cooked too many years for him an' assorted fishermen an' sailormen not to know V.O.F. cheese."

"Flour," Betsey went on. "G.L. What's that, smarty?"

"Prob'ly a brand name," Asey said, "like Gold Label, or somethin'. See, she's got F.G. after the sugar."

"I've made out grocery orders," Nell said, "for more years than I care to recall, and I never in my life asked for F.G. sugar. What is it?"

"Fine granulated," Asey told her gently.

"How perfectly foolish! I don't believe F.G. or G.L. or any of those things are so easily explained. Why, if this order means anything, and you seem to think that it does, they must be code, Asey. They *are* code, if they have any meaning. What's B.H. gelatine, now?"

"Bunker Hill," Asey said. "They make it in Boston. I know that, 'cause Timmy Higgins's son runs the place where they make it. I get it myself, though it ain't no great shakes."

"One quart Major Grey's chutney," Betsey continued to read the order. "One quart Colonel Skinner's chutney—lord, I should think they'd burn up. Asey, what are W.B. nutmegs?"

"Whole brown," Asey said, "n'en you grind 'em. Or grate 'em. Ever hear of a nutmeg grater?"

"I spent a year at cooking school," Betsey said, "and I always thought I was pretty hot stuff, but—let's see. Pepper. Caraway seeds. Cardamon. Poppy seeds. Foie gras. Antipasto. Partridge paste. Acquainted with partridge paste, you old epicure, you?"

Asey shook his head. "That's a new one on me. So is one tin Nixy-naxy. What'n time, Bets, is Nixy-naxy?"

"Cocktail cracker," Betsey said. "It—"

"It sounds," Hank Thorn said, "something terrible, like strained stewed prunes in cans for babies, and what not. Well, I can tell you one thing about that order. They were about to throw a party. See, there's still more hors d'oeuvres. Prawn paste and bloater paste, and all. What's that last item?"

Betsey made a face. "Irish oatmeal. Asey, what does this all mean? It's a large order, and an expensive order, but no more than you'd expect with that establishment. Does it mean anything? Do you suppose it's the order we want?"

"I'm sure it is," Nell said. "Genia used to keep her list until the things came, and then she personally went out and checked every single item herself. This one hasn't been checked. I know she always did. See, she has the prices jotted down, too. No one ever over-charged her a penny. If things were regularly fifteen cents apiece, two for twenty-nine, and if they charged her thirty cents for the two, there was war till that penny came off!"

"So this was an order," Asey said, "that was never sent. Huh. How would an order of got into that book? Can any of you think of the reason for that?"

Nell beamed triumphantly. "I can. You know I told you I remembered something about an order. Char spoke about it a long time ago. She said she found an order of Genia's in some odd place. I can't remember exactly where. I don't know if she even told me, specifically. Char was not a very specific person. Anyway, she mentioned it, casually. Everything was in order when Genia died. She was *so* orderly. But Char remembered this order was the only thing not tabulated and in place where it should be. Char just spoke of it that once, in passing, and I never thought of it again until tonight. I don't know why I should remember it now, except that I told Char at the time it was rather nice to know she left one thing out of or-der—"

"What a horrid pun!" Hank said. "What an atrociously bad pun."

"I never—a pun? Oh, is it? Well, I said it was nice to know that she was human. It was simply uncanny, the way that woman took care of things, you know. After she died, and Char took over the running of the house, the servants nearly went mad. I found Edward crying, one day. He said he couldn't stand the disorder. Char had to raise their wages. She was *so* easy-going."

"How," Asey said, "d'you account for this order that never was sent, bein' in this book? If she had the order made out, why wasn't it sent? What's it doin' in this book, if she was so orderly?"

"Well, it's my book, of course," Nell said, "that Char borrowed. She started an herb garden, you know, and it was the pride of her life. I barely saw this book before I lent it to her, and you can see it's been well thumbed. It looks," she added critically, "as though she'd left it out of doors more than once, too. Anyway, Char always left things in books as book marks. Why, just flip through those pages, Asey! There's a ticket for the Irish sweeps, and there's a clipping about the Republican party's prospects, and an invitation to be a patroness at the orphanage. And cards of all sorts. Cleaners and dyers, and all. It always hurt her to part with things outright. She stuck odds and ends in books, always."

"She did, huh?" Asey nodded slowly. "An' she found the order, an'— Huh. Well, well, well. I wonder."

"What do you wonder?" Hank said.

"Why the order wasn't sent. I—"

"Granting," Betsey interrupted, "that this is the order Charlotte Babb spoke to Nell about, and that she put it in the book with the rest of that junk in it, and granting that it's Genia Crane's order, how do we know that it's *the* order? I can't see anything to it that would inspire fifty thousand dollars' worth of bets! D'you suppose it's an acrostic, Asey? Or code, or secret writing? Or what? Or do you really think it's the order that Harper meant?"

"Well," Asey said, "it's the only gro'cry order of Mrs. Crane's that we come across. Edward didn't have no specimens over to Dixons'. If there was an order, it seems like this was it."

"All I have to say," Betsey announced with asperity, "is that it's crazy. Everything's crazy. Whoever named this place Blight was a prophet. Why, I hoped something would come of that order. I banked on it. I thought if we found it, we'd solve all sorts of things. Potatoes, carrots, chutney, cheese, flour, sugar, molasses—why, I could do it myself! I do do it myself. Six days a week, fifty-two weeks of the year. Except," she caught the twinkle in Asey's eyes, "when Aunt Prue's at the house, and she enjoys ordering. She says so."

Asey laughed. "Hard worked, that's what you are, Betsey. Pinin' your youth away over gro'cry orders. Yup. I know. Slave to Bill Porter's stomach."

Betsey stuck out her tongue at him. "Well, I'm going to bed. I never was so disappointed in all my born days. I could cry. All I've hoped for out of that order, and what does it turn out to be? A grocery order. Nothing more. Nothing less."

Asey pointed out to her that if she were hunting for a grocery order, she might expect to find a grocery order, and not a coach and four.

"Or a rattlesnake, or—"

"Don't mention rattlesnakes," Nell said, "they're about the only thing that hasn't happened. I'm going to bed, too, Betsey. Leon, you scamper back, too. Corral him, Hank. Gerty," she added as Gerty sleepily stuck her head in the doorway, "you might as well turn around and go back upstairs before you really wake yourself up. It's all over. We've found the order—"

"And it is ours," Hank said. "It's an order. Just an old grocery order. Good night, Asey. I take it all back about a grocery order being a nice touch. It isn't. It sounded well, but it's pretty mediocre."

" 'Night," Asey said. "Sleep tight."

"Aren't you coming to bed?" Nell demanded. "You need a good rest, you do! You come right up to bed this minute! I'm sure there's nothing about that order to keep anyone awake a second. Aren't you going to bed?"

"Your pr'scription," Asey told her, "about havin' Frank knead me was so successful, I feel it's tomorrow already. You folks forget I only got tomorrow on this. Day after, I got to produce r'sults."

"Nobody's going to hold you to that silly bet," Hank said. "Don't you think so for a moment—"

"I ain't thinkin'," Asey said. "That's my main trouble. Only when I make bets, I don't renege. Hop along, all of you."

Leon lingered behind.

"Can't I stay?" he asked plaintively. "I've been awful good an' quiet, ain't I? Say, you know what Mrs. Porter told me? She said I talked too much. I promised her I'd try an' keep quiet. Say, ain't I?"

"Just a golden glob of silence," Asey said, "that's what you are. Eighteen carat an' a mile high. No, you—yes, on second thought, you can stay."

"I bet," Leon said, "it means somethin' to you, don't it? That order, I mean. Dick Tracy always catches on quick, too. So does Durward Vane. You know what it means, don't you?"

"Hate to disillusion you," Asey said, "but I don't."

"But you got an idea," Leon said complacently. "I can tell. Say, did you ever think about that fellow I seen in the garage? Do you suppose it was the same fellow you chased tonight?"

"Both of 'em," Asey said, "are rippin' an' tearin' through

my mind. The fastest thing on wheels couldn't catch 'em. Leon, for a brief time will you be so kindly as to allow 'em to rip an' tear without interruption?"

"Sure." Leon produced a pack of cards from his pocket and shuffled them with the snare drum effect Hank had mentioned. "I'll just play me some Idiot's Delight. Too bad you can't play. Of course, I could get another pack," he added hopefully, "and we could both play solitaire. I—"

"Idiot," Asey said, "d'light yourself, an' do it quick."

"Okay, Asey."

Asey unbuttoned the neck of Hank's fancy pyjamas, found one of Hank's pipes, and sat down in an easy chair.

The whole business was beginning to clear up. If only he could get the connecting links.

He got up and started to pace around the room. After half an hour, Leon gave up his card game on the rug and leaned back against the couch to watch in fascination that slow measured promenade. He wanted to tell Asey that it took him just the same number of steps every time, from the door to the window, from the window to the piano, from the piano to the fireplace, and the fireplace back to the door. Several times he had his mouth all open to speak, but he had a queer feeling that Asey wouldn't have heard him if he did speak.

At two o'clock, Leon began to feel sleepy; just as he settled himself on the couch for a nap, Asey stopped short.

"Gee, say!" Leon was startled. "Usually it's when someone starts movin' that you think somethin's goin' to happen, but— say, Asey, what's goin' to happen now?"

"What've you got on under that flannel thing of Hank Thorn's? Pyjamas?"

"Naw, I'm dressed," Leon said. "He told me to get undressed, but I didn't."

"I wasn't so lucky," Asey told him. "Wait here. I'll be right back."

Before Leon had shuffled the pack of cards to his liking, Asey returned, fully dressed.

"How hungry are you?" he demanded. "Pretty much, huh? I'm empty, too. Let's forage b'fore we go, an' see'f we can't find a little pem'can to take along. We may find it handy."

"Where—"

"You are about to go," Asey said, "on a long, long journey, with a tall darkish man. Feel up to it?"

"You mean, with you? Sure. I was kind of sleepy, but that," Leon explained, "was just on account of I didn't have nothing to occupy me."

"Let's go." Asey took his arm. "Say, you happen to know anyone named Penn around here? Jerry Penn?"

Leon thought for a moment. "There's a family named that over near Whitefield. They're sort of crazy people. They come over here to the ski jump. They live in a big place near the country club."

"Fine. Leon, who do the Dixons trade with? For gro'cries, I mean?"

"All the folks in Blight trade with Schmidt," Leon said. "For fish they go to the Brandts, for fruits and stuff they sort of buy around. Most the vegetables they raise themselves. Tim says it costs 'em ten times what they'd pay to buy the same thing at the A & P."

"Schmidt live around here?"

"In Monkton, but say, do you want to see old Schmidt himself? Because you'll have a hard time. He's in the hospital, way over in Leicester."

Asey waved a nonchalant hand. "Don't let that worry you none, youngster. With all the things you an' me is goin' to 'tend to, that don't signify attall. We may land up in the hospital ourselves, if we take a whack at all of 'em. C'mon. We'll see how this half baked notion turns out."

Nell Westcott was the only one to take their absence seriously the next morning.

"I won't," Hank said flatly, "start any more Asey Mayo Rescue Projects. I wash my hands of him. He always comes back alive and grinning, and apparently in the best of spirits. I think these messes he gets into give him an inordinate amount of pleasure. Am I right, Betsey?"

"Well," Betsey said, "so far he's always chuckled his way out of things, but Bill and I live in a sort of holy terror that he won't, some time. Take last night, when he dashed off after that man with no more vicious weapon than an electric hair drier! Think of that!"

"If you could see what he done with that drier," Gerty told her as she poured cream in her coffee, "you wouldn't sniff at it. If you ask me, he takes his weapons where he finds 'em. He'll be all right."

"And he took my car, did he?" Betsey asked Rochelle. "The bum. I'm sure he said that Frank or someone had fixed his own. Well, I'll just take his. Will you ask Frank to dig it out for me?"

Rochelle departed to return in a few minutes with Frank.

"I'm sorry, Mrs. Porter," he said, "but Mr. Mayo took the keys of the other Porter with him, and he left a note on my door saying that no one was to touch any car but Mrs. Westcott's own. The big sedan. He—well, he's taken the keys to all of them," Frank added. "He even got my duplicates, from my tool chest. The tool chest was locked, too."

"Are you sure it was Asey who took them?" Hank asked.

"Yes, Mr. Thorn. He said he was sorry to break the lock, and left a dollar for a new one! I couldn't even see where he forced it, but he did."

"He can do anything with a lock," Betsey said. "He had a bo'sun once who was a reformed cracksman. Comes in very handy. Every year when we go to Cape Cod, Asey drops over and sees to the trunks. Bill Porter never kept a trunk key over five seconds in his life. He loses them constantly. I think myself that he just depends on Asey."

At noon, Dr. Stern dropped over.

"Have I seen Asey Mayo? Don't talk. Don't say a word! He had me out of bed at five o'clock this morning, that man did! He was in the Leicester hospital. He—"

"There!" Nell said triumphantly. "I *knew* he'd get hurt! I knew it! What's the matter, did someone shoot him at last?"

"He was in the Leicester hospital," Stern said, "trying to make them let him see old August Schmidt, the grocer. Believe it or not, he'd persuaded everyone he should except for that old war horse of a head nurse, Bickum. She was wild, the old hatchet face. I had to call three trustees and Gardiner himself before she melted. And an hour later, Bickum called me back and practically apologized, and said my friend Mr. Mayo was very charming, and that they'd spent the Christmas of nineteen-seventeen only forty miles apart in France! You have to have caught sight of Bickum to appreciate that. She makes cast iron look like a bowl of corn meal mush."

"So does Asey," Hank said, "but from a different point of

view. I'll bet he's delving about the grocery order. I still can't
see why."

"I wish," Betsey said, "he'd come home!"

After luncheon was over, Hank took Nell, Betsey and Gerty
over to the movies in Whitefield.

"But suppose he comes back," Nell said, "while we're away?"

"I'd say," Hank remarked, "that it served him damn well
right. Come ahead. I'm sick of seeing you fidget. All of you.
You can fidget all you want to in the movies, but I'll mercifully be spared the details of the process in the theater. Come
on."

Half way through the second picture, he shepherded them
out.

"Just two seconds," he told his sister irately, "before that
usher gave you the bum's rush! I'm ashamed of you, Nell Westcott! The whole audience is seething with rage at you, and it
serves you right! You too, Betsey Porter. You were every bit as
bad as she!"

"Well," Betsey said, "Gerty never said a word. Not a word.
She made up for us."

"No," Hank rose to heights of irony. "Gerty never said a
word. No. She just let out a sigh like a noon factory whistle
or the siren at Sing Sing, every four and a half minutes by
actual timing. Tick-tock, tick-tock, tick-tock, then wheeeeeee!
That's all. For God's sakes, come home! You can fidget all you
want to there, and make all the noises your souls seem to crave,
and I'll retire to the attic. Come on. Betsey, come! Oh, my
God, this is no time to pick up stray males!"

"He's not a stray male," Betsey said crossly. "He's someone
I know. Jerry. Oh, Jerry Penn! Come here!"

Jerry Penn paused with one foot on the running board of his car.

"Hi, Bets! What're you doing here? Hullo, Hank. I say, who d'you suppose I saw today, Bets, of all people? Friend of yours."

"Who?"

"Asey Mayo. Bill's pal. Dropped in out of the blue, he did. Had lunch with us. Most amazing kid with him. Never saw such a boy."

Betsey, Hank, Gerty and Nell all exchanged glances.

"Oh, he did, did he?" Betsey said. "He and Leon had lunch with you, did they? I hope it was a nice lunch."

Jerry Penn looked at her oddly. "Well, mother's got rather a good cook, you know. I say, Asey was in superb form. Simply superb. He—"

"He wowed you, I bet," Betsey interrupted. "Oh, I just bet he did!"

"He wowed Penn Senior," Jerry said. "Told him about being in Sydney when they had all the fuss about the sea serpent, and winning with old man Porter's yacht at Cowes. Kept Penn Senior in stitches, and that, believe me, is no small item. My paternal parent is a tough lad to move."

"Isn't that peachy," Betsey said. "Did he tell you about Abner Dyer's going to heaven on a step ladder? That's another that always wows the outlanders."

"Betsey," Jerry said, "how peevish you are! I say, Hank, you're losing your memory—"

"No," Hank told him, "just my mind. So would you, if you'd sat in that theater—"

"No, your memory. You told Asey it was a year ago last fall.

That Mexican trip, you know. But I set him right. It was two years ago last fall that you and I washed down tamales and enchilada with pulque. Good old pulque. I say, Hank, are you going to be sick, or something? Don't you feel well?"

19

AT ten o'clock that night, Hank and his sister, and Betsey and Gerty all sat around the log fire in the living room, still waiting for Asey to return.

"I find myself," Betsey said after an extended and cheerless silence, "rather longing for Leon. I could do with a good game of double solitaire. Anyway, we know that he and Asey are still alive, and that's something of a consolation."

"Alive, but mad, poor things," Nell Westcott said. "I'm resigned to that. Think of them scavenging in the dump! In the dump! I really didn't believe Frank until he called in Rochelle to uphold him. The dump! Scavenging in the dump!"

"If they have to scavenge, it's undoubtedly the best place, Nell," Hank said. "I'd pick a dump myself if I felt the scavenging urge."

"Well, you know the answer to that one," Gerty said. "Harper told Joe at the garage to sweep up what was left of his car and throw it in the dump. Asey's after Harper."

"He's after me," Hank said. "Why else would he go pump Jerry Penn about me and that damn trip? My God, I wasn't trying to lie to Asey. What if I wasn't in Mexico? I was in California, and I can prove it. Either place, what's the difference, just so long as I wasn't here!"

A knock at the front door raised their hopes, but it was only Ernest Vail, who came in beaming from ear to ear.

"Splendid, isn't it?" he said heartily. "I'm so pleased. Very pleased. Delighted."

"At," Betsey demanded, "what, I'd like to know?"

"Asey, of course. He just told me this would be all settled tomorrow. I'm so glad. I've lost so much time on my book, since Saturday."

"Did he say that, in so many words?" Hank asked.

"Well, no. No, to be exact, he didn't. He said, in one way or another, he would be through tomorrow. And d'you know, he thinks he has the solution to the ransacking of my books and papers. He thinks someone was hunting for Mrs. Crane's grocery list that Mrs. Babb had put in that herb book. You know, he has a most unusual mind, Asey has."

"Where'd you see him, at the dump?"

"Dump? My, no. No indeed. At the hardware store this evening, earlier. He was contemplating the purchase of a pick axe or two."

"Utterly daft," Nell said, "utterly daft, poor thing! Did he offer any explanations about the pick axes?"

"I was led to believe," Ernest said, "that he intended to dig. Er—d'you mind awfully if I wait here for the end of this? I mean, having been in on so much of it, as you might say, I feel I'd rather enjoy participating in the finish."

"Wait as long as you like," Nell said, "but I rather think you'll be paying us a very extended visit."

"Oh, with all those men," Ernest said, "I'm sure it will take no time at all. All," he added hurriedly, "those new police officers and experts and all. The Dixons' place is quite seething with people. I've just been there returning some books I found I had at the cabin. That is, books which belonged to them. Both Pete and Harper are busy with some lawyer, and some-one is there with an inventory of Mrs. Babb's jewels, and Sue Vail is helping. Really it's seething. Quite a beehive of activity."

"A seething beehive, is it?" Nell asked thoughtfully. "You know, I think I'd enjoy a seething beehive—after all, haven't we some right to be there, Hank? You and I and Gerty are all mixed up in things. D'you think they'd throw us out, Ernest?"

"Why, I can't see any reason for them taking any such—er —violent action," Ernest replied. "They were most cordial to me. Most. But don't you think it might be wise to wait for Asey to return?"

"If you had waited for Asey as much as I've waited for Asey during the last few days," Nell informed him, "you'd know it was a grossly overrated pastime. Come on, Hank, get the car out. We'll all go over."

As Mrs. Westcott's big sedan rolled down the drive and onto the main road, Asey started up Betsey's roadster, which had been parked beyond the entrance to the Westcott house.

"Good for Ernest," he said to Leon. "He done that quick an' efficient. Grip onto them cans of paint, kid. They're precious."

"Say, did he get a kick out of doin' that for you?" Leon said. "Say, was he thrilled! What you waitin' for now, Mackinson's signal?"

"That's right. I want to be sure we ain't goin' to have no slip-ups at this point. Ain't you done up, Leon? Ain't you tired?"

"I would of been, if I'd had to do that diggin'. Wasn't we lucky?"

"I was lucky," Asey said, "to pick an ex-golf caddy with sense enough to mark things. Leon, I owe you plenty. I—ah. There's Mack's horn. Two short, two long. Okay, kid. Pretty soon we can go to bed."

"Say," Leon said as the roadster purred up the drive, "what d'you s'pose all them folks thinks, right now? Gee, you told'em everythin', but I bet they don't get it. I bet they don't even know you told the prof or the doc to go see'em, or that you planted that Penn fellow for'em to bump into. I bet they think it was all accidents."

"I done my best," Asey said, "without tellin'em too much. Bring in the paint an' them brushes, an' I'll bring in the rest. Go get Frank an' tell him I want that tool kit of his. We'll need him, too. Think of it, no carpenter in this whole burg! It ain't natural. Now, if only Mack an' Ernest an' Crump can keep that bunch int'rested till we're ready!"

At two o'clock that morning in the Dixon house, the seething beehive was still in action, but with diminished intensity. Mackinson was beginning to look worried. Dr. Stern had taken off his wrist watch and propped it up in front of him. Stephen Crump looked at it at five minute intervals.

"The hell with Asey," Harper said at last. "I'm going to bed!"

"You're staying right on that couch," Gerty told him, "like the rest of us are staying right here. Who d'you think you are?"

At two-thirty a car pulled up in the driveway.

"It's the roadster," Betsey said. "It's Asey!"

At the threshold of the living room Asey paused and drew a deep breath. Then he walked in, perched on the arm of Betsey's chair near the door, and tilted Hank's yatching cap on the back of his head.

"I'm 'fraid," he said to the roomful in general, "I've kept you up. I owe you an 'pology, I guess. I thought I had somethin', an' I was wrong. Pete," he reached into the pocket of his coat and drew forth a check, "here's the bet I owe you. Don't say you won't take it, 'cause you're goin' to. All I ask is that you wait till Sat'day b'fore you cash it. I got some liquidatin' to do. Anyway, I 'pologize, all around."

His voice was weary and flat. Betsey tried to look up at his face, but his elbow pressed against her shoulder and she couldn't turn her head. Asey increased the pressure of his elbow. Maybe he could pull through this, if he kept his eyes off Steve Crump. If Betsey caught on for a second, he was lost. She simply had to be made to believe that he was speaking the truth. Her face was almost more important than his.

"I'm sorry," Asey said again, even managing a little catch in his voice. "I busted into this, and there you are."

"The Mighty Mayo!" Harper said. "Someone else found the grocery order for you that—well, I give you half credit. I didn't know it existed. But even with *a* grocery order, you couldn't get to first base, could you?"

"Well," Asey said, "not exactly. That was a staple order. Barrel of flour, hundred pounds of sugar, 'bout fifty odd pounds of cheese—"

"It didn't say those amounts," Nell protested. "It—"

"Oh, yes. Nutmegs, an' chutney, an' caraway seeds an' all

ain't things you order ev'ry week. B'sides, them prices marked on the list told the story, for the flour an' sugar an' all. Anyway, it was a staple order, mostly. Seems Mrs. Crane give one more or less just like that every month, on the fifteenth. Funny thing, Schmidt said the staple order was due the day she died. The fifteenth. She always gave it then. But he never got it. It was all made out, an' ready to be given to him, but it never did get to him. Schmidt keeps nice records, an' he ain't thrown away his old ones because of some unpaid bills. Schmidt said it was the first fifteenth of the month in twenty years she hadn't given him almost that exact same order, 'cept for what he called seasonal changes."

"What of it? What of that?" Harper demanded.

"Oh, nothin' much, it's just sort of funny. Mrs. Crane makes out her usual fifteenth of the month order on the fifteenth, but it never gets to Schmidt, an' it never comes to light around the house. Matter of fact, Mrs. Babb finds it 'mong a bunch of securities that come out of Mrs. Crane's safe deposit box. Funny, considerin' Mrs. Crane hadn't no chance to put the order there herself, because she died that day. Kind of a hiatus, like."

"What do you mean?" It was a chorus.

"Crump's old bookkeeper, Lucius, he remembered. He got the things from the box. That order's listed twice in the office, Lucius says. In the things he took from the box, an' among the things he give Mrs. Babb. He says she never read lists, though."

"But see here," Hank Thorn said, "how did that order get from here to the box? If Eugenia died that day you seem to think the order was due?"

"I don't think it walked by itself," Asey said. "I think Mrs.

Crane, she give the order to someone else, to take to the store for her. But that person had other things on his mind than orders. He went straight to the safe deposit box, after she died. He left it there. By mistake, of course. Prob'ly didn't know it was lost till later, an' then didn't know where. Well, that's that, Harper. You see, I got to first base. That—"

"Asey Mayo," Betsey was beginning to catch on to his tactics, "that wire sent you about Blight! Did Jerry Penn send that?"

"No, didn't he tell you? He was s'posed to."

"Asey," Harper said, "do you—are you insinuating that Aunt Genia was killed? Is that what you're talking about? You're crazy! You can't prove it!"

"Aunt Genia?" Pete looked at Harper and his face grew black with rage. "You—"

"He can't prove it!" Harper shouted.

"Oh, my, yes," Asey said. "Yes I can. Leon!"

Leon, feeling almost a little stage fright although he had mentally rehearsed for hours, strolled into the room and placed a charred oak bucket with metal bands on the exact center of the rug. He looked at the bucket fondly, as if it were a masterpiece. In a sense it was. It had taken three hours for Asey and Frank and himself to piece a new bucket with charred parts of an old one, to paint it with quick drying enamel, to get the white part charred and burned looking with Frank's sodder light and small blow torch. The green stripes had been the worst. They hadn't dirtied as they should, and they'd had to sweep the Westcott barn to get proper dirt. Fitting on the old burned metal bands had been another job. And the old handle had even Asey cussing. But for a spur of the moment job, it was, as Asey said, a wonder. Probably it did look to these folks more or less like an old bucket dug up out of a hillside. On a spot that he himself had marked when the man had carried the original bucket there, and set it on fire, and buried it.

It was certainly making all these folks sit up and take notice, too, as Asey said it would. Mackinson had just wanted to show the old handle and the strips of metal and the charred bits, but Asey knew best. A lot of little pieces didn't mean anything. This old patched bucket did.

"That's one of Genia's buckets," Nell said. "One she used for her horses. Each horse had his own green striped bucket, with a number corresponding to his stall. What—"

"Them buckets is still out in the barn," Asey said. "They're all painted dark green now, includin' the numbers. Number three ain't there. This here bucket is number three."

Dr. Stern caught Asey's eye. He was so excited that he had nearly forgotten his cue. "Eugenia Crane," he said, "was drowned, just as Charlotte was. That bucket there," he made a little gesture toward it, "well, that's—well, it's the bucket."

"Just so." Asey was beginning to purr, and Betsey could have cried for joy. She knew that soft even voice, and what it meant. "Uh-huh, just so. Y'see, when you murder someone with a gun, you are apt to throw away the gun. Partly to keep b'listics experts from annoyin' you, an' partly to ease your conscience. The person who murdered Mrs. Crane by holdin' her head into that bucket, filled with water, he apparently acted the same way. Seems like he had a conscience too. He wanted to get this p'ticular bucket out of the way. So he filled it with ker'sene oil, an' carried it out to the hills, an' set it on fire. Burned it. Then he buried what was left. But I think on the way he was nervous, an' he spilled out a lot of the oil. I think he was too nervous to let it burn up thorough. Oak buckets with metal bands don't burn easy. N'en if you think you're bein' watched, as this feller did, you don't linger none to make sure. This feller was scared, an' nervous, an' as he lighted matches an' his ker'sene oil burned out, an' the bucket still not burned up, he was sure someone was watchin'. Matter of fact, someone was."

Harper leaned back on the couch and covered his eyes. Pete looked at him, his face white.

"My, yes," Asey said, "someone was really watchin'. 'Course, it didn't mean much more'n someone crazy doin' a crazy thing. But the feller who did the watchin' was no fool."

Pete Dixon's mouth was working hideously, and his throat made croaking sounds. Betsey felt sorry for him, and for Gerty. Of course Harper had done it.

Pete broke down altogether, and in a flash Sue Vail turned on him.

"You fool you, shut up! You jellyfish! He can't prove a thing—he—"

"He has!" Pete shrilled. "He—who watched me? Who? Who was it on that hill—"

"Grab'em, Mack," Asey got up from the chair arm. "That's right, Harper, help. You had plenty experience with Pete. Wa-el, this come a lot easier'n I'd hoped for. At that, Lady Macbeth done the trick herself, didn't you, Miss Vail? You cracked as soon as he did. I'm almost kind of sorry," he said regretfully. "I had a pretty good story all ready, an' I was goin' to play you two like a couple of pianos. Tell me, Miss Vail, did that barb wire hurt your hands last night as much as it tore mine? An' to think I didn't catch on till I seen them girls in ski pants, up in the town! One way to tell a woman paradin' as a man is to git her to throw a ball. 'Nother way is to have her clamber over walls an' gates."

He held Sue Vail's wrists while Mackinson expertly snapped on a pair of handcuffs.

"Was she," Gerty said, "was she the man who you chased last night, that was lurkin' around my place?"

"M'yes. She hopped back to your store an' changed her clothes on the way in her car, I guess. Least, she took off her pants an' put on a skirt. Mack kind of c'nfused me, sayin' she'd been there a long time. It was b'cause he'd been there only a short time himself, an' she was there when he come. Yeah, she planted that stuff on you, Gerty, an' the pearls on the prof."

"Had *me* fooled," Mackinson said. "By the way, Asey, that maid pretending to be Miss Vail over the phone last night, she's an old friend of our department. Only out on parole. I—"

Suzanne Vail proceeded to let loose.

"Take Lady Macbeth out," Asey said. "That chatter's kind of tirin'. Take Pete out too, an' better take care with 'em."

"My, my! My goodness me!" Ernest Vail's eyes were bulging. "And I thought of course it was Harper! Why, why! How did you know, Asey?"

"It got easier," Asey said, "when I b'gun to think of two people in this 'stead of one. No one person fitted to everythin'. Two sorts of things was goin' on. One neg'tive kind of things, like wipin' fingerprints, an' openin' that window, an' stickin' jewels into the safe. Coverin' up, like. N'en there was the down-right violent things, like Sue shootin' me on Sunday. Sure, Mack found the 30–06 in her cabin, back of the clay bin. No rusty triflin' about that gun! Yes, Hank, I know what you're goin' to say. She was with us when Harper was shot at; an' that was Pete. Mostly he did the neg'tive things, 'cept when she made him do otherwise. Mackinson's got times checked, an' that maid'll clear up the time d'tails. Harper, they darn near got you in that crash, didn't they?"

Harper nodded. "They've been trying that stunt for years. Usually I go over my car before I start out, but I didn't that night, thinking I was safe with the cops around. The tie bolts those two have played with! They—"

"Asey," Hank said, "did they tinker with *our* cars? Was that why—"

"Yup. Sue was Leon's man with a bomb, only it was a few tools she had. I had a hunch about that, an' looked around the cars b'fore we set out this—no, I guess it's yest'day mornin' Leon an' I set out. Harper, you've had an eventful c'reer as pres'dent of the Give-a-Dog-a-Bad-Name-Club, ain't you?"

"Eventful is a mild word," Harper said. "I thought they had me the other night. The shots, and oh, when I turned that corner and felt things go, and saw that wall coming towards me! I'd felt so secure, with you and the cops here. Then I went to pieces. That's why I insisted on staying at your house, Nell. It wasn't temper. I knew I was safe there. Incidentally, Asey, I tried to warn you, via Gerty, after Pete returned your coupe to you, in case he'd played with it. It didn't work, though, and luckily you took the beach wagon. Asey, did you guess about me and my crash that night?"

"I thought it was a made accident, but I wasn't sure if you or someone else made it. That was such a complete kind of wreck—"

"D'you mean to say," Nell sounded incredulous, "all your accidents Pete said were drunken driving, and all—"

"All his and Sue's work. Gerty knew. She yanked me out of a burning car once, and she knew I was sober. You see, I was safe if I seemed drunk, so I played drunk. Asey guessed that, because I coordinated so nicely."

"My God," Stern demanded, "why didn't you tell, if there was a conspiracy against you? Whyn't you say—"

"Why? With the reputation Pete's been building up since he began to think, and began to be sensitive about his size, and all? Listen, how could I—"

"Ooh," Betsey said. "Ooh. I get it! I said to Asey that you eclipsed Ernest so, and made him negative—sorry, Ernest, but he did! Of course, that's what he did to Pete, and that's why Pete—ooh. I see! But Harper, couldn't you have told someone?"

"How? Who'd believe me? I was big, I was a bully, a cad, a drunk. Swell build-up. Pete's so damn honest looking, and I'm dark and villainous, huh, Nell? Asey didn't believe me when I told him the truth up at Vail's cabin. Stern wouldn't have. He'd have slid me into a psychopathic ward. And—do you happen to know that Pete controlled my money, most of it, until I was thirty?"

"And to think," Nell said, "I thought it was a good idea! I told your father so!"

"There you are. And I'm thirty on March first. I tried to get that across to you the first minute I saw you, Asey. I thought you might have palavered with Crump before you came. That didn't work, either. Anyway, if Pete'd got rid of me by then, he and Sue would be sitting pretty."

"And it was you who sent that cable to Asey the night of the game, and not Jerry?" Betsey asked. "Did you know about the order, really? Did you—"

"I lost my head that day," Harper said. "Pete chucked something into a drink of mine, but I was sober, and I knew. That got me. Poison—well, I stuck that cable on Root's desk. I hoped it might get off as a drunk message. A lot were. Don't you see, I couldn't do anything overt—"

"Did Pete know about the cable, or that you sent it?"

"Mercifully when he found out, he thought it was Jerry. I had to keep him guessing all the time, don't you see. I couldn't do anything openly. Suppose I went to Stern or the cops, and said Pete was trying to kill me because he was jealous of me, and wanted all the family money for himself and Sue. Pete, the good Dixon, trying to kill that lout Harper? It even sounds foolish when you say it. To the psychopathic with Harper would have been the instant reaction. I think they hoped to get rid of me that way, once. I suggested it to Gerty, and she thought I was crazy. I couldn't get a private detective. The second Pete found out, don't you see, whang would go the money of mine I controlled. He didn't have to give it to me if he had any excuse not to. He had complete control over me that way. I went to the big game last fall with just one thought, a thought I'd been brooding over as the only solution. To get Bill Porter sore, and somehow drag Asey Mayo in. I heard about Bill avoiding me, and what with the poison in my drink, and apparently no chance to get at Bill, I made the only open gesture I ever attempted and sent that cable. I hoped it might puzzle him, and I intended to send a series. Then I found Bill in the writing room, and I could have screamed for joy!"

"Then you weren't drunk then?" Betsey asked. "Oh, will Bill burn!"

Harper smiled. "I didn't know a thing about the order, really, except Char said once that she had found an order among some of Genia's bonds. You have to have known Genia to know how queer that was. Char only found the order last summer, but I kept wondering about it. There was a hiatus, as Asey said. Genia's order, sent or not sent, filled or not, would never be among bonds. Now, I was morally certain that Pete had killed Genia, but I had no proof. A grocery order was no proof. It was just queer. I made that bet with Bill—took every cent I had, Bets, to pay it!—hoping just to get Asey here about something queer, and thinking if I could once get him here, I could goad him on to the rest. Maybe save myself, too. The only things I could do to force this business on before he got me were to goad and prod."

"You did," Asey recalled his actions Sunday afternoon, "just that. It was wonderful goadin'. But you couldn't of gone ahead on just that!"

"No, there were other things that began to occur to me last fall. Pete never spoke of a grocery order. He balked at the word order. When he talked over the phone, he scrawled 'order' over the pad, with curleycues around. That sort of subconscious stuff. It was a wild guess, but what could I do? I wanted to live."

"I r'call that," Asey said. "Pete said groc'ry list, when he asked me to investigate. Clever of him, puttin' me onto it, so's he could find out anythin' himself. What did he think about it?"

"The order? Well, I convinced him I was drunk when I made the bet. I think Genia gave it to him that day—he was supposedly at the races, incidentally, that day. With Sue. I think he came back, and Genia gave it to him, and he killed her, and went off. And—"

"And while he was prowling around the bonds and her box," Asey said, "he lost it among'em. He was there the next mornin'. Lucius called the bank an' got the vault record. He signed it."

Harper nodded. "Probably that's it. Probably he never bothered with it. Or thought of it. And he knew I didn't know much about it, or I'd have done things before. Say, Ernest, that's why I threw books, you know. I felt if the order still existed—by the time I'd brooded enough to ask Char more about it, she said she'd thrown it away, but I knew her habit of sticking things in books—I felt if it still existed, it was stuck in a book. I'd gone through the entire library at one time or another, but I hurled 'em around that night, hoping a miracle'd happen, and it would come to light."

"Did Pete an' Sue get wise to it then?" Asey asked, mindful of their "confession" the next morning.

"I think they worried more about what I might have said, or might have guessed, after my smash-up. Their confession to you was swell stuff."

Hank nodded his approval. "A grand touch!"

"So was Sue's sendin' Ernest to tell me of the 'man' on skis that was her all the time," Asey said, "an' Pete's callin' for me Sunday night, but really to see'f he'd got me. An' Sue's offerin' to call Pete after the smash-up, to tell him it was another failure. Bright, both of'em."

"That confession was best," Harper said. "They'd planted the pearls on Ernest then, and gone through his stuff, and hoped you'd go for him. And on Gerty. And—"

"My cap," Ernest said. "What about that?"

Asey laughed. "Prob'ly picked it up long ago, an' kept it for emergencies. That is, most likely Sue did."

"Sue's the one that thought of this," Harper said, "and egged Pete on. She's the most lavish spender in the world."

"I gathered that," Asey said, "with her guests, an' parties, an' guest houses, an' cabins an' all."

"That's only half. Really, all the money there is would never satisfy Sue. She was brought up in the lavish tradition. And she had Pete wrapped around her little finger. My God, she wore low heels to make him feel big and tall! Poor Pete, his size always bothered him so. He was little, and he wanted to be big. It never dawned on him that bigness wasn't anything physical."

The professor coughed nervously.

"But the bucket!" Harper went on. "That—how did you think of that?" He got up from the couch and examined it. "My God, it's a fake!"

"Pretty good fake, I think," Asey said. "You see, I was sure, but we couldn't prove nothin'. I hoped this might kind of make things jell. Leon seen the burnin', but he didn't know it was Pete. He told folks, but no one b'lieved him. Lots of folks heard about that bucket burnin', an' said Leon was crazy. Only I found that Leon told the truth quite often, an' if Mrs. Crane was drowned—well, buckets hitched up. I got a gang to dig where Leon said, an' we got the handle an' bands in two hours. I kind of hoped to make Pete break. Didn't have much hopes of gettin' the girl, but she was so anxious about Pete's breakin' that she busted too."

Harper asked Stephen Crump if he had figured out anything from the wills.

"Asey did. Genia was about to change hers—I wonder, Harper, if she didn't suspect Pete? And she died intestate. Char first left everything to Pete, and then I think she began to wonder too. She made a change in favor of you. Pete didn't know that. But he somehow learned she was going to make *a* change—probably another in favor of you—and she died. That way, almost everything went to him. What went to you,

Harper, he could bide his time about. He was sure of it all, sooner or later, but he wanted it all to come to him legally."

Outside in the hallway, Sue Vail's voice rose.

"The lipsticked cigarettes Leon found," Gerty said suddenly. "Sue Vail had some of that lipstick!"

"Uh-huh. We found it. An' when she stuck a hand on my head Sunday, as I lay out on the hillside there, I got a whiff of perfume. I got it again when she kissed me—Betsey, stop that! Stop. She did, the other day. I was too dumb to figger from it, but it fits in now. She's kind of actin' up—s'pose we kind of finish up. Harper, you want to see Pete b'fore—"

"No." Harper said. "I might forget my bad arm. That may sound unbrotherly, but this big bully mightn't contain himself—"

"My God," Stern said, "I still can't believe it! But you were so damned nasty, Harper!"

"If you," Harper said hotly, "had lived with a smaller, older brother and been in wrong—oh, nuts! Do you need blue-prints? Can't you see? Can't—"

"Turn it off," Gerty said. "You got a lot of renovating to be done, you have!"

"I can't believe it," Stern said. "Even now!"

"Who can?" Nell demanded. "It's perfectly diabolical! Genia, and it was all so natural, and then Char, and that seemed natural, too, and then trying to make Harper smash himself up!"

"Almost," Asey said, "a massacre."

"Diabolical." Stern stifled a yawn. "I—oh, this has exhausted me. I've got to get home. Sounds heartless, but the radio says there's another storm coming, and somehow everyone waits for a storm to be sick in. Always."

"You'd better all go out," Asey said, "the back way. Mrs. Westcott, take Harper an' Gerty in t'night, an' the p'fessor. He—"

"Now let me see," Vail fitted his fingertips together, "if I have it straight. Pete killed Mrs. Crane by drowning her, killed Mrs. Babb by drowning her, and made both deaths seem natural. Then—"

"Betsey," Asey said, "take him in hand. I'll be over shortly. And Leon—where'd Leon go to?"

Betsey pointed to a chair in the corner. Leon was fast asleep.

"I'll look after him," Harper said. "I don't know what he yearns for most, but he'll have it. Help take him back, Hank."

Nell Westcott lingered behind the others.

"Can we depend on your coming back, without—"

"Without bloodhounds? Yes. You can."

It was nearly five o'clock in the morning before Asey returned to the Westcott house, having settled all the details with Mackinson, and having extracted without effort a full confession from Pete Dixon, who was, as Sue Vail repeatedly stormed, a pulp. Asey was glad that Mackinson and not he had the job of looking after the girl. She was at the snarling stage.

The telephone rang insistently as he entered the hall, and he answered it.

"Yup, Asey Mayo speakin'. Who? Oh. Yup. Uh-huh. I see. Oh, I guess so. Yes. That's right. You do that. Okay."

He hung up the receiver and went into the living room.

Newspapers had been spread over the floor before he and Leon and Frank had set to work on the fake bucket, but the place was a mess of paint cans and tools and shavings.

He looked at them, and grinned, and then set to work.

There was something wrong with her room, Nell Westcott thought, as she awoke the next noon.

A northeast wind raged outside, but her windows didn't rattle. The blind wasn't slatting. The—

She sat upright in bed.

A note fluttered from the mirror of her dressing table. Ignoring her slippers and robe, and the frigidity of the room, she slipped out of bed, grabbed it and slid back under the covers.

"Dear Mrs. Westcott," said the note, written in a carpenter's blue pencil, *"I fixed up your windows and hope I didn't disturb you none. I fixed the blind, too, and I went over the electric plugs. You need a new beater on that electric mixer. I fixed up the ice box. It was just oil it needed. I fixed the spring on the toaster, too, so it won't hurl toast so. I cleaned out the spray on Hank's shower bath and put new washers in most of the faucets. I put a little piece of weather strip on your front door too."*

Nell's mouth worked, but no words came. She turned over the page.

"I also," said the note, *"fixed a couple of radiator valves and soaped up some bureau drawers Rochelle and Hank said stuck, and I planed up some doors that stuck and put new hinges on your back door. It sagged terrible. I'm leaving a stack of rubber wedges I found in the barn to take care of the rest of the window squeaks. I puttied some panes, too.*

"You been real good to take me in like this and I wish you'd take that Porter coupe for yourself, only have the Porter dealer

reclaim it some first. It ain't a bad job, but I phoned him to fix
it proper or else. I also left a check made out to the phone
company for all my phone calls and radiophoning to Root.
You—"

The bedroom door burst open, and Betsey flew in.

"Nell! He—"

"Don't tell me," Nell observed, "and put that blanket over
you before you catch your death! Don't tell me, I know. He's
gone. He says the pilot who brought him up wanted to get back
before the storm came, and he—did he leave you a note, too?"

Betsey passed it over to her.

" 'Someone,' " Nell read aloud, " 'will bring your car back
from the airport. Tell Bill to fix the brakes. I don't like to say
so, but a good housewife would know a staple order when she
seen it. Now—' "

"Wait," Betsey said. "I hear Hank. Hank, are you there?
Come in!"

"Asey's gone!" Nell said. "Hank, he's gone back to Jamaica!
Hank, you don't seem a bit surprised. Did you know? Did he
tell you? Did he leave a note for you?"

"No," Hank said. "He didn't tell me, but I knew."

Betsey and Nell stared at him.

"Don't you see," Hank said with finality, "if I'd been writing
it, he would have. That's all. That—"

"Hank," Nell said, "where are you going with that dreamy
look on your face? Where—"

"Why," Hank said simply, "to write it, of course!"